the Little Known

A good-hearted boy.
A segregated town.
A stolen fortune.

When twelve-year-old Knot Crews, an African American boy growing up in the segregated south Georgia town of Statenville, discovers a bag of bank-robbed cash in an alley, he is nearly overcome with happiness and terror. All that money—a hundred thousand dollars—could be the ticket to everything he's ever wanted, but he knows he can't spend it, not only because his conscience won't let him, but for fear of being caught.

He decides to do what he can for his needy neighbors, both black and white, and begins mailing them hundred-dollar bills anonymously, but it irks Knot daily to discover that most of them squander it and don't use the money as he had intended, and that the money doesn't change their lives for the better. It turns out that the weight of Knot's world can't be lifted by cold hard cash alone.

Set during the turbulent 1960's, *The Little Known* is a coming-of-age story full of hope and forgiveness.

ABOUT THE AUTHOR

Janice Daugharty's 1997 novel, EARL IN THE YELLOW
SHIRT, (HarperCollins) was nominated for a Pulitzer Prize.
She is the author of seven acclaimed novels and two short
story collections. She has served as writer-in-residence at
Valdosta State University, in Valdosta, Georgia, near her
home.

Visit the author at www.janicedaugharty.com

Praise for Janice Daugharty's Writing

"Daugharty does a fine job of demonstrating how ordinary
men and women are affected, in unpredictable ways, by race,
poverty and geography and by the enduring legacy of
important historical moments."
  - Francine Prose, *People* Magazine

"Daugharty creates a forceful character and a compelling,
often even humorous narrative."
  - Washington Post *Book World*

"Daugharty's ear is excellent, her language concise and
precise . . . shrewd and colorful prose."
  - The Atlanta *Journal-Constitution*

" . . . fans will rejoice to see Daugharty do what she does
best: showcase one character, setting her off against a
thousand daily details, like a diamond nestled in the shards
of lesser gems."
  - USA *Today*

"Swirling with details that become more disturbing the closer you look, Ms. Daugharty's portrait of Cornerville is both intimate and unsettling."
    - The New York *Times* Book Review

"Janice Daugharty is a natural-born writer, one of those Georgia women like O'Connor, McCullers, or Siddons who are best grown in small towns, a long way from city lights. There is a lot of red clay and long nights in every line she puts on paper."
    - Pat Conroy

the
Little Known
Janice
Daugharty

BelleBooks, Inc.

BelleBooks, Inc.
PO BOX 900321
Memphis, TN 38130
ISBN: 978-0-9841258-5-2

Copyright © 2010 by Janice Daugharty

Printed and bound in the United States of America.

We at BelleBooks enjoy hearing from readers. You can contact us at the address above or at BelleBooks@BelleBooks.com

Visit our websites—www.BelleBooks.com
10 9 8 7 6 5 4 3 2

Cover design: Debra Dixon
Interior design: Hank Smith
Photo credits: Bicycle - ©Soubrette | iStockphoto.com
                 Sky - © Rolffimage . . . | Dreamstime.com
                 Money - © Christopher Rawlins | Dreamstime.com

:Lc:01:

the Little Known

CR • ဆ

Chapter 1

It is all happening so fast it feels slow, runny as the midday heat in the alley, and for a fact Knot can see the sun beaming down from the top of the world. A block of sky like bought ice in the shimmer stage of melting. Shimmery too, at the other end of the alley, is a giant with a warped booger-man face. He is hugging a brown paper sack and running Knot's way, coming to rob him maybe of his play-cousin Lee's bicycle. Knot starts panting like a dog to the strumming of haywire on the front wheel spokes.

No brakes on the bike and Knot has to drag his hurt foot over the hot cobblestones to stop, eyes on the man likewise stopping before the green dumpster midway up the alley between Patterson and Ashley streets. Shucking off what looks like one of Aunt Willie's stockings from his head. Yes, a stocking. Black face, stung lips, teeth white as his eyes. Running again, the big man, big as Winston Riley, back home, makes straight for Knot but keeps close to the rear walls of the street-front stores.

Knot starts to drop the bicycle and run the other way, back toward Patterson Street where he had been cruising, cool and easy, but he can tell the man isn't after him by the way he kind of slinks along the wall, slow now, cool and easy, with his left hand in the pocket of his brown jeans and his right arm encircling the stuffed brown paper sack with the top neatly folded. He looks scared, maybe afraid of Knot because Knot is so ugly—buck teeth, ball head, skinny as a tobacco-stick scarecrow.

Sudden sirens rage along Patterson Street, all around, like peepers before a rain, and the man loops around and heads back the way he came, running hard, and the paper sack slips from his arm and drops to the cobbled brick.

"Hey, mister," says Knot, "you drop yo sack." He just says it because he should say it, to be polite like his rich pretend-kin he's been visiting all summer, but doesn't yell it out and anyway the man knows and the man is turning the corner onto Ashley Street, gone, and Knot is glad he's gone.

Still straddled the bicycle, Knot walks it over to the spot where the sack landed—top still folded down. The kind of sack Aunt Willie carries her groceries in from Harvey's downtown all the way over to Troupe Street. Sirens shatter the time-ticking of haywire on the bike spokes. "I ain't into this," Knot mumbles, "I ain't into this." And Knot is pedaling fast up the alley, good foot bare and nail-jabbed foot in a white sock, then north along Ashley Street, past the stalled cars with horns beeping and shoppers dodging his bike. One block away from the screaming of sirens that makes his gums itch.

So hot, and he would like to be on the east side of town, where he longs to belong, in the shady quiet of row houses whose front yards spill children onto the gravel street. But at the next intersection, he steers the bicycle west, rather than east, and pedals along the sidewalk toward Patterson Street, where not ten minutes before, which seems more like a long fevered sleep, he had been minding his own business: cruising over spilled cola steeping on hot concrete and exploding pigeons the color of courtyard statues.

"I ain't into this," he says to a stout blue-haired woman weighted down with shopping bags. She is scurrying toward a parked car the color of her hair, trying to unlock it while gazing off across the street at the train of black and white police cars with lights flashing and sirens wailing. People are gathered around the door of the bank—FIRST NATIONAL BANK, according to the sign on the white stone facade atop the building at the corner of Patterson and Hill.

One more turn down the alley and Knot brakes with his socked foot, stopping next to the paper sack and scooping it up, packing it into the bicycle basket, then pedaling again, up the alley again, onto the sidewalk running parallel to Ashley Street, turning east this time and flying away from the sirens and car horns with pigeons the color of courtyard statues.

He should look, he should look in the sack, but he is afraid he will find money, afraid he will not find money. Looks like old magazines, the squared-off corners of the sack do. "How do?" he says to the brittle old black men seated on the store-front bench, corner of Troupe and Gordon. Hieing south, toward Aunt Willie's house. He knows that the man in the alley was a bank robber, that what is in the sack has to be money. He doesn't have to look, can't wait to look. Instead he looks behind, pedaling regular and sure, south along Troupe Street, and his looking behind causes the bicycle to veer left where three black children are playing with a litter of black puppies. The happy kind, regardless of their station in life.

A tiny girl stands with a puppy hugged up to her bowed belly, hard tail switching at her stubby brown legs.

"Go on, Knot," says her brother, an eight year old with square hair. "This our dogs."

"What I want with no old *dogs*?" Knot pedals straight up the street to prove he can drive this bicycle right. "What I want with no old *dogs*?" he repeats to himself and laughs. Then cries. What he wants is to stay at Aunt Willie's house.

He doesn't really belong to Marge, so why can't he belong to her sister?

An old auntie is sitting on one of the row house porches, fanning with a hand fan. Her stockings are rolled at her parted knees. High floors, up and down the street, so high that a boy can play underneath and hear the grownups walking around and talking inside—somebody older over him to protect him from the po-lice, mad dogs, and himself. Big square houses with peeling paint and metal gliders on spacey front porches where people sit in the sunshine after supper. Scraggly crepe myrtle trees with frilly cerise flowers that decorate the order of things that Knot can't name. Just summer on Troupe Street.

Again he checks behind him, for the black and white cars downtown, stretching the distance between them and him and the street opening up ahead, and checks too for anybody who might happen to be listening—he has to keep talking to himself so that the words won't bank in his overloaded head.

"I ain't ask for no money, don't want no money. What business a lil ole knot like me got with money?" All lies ticking off through his teeth to the tempo of the haywire on the wheel spokes.

He can see Marge's celery and rust car parked in front of Aunt Willie's roomy old house, waiting to take him back to the one-room shack in the quarters of Statenville, twenty-five miles east of Valdosta. That's where Marge has to live till she gets cured of drinking and cussing. All of Knot's rich pretend-kin are on the front porch: Aunt Willie sitting in one of the high-back rockers, taking the hem on Cousin Judy Beth's white baptism dress; the old granddaddy in the next rocker with his puffed pinkish lips and white hair; Lee on the end of the porch, watching for Knot and his bicycle around the twine trellis of nooning purple morning glory. Marge, rawboned and tall, is standing on a baluster of the doorsteps in her walked-down black shoes and the black-and-navy striped dress that looks all-black, which she always wears to town. Won't wear color, Marge won't. The women are laughing, hooting, and Aunt Willie play-spanks the seat of Judy Beth's flare-tailed dress. She scoots forward with her bony shoulders slumped and arms limp alongside, play-mad, and stomps through the front screen door, slamming it.

Knot swerves the bike onto the sloped dirt drive, north of the house, and coasts on toward the back yard.

"What you got in the basket?" calls Lee.

"Books," says Knot, passing the chimney with mortar sifting like hour-glass sand from between the red bricks.

"Bunch of old books."

Say *books*, Knot has found out, and nobody will look inside a box or bag.

"That boy do love his books," says Marge and hums a laugh. She tells everybody that, and though she doesn't read herself, she is proud he does read, proud of this lil ole knot, as she calls him, who she had taken to raise after somebody fished him out of the trash twelve years ago. "Get yo stuff, Knot," she yells, "we gotta go."

"Knot step on a nail yesterday, stick it in his foot," says Lee, who figures Marge might care for a change.

Knot is in the back yard, at the sloped edge of the porch, standing straddled the bicycle. The uneven boards of the hip-roofed house used to be painted either green or red; you can't tell which because the paint is scaling, blending, and the effect is a rich tapestry. The fact that Knot is long-gone, hiding out from the po-lice with his stolen money, makes no difference to his family out front. They are still mouthing at him as if he is right there with them. Get Aunt Willie and Marge together and they'll talk.

"What all them sireens about?" calls Aunt Willie.

"Ain't *seen* no sireens." Knot wipes his eyes on the sleeves of his brown striped shirt, then lifts the paper sack from the basket and lets the bicycle drop on its side. Wheels spinning and haywire clicking on the spokes.

Up the tall wood doorsteps, past the daisywheel of yellow cats eating oatmeal from a bowl and through the door to the sunny yellow kitchen. Toasted bread smells—one more thing Knot loves about city living, about being at his rich pretend-kin's house. Money buys the smell of toast and money buys color. He will buy Marge a toaster and some color for her shack.

ॲ • ॐ

He is still holding the sack of money, or maybe books—now that he has said it he wonders and wouldn't be surprised or even disappointed if it were books. He stands on the curb next to the old car that reeks of mildew and burnt motor oil.

Aunt Willie and Marge are loading paper sacks of Lee's hand-me-down clothes into the trunk.

"Be enough clothes to start him back to school," says Aunt Willie and rubs his head hard. "Like Daddy always say, Marge, put a brick on that head if he keep growing."

Mourning doves purl, locusts hum. Way-off rumble and toot of a freight train Knot has seen with his own two eyes. The three black children with the black puppies linger along the street. A slow car passes. Their mother steps to the edge of her wide front porch with her hands on her hips. "Git off that hardroad fore a car run over you."

"You gone nuss them books all the way home, or put em back here?" Marge asks Knot. She has one hand on the raised trunk with a long brown finger hooked through her key ring. Bunch of keys. Though only one serves a purpose. She slams the trunk, hugs and hums over Aunt Willie, Granddaddy and Judy Beth, then goes around to her side of the car.

"Kiss em all bye, Knot," she says.

He hugs the books and kisses Aunt Willie and Judy Beth on the cheeks as they pass along the curb before him. "You behave yourself," says Aunt Willie.

"I'm gone miss yo ugly mug," says Judy Beth.

"That boy be a fool bout them books," hums Marge over the car roof.

Knot is truly ugly, and he likes Judy Beth—maybe loves her—because unlike everybody else she never pretends that he's easy to look at.

The old granddaddy pokes over with his cane and slaps Knot on the shoulder. He wears a suit of gray twill work clothes, starched and ironed. His skin is the gray of his clothes. "You be back here fore you know it. Mind Marge, you hear?"

"Yessir." Knot likes him too—no, *loves* him—wishes he were his real granddaddy.

Lee is inside, outside, somewhere. The fact that he doesn't come to say good-bye says how sorry he is to see

Knot go. All summer they have quarreled over the bicycle, drove Aunt Willie crazy, but now that Knot is leaving, Lee is sorry to see him go. May be crying right this very minute. Knot grins, shining his great white teeth.

ଔ • ଔ

Knot is almost safe, almost free, perched on the front seat with only his eyes moving. But Marge has to run by the drugstore downtown to get her blood pressure medicine. Knot cannot believe that he is downtown again, traveling along Patterson Street again. Light traffic slow-motoring along all four lanes of the one-way street and not a cop in sight.

It has to be books in the sack. Old magazines, probably.

Marge is changing lanes, merging left, turning the celery and rust car onto West Hill, pulling up and backing into the corner parking space with the bank on the northwest corner behind them.

"You coming in with me?" she says. "Too hot out here in the car."

"I'll just sit here."

"You ain't sick?" She feels his forehead with the backside of her hand. "You just sad," she says. "Hating to leave everybody, right?"

"Right."

"Cause they rich, right?" She hums a laugh because she doubts that. "Well, read you one of them books while I'm gone." She opens the door, checks for traffic, lumbers out and around the rear of the car.

He watches her pass through the glass side door of Bel-Lile Drugs next to the stairs that lead up to the doctor's office where Marge took Knot when he had what's called coronals on his neck, and where there were two waiting rooms—one for blacks and one for whites. Long time ago, and now he goes to school with the whites who treat him okay because he is clean and honest, makes good grades, and never says po-lice, sireen, loot or cop.

Now he can look in the sack; he has to look. Is afraid to

look.

He stays stiff, unblinking, as he unfolds the brown paper cuff, peeps inside. He looks up and blows. "Ain't books," he says, biting back a grin.

Stacks of dirty-green hundred-dollar bills with narrow bands like brown paper-sacking marked "1000" in red print.

He blows at his forehead again. Folds the top of the sack down, grips it tighter. Stares straight ahead. He wonders how much money he has. Starts to get out and leave the sack with the loot on the doctor's stairs. Waves of high tight happiness and terror pass over him like hot and cold water.

Suddenly, the driver's door swings wide, and Marge is getting into the car with a white cup of fountain soda in one hand and a white sack of rattley pills in the other. "Here," she says and hands him the cup. "Perk you up."

"Thank you," he says.

"Say somebody rob the bank this afternoon, get 25,000 dollar."

He is sipping the fizzy cold cola and has to bite down on the cup lip to keep from gurking. Sinks his buck teeth into the Styrofoam leaving horseshoe impressions he can see with the tip of his tongue.

Almost out of town, juddering south past the ABC Liquor Store on his right and checking Marge's long brown hands on the steering wheel to see if they will turn the wheel right. Then over the railroad overpass, from which point he can almost see Aunt Willie's fine house and can see her church with the fancy white steeple and cross. He will buy a house like that, he might even buy a church like that, but knows he probably never will—even with all this money—when Marge stops at the Dixie Station and has to count out her dollars and dimes for gas and he cannot so much as hand her one of the hundred-dollar bills from the sack for fear of getting caught.

C꙰ • ꙮ

Knot dozes with his left hand on the paper sack of worthless money between his cot and the unpainted wall and window of Marge's shack in the quarters. It's too hot to sleep.

But Marge, in the next bed, is snoring—sounds like a small engine sputtering—and next door, in the shack on the right, Winston Riley is beating up his wife Boots. Children scream, flesh splats, a chair overturns, Boots hollers, "No, Winston, no!" In a minute, she will be over here. In a minute, Marge will be doctoring her battered head while preaching to her about leaving Winston.

A door slams. Knot sits up, swings his feet over the edge of the cot and waits for Boots, waits for the heat to let up. Dim light through the screened window facing the woods—starlight thick with the ringing of katydids and the hulled whine of mosquitoes. Rooty smell of hogs in the pen out back, or maybe it's the rotting potatoes in the bag by the front door. Ask Marge why she doesn't clean up the combination kitchen-living room-bedroom and she'll tell you quick that she gets enough of cleaning other people's houses. Besides, she adds, my own dirt, me and mine, don't bother me. Knot feels good when she says the part about "me and mine," because then and only then does he feel he belongs. She's never even hugged him. But she has let him borrow her last name—Crews—same name as the old gray granddaddy.

Knot slaps a mosquito on his arm and scratches the itch till it smarts. Marge has quit snoring, is waiting too.

Feet bound on the porch floor, shaking the entire shack and rattling the windows. *Bap bap bap* on the door. Ragged breathing, mewling. A baby stifles crying.

Marge moans, stands, pulls the cord on the overhead light. White light showers down on her broomed peroxide hair. She is almost forty, but looks younger because she is skinny, all legs in her man's white T-shirt (Knot cannot remember which man, only that once upon a time there was a man), except for her belly, which is bloated and tight from what the doctor calls liver trouble.

Long bare feet in motion, Marge lumbers over to the front left corner and picks up her old rabbit-eared shotgun, then goes to the vertical-board door and flips the metal latch. Boots with her antennae braids and wild eyes, and a baby on one hip, shoves past Marge and into the room. Three guinea children are clinging to her legs. Boots's nose is leaking blood to her blue cotton smock trimmed in red rickrack; her broad flat nose looks flatter, spattered.

Rotten potatoes scatter and roll across the filthy wide floorboards and out the door where Marge is standing with her shotgun pointed barrel-up to the night sky. She breeches the shotgun and fires. A flashette of orange, the color of her hair, then smoke curling back into the room with Marge. "Come on over here, Winston," she yells in her braying night voice. "I'm waiting on you." Much cussing. Then quiet outside as she slams the door and sets the latch in its hook.

Inside, the children are sniffling, whining, drying up their crying. And Boots has one forearm pressed over her nose, blood leaking over and around it and drip drip dripping on the floorboards.

Marge ambles over to the corner and leans the shotgun against the unceiled wall, then picks up a white washrag from the second-hand yellow dinette table by the door and tosses it to Boots.

"He oughta break your neck for you staying with him."

"I got younguns to feed," Boots says, burbling blood. Then presses the rag to her nose.

Winston shouts through the double walls of his shack and Marge's shack: "Boots, you better get yo ass back over here. Don't, I come in there after you." Sounds like he's in a next room, though neither has a next room.

"Come on," Marge shouts back. "We waiting on you."

"You ole mess-making bitch!"

"Shut up, you S.O.B! Go to sleep."

Winston quits shouting and starts mumbling.

Marge takes the baby from Boots. He wraps his thin, sore-crusted legs about her waist and rests his curly head on her bosom, sucking his thumb. "You babies climb on up there in my bed," she says to the other children, who are variously wandering, gnawing on fingers and staring fix-eyed at their mother. "Boots, you sit here." Marge points to one of the chrome-legged chairs at the dinette table by the door. "Let Doc Marge see to that nose," she adds in a kinder tone.

Boots sits, tilting her horsy face up and holding the towel under her chin to catch the drooling blood. "Yeah, look like he break it this time," Marge says to her. Then to Knot, "Here, buddy, come take this baby."

Knot crawls across his cot in his underwear, goes over and takes the baby. Wet diaper settling on his left arm. The baby cuddles close as Knot pats his warm brown back. There is a living wreath of night beetles and moths around the light.

"Hold still now," Marge says to Boots and stands straddle-legged before her knees, sighting the nose-bone alignment with the precise center of the wide bridge between Boot's inky eyes. Marge yanks hard, Boots grunts. Marge holds the nose between both hands like a caught bird, then steps away. Sighting again.

"I ain't taking it no more," says Boots and sprawls in the chair.

"Yeah, you will," brays Marge. "You gone take it till the undertaker take you."

"You a hateful old thing," says Boots, dobbing blood from her precious fixed nose.

"How come I ain't beat black and blue and you are."

The baby is limp, heavier asleep in Knot's arms; he lays the leggy boy on his wallowed-out cot and lies down beside him. Bony knees and elbows in his back as he turns facing the black window and the paper sack of money. He listens to the two women talking low and the children in the next bed breathing shallow, regular. All but one who is snoring: bad adenoids, according to Marge, who would know, because she used to work for a baby doctor in Valdosta before she got fired for drinking on the job. Then, she had lived in the house with the old granddaddy and Aunt Willie and was welcome as the flowers in May, they said, as long as she didn't drink and raise sand. It has been at least six months since she pitched her last drunk, but the fact that she stays on in the quarters of Statenville means she could very well pitch another drunk at anytime.

Knot lulls himself to sleep with thoughts of moving in with Aunt Willie and her family and how to use the money without getting caught.

❧ • ❦

When he wakes the next morning, everybody is gone, his bed is wet, and sunlight is streaming through the double east windows each side of the door. One pane is missing from the window on the right and in its place is a cardboard patch, a blank square in the fifteen-pane window stencil spread across the fused junk and clothes on the wide floorboards. Smells of blood and urine, like mold and ammonia.

Beyond the wall at the head of Knot's bed, Boots is fussing with the children. Back to normal. Winston has gone to work in the pulpwoods, and for two or three days they will get along, then BOOM! all over again.

But life is good now: dogs bark, children play, women hang out their wash, and Knot has finally come up with a way to use the money.

Wearing the same khaki shorts and brown-striped shirt he wore yesterday, same white sock on his injured foot, he limps to the door, out the door, with two of the stiff hundred-dollar bills in his left pocket—one for Marge and the other for Boots—plus chiming coins from Marge's change jar for postage.

It is about ten o'clock and already the sun is heating up the quarters, shining through rags of moss in the oaks. Flocked shadows on the packed gray dirt that hatches broken glass and trash like fleas. Locusts hum and bandy-legged children scamp yard to yard of the unpainted, close-set cabins. Old women on porches rock and swat flies and wait.

Knot takes the gravel horseshoe road along the west curve where the yellow buses will soon circle the school grounds. The softball field on his right is grown up in red bitter weeds, looks like tilled clay. Hands in his pockets, he limps along, past the giant oak that divides the road at the side entrance to the schoolyard. A checkmark breezeway hooks the old portwine brick building to the new red brick building that still smells of wet cement.

At the end of the road, he turns left along the sidewalk, passing the row of white people's white houses, where Marge works now but won't have to work after tomorrow. He doesn't cross Highway 94 to the other side till he gets to the red brick, flat-topped courthouse, directly across from the red-brick, flat-topped post office.

ʘ • ⁊

Just as he'd expected, on Friday evening when Marge gets home from work, she is scooting in her black shoes with the walked-down heels and saying "Hoo-oo-oo!" Hum-laughing. Around the rear of the parked car, across the yard, and onto the porch, calling "Knot, Knot . . . hoo-oo-oo!" Through the open door with the white envelope Knot sent yesterday loved-up to her flattened breasts.

It is sunset in the quarters and the orange light slanting through the west woods outshines the trash fires. Smells of smoke and supper cooking as if from the same pot. So hot that the heat seems textured of the locusts' hum. Pickups come and go, delivering the men home from work. They wander cock-sure through the knots of merry children and dogs. The old women on the porches wait for tomorrow, when it will start all over again. That kind of evening.

"Honey, you ain't gone believe what's in here." Marge speaks secretive and low. She dances in a circle with the envelope in the air. Shuffling her big feet to an imaginary beat. "Hoo-oo-oo!" An old-timey dance shuffle that used to embarrass Knot, but now with only the two of them around makes him proud. He feels like Santa Claus.

How many times has he daydreamed about finding money, giving Marge money to make up for her sacrifices: all those cold nights when he'd be sick and she would get bundled up like a witch in her black coat and headscarf and go out to find wood to feed to the hungry black heater.

"What is it, Marge? What?"

"Money, baby, that what."

"Where you get it, Marge?" he says. "How much?"

"A hunderd dollars, baby. *One* hunderd dollars!" She takes the clean dollar-green bill from the envelope and kisses it. Then fans it at him. Has forgotten the first part of his question.

She dips up and down like a carnival duck, then holds her knees. "We in the money, honey," she says. "Gone get you some new shoes, gone get my hair back like it was— gone get it dyed black, baby." Her brittle orange hair stands out, looks gnawed or singed, for a fact. "Gone get us a TV, baby. Gone get us some new tires on that old jalopy out there."

"And a bicycle," says Knot.

"And a bicycle," she shouts, then shushes herself.

He doubts that one hundred dollars will buy all that, figures he'll have to mail more to her—if all goes well. After all, Christmas is coming up. As for her hair, he doubts that black dye will cover the orange. Last summer, she had gotten Boots to peroxide her hair. They left the bleach on too long because the man who owns the water system in Statenville was waterlogging the pump and Marge couldn't wash it out.

Knot, in the yard, had watched Marge sitting on the porch with her hair growing lighter, brighter—strange shades ranging from sulfur yellow to fire red. She had a round mirror in one hand, and with the fingers of her other hand she was plucking at strands. Boots behind her chair had been warning her that it was time to wash out the peroxide. Lots of yatter and back-and-forth.

"That bleach liable to burn up yo hair."

"Naw—ain't light enough yet."

"It's yo head." Boots laughed and scooped a dollop of white foam from the small blue bowl she was holding and plopped it on Marge's tangerine crown. "It done about all it gone do. Ain't never hear tell of nobody leave it on over a hour."

From the yard, Knot could smell the gunk like the Red Devil lye women used to scrub their porch floors. Marge stank and she looked in pain. Forehead wrinkled and eyes red and watering. Her spiked hair changed before his eyes from tongues of fire to orange Jell-O. Even the gnats wouldn't go near her. Boots had given up on her and taken the children next door for lunch. Still, ever so often Boots or one of the children would pop through their door to look at Marge in agony for the sake of beauty.

Finally, she stood and walked into the house, and next minute she began cussing and screaming. "That sorry SB pick some time to turn the water off." Stomping the floor, she yelled out, "Knot, hurry, run go tell him to turn the water on. Run."

Bare feet digging into the dry dirt of the yard, spinning dust, Knot took off toward the paved road, westside of the school. Behind him, Marge was still shouting and cussing, Boots trying to calm her. Knot's heels were kicking high, elbows pumping for speed. He could feel bugs peppering his face like BBs, hot air whizzing in his ears and his heart keeping time with the slapping of his feet. Breathing, breathing, running to save Marge's hair from burning up.

He used to run all the time, it seemed, until Marge pointed out that running kept him skinny.

When he got to the sidewalk, leading uptown, he took the bend without slowing, outrunning a pulpwood truck rocking west along 94.

Almost to the house of the man who was master of their water, Knot began yelling, "Turn on the water, sir. Pleasesir, turn on the water."

He could see the slight bald man, dressed in khaki twills, at the concrete block pump house behind the white frame house where he lived. He was leaning in the doorway, watching Knot come.

When Knot reached him, trying to catch his breath to

explain, the man said calmly, "Now, boy, what's all that fuss? Y'all got a fire around there or what?" His spoked blue eyes were like marbles but didn't roll.

"Turn on the water, mister. Boots put peroxide on Marge's hair and she can't wash it out."

The man smiled. "Don't say." Behind him, inside the pump house, water trickled; it was cobwebby, dim and hollow as a tomb. Cool air breezed through the door.

Then Knot recalled Marge blessing out the waterman last time he had drained the pump. Knot had made a mistake—a big mistake—but one he'd never make again. He learned never to give ammunition to the enemy. They had no water for two or three hours.

So, having hair that barely grows, Marge is stuck with the cap of blinding orange hair.

She grabs Knot now, waltzing, humming, around the walk-space of the small room being daily reduced by junk. Suddenly she stuffs the bill into the bosom of her brown blouse and says, "Now you stay here. Mama Marge gone go get us something fitting for supper—ain't gone eat no beans tonight, baby," and she is out the door, shuffling toward the old celery and rust car. Gets in, coaxes it into starting, and is gone.

 catch • so

She doesn't come back and she doesn't come back, and it grows dark, darker. Knot had been expecting that too.

And expecting that next door all hell would break loose when Winston got home and found Boots and the babies gone. Hell is breaking glass and wood.

Knot latches the door, turns off the light, and sits on his cot with his socked, throbbing foot atop the money sack, and listens to Winston slam about the house, cussing and threatening to cut out Boots's liver when he finds her.

Knot smiles.

catch • so

He stops smiling when he wakes during the night to Marge pawing at the front door and calling him. Her braying night voice now slurred.

He pulls the cord on the overhead light, unlatches the door, and she wobbles in with her eyeballs rolling up and her lids rolling down. She starts to cry as he leads her to her bed, helps her lie down, and takes off her shoes with the walked-down heels. The second toe of her right foot overlaps the big toe. The paler soles of her feet are grained like wood, smell like scorched ironing.

"I forget you, baby, didn't I?"

Knot nods.

"I spend all my money and forget you."

"All of it?"

Right arm bent at the elbow, she rocks her hand side to side. "Give it away, throw it away—I ain't have it nomore."

To stop her blubbery crying, he starts to tell her not to worry, there is more money. He starts to show her how much more. Is already walking around the spindled iron foot of her bed, but stops. Knows he'll never give her more money, can't give her money. He looks around at the colorless gloom of the shack, at the dingy light showering down on Marge's few dark dresses and coat hanging from the broomstick rod in the right corner, next to the bathroom door. Even the bloody rag with Boots's blood on it, in the middle of the floor, looks like a dead rose. If he gives Marge money, she will never be welcome as the flowers in May at Aunt Willie's house.

"Poor lil ole Knot," Marge says and places her forearm over her eyes so that her whiskey breath smells stronger, her triangular lips look greedier. "First I chunk you in the trash, then I take off and spend my money on liquor and men."

"Marge," he says and goes to the head of her bed again, "you ain't chunk me in no trash. You the one take me to raise when somebody else fish me out and bring me to you."

Arm still over her eyes, she says low, "Ain't how it went, boy. I had you, didn't want you. That the truth of it." She moves her arm, smeary brown eyes full on him.

"Why you act like I ain't yours then?" He kneels on the floor beside her. "Why you make up that story bout me belonging to somebody else? Say how sorry my real mama be."

"You know me . . ." She moans, cries, chugs crying, then, "Know me like my ownself, and know I ain't never want to be tied down to nobody. Be easier, better, to make you think you don't belong to me."

She rolls over, facing away from him, sobbing. Bony back shaking under her sorry brown shirt. "At first, I don't tell you mine cause I don't want you to know I stoop so low. Then, I don't want you to know for the same reason I chunk you in the trash in the first place." Her hot hoarse voice goes suddenly cold: "Now go on. Go on and stay up yonder with Sister and them. I ain't have no claim on you."

"You just sorry for yourself, Marge." He is the one crying now. "You just looking for a excuse to get drunk and stay drunk."

For a fact, she always blows up at him when she is drunk, and for a fact, the next day all is forgiven and forgotten, but this time is different.

Chapter 2

When the train of yellow school buses began circling the quarters, after school started, the children and the bus drivers saw red tricycles and blue bicycles, rainbows of clothes on the lines, and vari-colored plastic flowers in pots on the shack porches. All except one. But that was okay.

It was okay and even better than okay, as far as Knot was concerned. Almost a whole month and Marge hasn't had a drink—not even a beer!

And soon, by Christmas maybe, Knot would be with his new family on Troupe Street, in Valdosta. And if there was any money left over—barring more unforeseen wants disguised as needs popping up in the quarters—he would take the sack of money back to the alley. He would borrow his true-cousin Lee's bicycle and take the money back and leave it there. Though, for a fact, he would be tempted to buy himself a new bicycle first. But he wouldn't cave in. He wouldn't cave in and spend the money on himself because he wouldn't need to. He would be rich then.

Well, that was the ideal, Knot's ideal. But Marge was not to be trusted.

It's bad enough that he is stumped, blocked, while working on this model-White essay—"What Did You Do Last Summer?" A question, and the correct answer isn't happening up on a sack of cash in some alley and finding it to be more trouble than it is worth, more drain than asset, less pleasure than pain. He could write a really fine essay on the many ways to spend such sudden money, all the sneaking around, and the heartbreak of not being able to personally benefit from a single dollar bill. He could write about suddenly "seeing" all around him the sorry lives of his neighbors, the whole mess, and how he could make it all better by dipping into his money sack and withdrawing a thin meager slip of green paper. And to be honest, he would have

21

to write that most of the time those very people drank it up or shopped it up as if gift money of course wouldn't be intended for teeth, medicine, freedom, food, or heat.

To top the list of Knot's problems, Marge shows up drunk at school.

Late September on a Friday afternoon, and she just bumps open the classroom door and stands swaying like a bed-sheet ghost in the wind, holding to the jamb. The waist of her faded black skirt has ridden up above her pooched belly, her white blouse is filthy. There is a brownish streak down the front, and spatters of the same on her skirt, where she has either spilled something or puked on herself. "Scuse me, teacher." Her words run together like syrup. "I needs to get my boy a little bit early."

She seems to have practiced this little announcement while gathering herself out in the hall. The way she said "boy" makes Knot feel like her little nigger.

"Knot," the teacher says low, standing watch over her students before her desk at the front of the room. She is backed by the green chalkboard and the title of the personal essay she's chosen for them to write.

The breeze through the tall open windows, to the left of Knot's desk row, is cured and mild, an autumn breeze. Beyond, on the school grounds, there's a softball game going on, the excited calls and crack of the bat drifting under a deep blue sky. One cricket is chirring outside the wall of windows, a steadying sound in which to order Knot's thoughts and keep him calm. Another minute and he would have been writing away about his summer at Aunt Willie's, a pumped up story in the vein of kid-normal about riding Lee's bicycle all over Valdosta, but skipping the alley and the stolen cash.

Knot would like to disown Marge in the doorway, but being one of two Negro students in the class, he figures he may as well get his books and get out before she lets go of the doorjamb and lands smack-dab on her face.

"How he doing on his rithmatic?" Marge is made brave,

apparently, by her having completed a whole sentence before.

"Well," says the teacher, walking in her new start-of-school bone flats to the door. Speaking low to silence Marge who is speaking loud. "Back to work, boys and girls," the teacher says because the entire class is staring at Marge, what they did over the summer forgotten.

Knot knows the teacher is making a mistake, a big one, when she places a finger on her puckered pink lips and shushes Marge, head to head, in the doorway. "We're working on our narrative essays if you don't mind."

"Do I *mind*? Why I *mind*? I *look* like I mind?" Marge, speaking at the top of her lungs, lets go of the door jamb and tilts forward so that the teacher has to grab her, prop her up. They dance back and slam into the last desk on the first row. The white-headed girl named Becky Bruce, seated there, leaps up and hops over an empty desk on the next row, making a big show of being frightened. She crosses both arms over her head to cover it. Then she begins to cry, her round face turning red. Everybody else laughs. Somebody says, "Boy, that lady's drunk!" The skittering of the desk has stopped the chirring of the cricket outside, and inside the students seem to have come unstuck. All turning in their desks and talking.

"Boys and girls! Quieten down." Usually the teacher would clap her hands, saying this. But her hands are busy propping up Marge. Regardless she manages to hold her ground in the spot where Becky Bruce's desk had been before the two women shoved into it.

Knot feels angry with the white-headed girl for over-reacting when Marge and the teacher reeled into her desk. She knows Marge; Marge cleans for her mother sometimes. Did she do it for a laugh? No, she wasn't clowning. But still...

The teacher is glancing back at Knot, a wild look in her slanted green eyes, as he dodges around the end of his desk row, not even looking at the sobbing girl as he passes. A boy named Scottie, who is white and would have lots of stuff to write about what he did last summer, says, "Phew! That smell!" and holds his nose.

"Come on, Marge." Knot takes one arm and tries to disengage her from the teacher, to head her out the door. She smells of fried meat, stale cigarettes, alcohol and sweat.

One on each side, Knot and the teacher guide Marge out the door to the hall. Inside, the classroom fills with laughter, yapping, skittering desks and bawling Becky Bruce.

The teacher on the other side of Marge is breathing hard, leaning away, but still holding to Marge's left arm. Together she and Knot push through the tall wooden door with panes of smudged glass halfway up to the top. Down the high concrete steps and across the trenched gray dirt, they walk Marge who is now rooting her nose into the shoulder of her white blouse.

The teacher takes Marge's sniffling as a sign of remorse and meekness. "You should be ashamed, embarrassing your son like this."

The bell dismissing school for the day goes off like a thousand buzzers, and students pour out the door, shouting. No doubt saving Marge from beating the teacher into the ground for their after-school entertainment.

He is so glad to get Marge in the car and away from the school and the normal-White kids now loading up on busses and those walking home along the tree-lined sidewalks left and right of Highway 94 that he doesn't even question Marge at the wheel weaving toward the red light at the crossing about where they are going and why she has picked him up from school. She has never picked him up before.

The light goes green before she gets there. But the fact that she hasn't slowed down means she hasn't seen the light, just takes a left onto 129, chugging past the Delta Store facing the courthouse, then the café facing the white frame houses with neat fenced yards. Becky Bruce, in dungarees and a green striped shirt, is walking slow, arms loaded with books and head hung. Knot hopes she is hanging her head in shame for having made such a big deal over Marge stumbling in drunk. But he doubts that. He hates her.

The open highway up ahead looks peaceful, though Marge is driving the forty-mile-per-hour Ford seventy miles per hour. Swerving off the highway and churning up the shoulders of seeding pale grass.

"I can drive, Marge," he says.

Her peroxide hair looks like Moses' burning bush. "Meaning I can't?"

"Meaning maybe you ought not to."

"Cause I be drunk, right?"

He doesn't answer. Warm wind through the open windows bats at his face and snaps the loose ends of lined notebook paper sticking from the books on his lap. Sounds like one of those cricket clicker toys that come in boxes of Cracker Jacks. He can smell wood smoke and there is a haze of smoke across the pinewoods. A smell he usually likes but now makes him feel edgy. The heavy patches of smoke up the highway seem to move when the car gets near.

"You go to work today?" he asks.

"Knock off early."

"Where we going, Marge?"

"The Line."

"For you to get some more likker, right?"

"Nope. For you to."

"*Me?*"

"Done been in there one time today. Old Fart say don't come back no more till I come up with the money."

"Then how'm I s'pose to get it?"

"Tell him your daddy's Winston Riley. He send you for it. Say he be by and pay up tomorrow."

"*Winston Riley?* Marge?"

"Old Fart don't know you from Adam's housecat."

"But Winston do."

"He at work—belong to be anyway." The last part she says out the window, as if Winston is her husband and she's depending on him for grocery money.

"Marge, he'll kill me if I do that."

"I'll kill you if you don't. Now do what I say do."

Already Knot can see the Georgia/Florida line sign, white with black writing, and the highway going from dark to light, separating Georgia from Florida. Box-like at a distance on the right the small concrete-block beer joint moves closer and closer. Bars on the two front windows and red neon Budweiser lights in twists like pretzels.

But when they get to the widened shoulder of sand and gravel—pullover parking for customers of The Line—Marge takes a left down a dirt road running through the woods. "Gone go up here a piece, put you out and you can walk back."

"It won't work, Marge." The car is bucking over ruts. "I'm telling you it won't." Since she's bound to drink anyway, Knot thinks he should go ahead and give her some more money. At least then he wouldn't be in trouble with Winston Riley, and maybe even the law. He thinks longingly of Marge's shack, in the quarters, after school, the tainted place he calls home. He could be doing his homework, safe and alone, on this dry crickety evening. Never before had he thought of his lonesome life like that.

Marge pulls over to the side of the sandy dirt road, on the edge of the ditch cut sharp and about a foot deep. The old Ford smells oily and makes a ticking noise, then a single sucking racket like a sigh as she switches the key in the ignition to off.

"Go on now," she says. "Ain't far and you can do with a little extracize."

"What if the man sics the law on me?"

"You some kind of nigger boy! I raise you too easy. Spoil you." Louder she says, waving a long bony hand, "YOU DUCK OUT THE DOOR, DUMMY. OUT RUN 'EM. NOW GO!"

Marge has never beaten him but she has slapped him. He pulls up on the latch and the door opens just a crack with a hum. He shoves it wide with a hideous squawking. "What I ask for?"

"A fifth of Royal. Crown Royal. If he say that too much money, ast for a jug of wine. Strawberry Hill."

The walk to the end of the road and the highway isn't nearly long enough, and the sun is shining in Knot's eyes from across the woods and straight-arrow down the stretch of fresh-graded dirt, and Knot is shaking as if he is cold. Inside, his body feels flushed, his heart gushing hot blood. His head feels light, emptied of thought, though his brain is ajumble with what he will say when he gets to the beer joint on the Florida line and what will happen when Winston Riley finds out that Knot is charging liquor for Marge in Riley's name. And too Marge has spent what dab of money she has made for groceries on today's drinking spree. Otherwise she would be buying liquor right now instead of sending Knot on this disastrous mission. But for once Knot doesn't feel hungry. That is something at least.

He is now near the end of the road and anybody looking out the window of the beer joint can see him walking up out of the woods if they have a mind to. Big trucks rumble north and south, out of Georgia into Florida, and out of Florida into Georgia; they drown out the sounds of katydids and crickets and frogs cheeping and blatting like sheep from a cypress swamp nearby, sounds he hadn't even noticed till they are banished by the roaring of the trucks. Up close now, standing off the edge of the highway waiting to cross, Knot can smell the oily tar off the asphalt and feel the hot wind off the truck wheels, their powerful suck and drag. WHOOSH . . . SCHOOM!!

Some crazy in a little red car lays down on his horn to warn Knot not to step out on the highway till he passes, which Knot has to admit probably saves his life, as he'd had all intentions of dashing across after the last semi had passed. Delayed fear surges in his chest and stings to his fingertips. This minute, he could be dead, minced on the asphalt and gravel he is now crossing over. Which under the circumstances seems like an escape.

He can at least take comfort in the fact that there are no pickups or cars parked out front on the tracked white sand before the building.

He shakes his head to get into the character of Winston Riley's son. He can figure that a boy of Winston Riley's—yeah, *boy*, not *son*—would be blare-eyed and timid, scared to death, so that will be easy to pull off.

At the rusty screen door, he can hear knocking around inside. Sounds like the owner or somebody is unpacking a crate of bottles, arranging them maybe in the standing cooler along the back wall, which Knot can see in the dim light through the screen of the door. He can see the man, Mr. Fart, tall and apelike, pale in a long-sleeved plaid shirt. He has a wide mouth and dark hair growing low on his forehead. His hands are big as feet. Bending behind the counter, he picks up two brown bottles in each hand, stands and places them on a rack in the cooler behind. He is just about to bend again when he stops, staring at the door.

"What you after, boy?" The man sounds gruff, mean, like a white Winston Riley.

Knot opens the door. "Hey, mister."

"Where you come from? Who sent you?" Talking the man turns and sticks one hand under the counter. Reaching for a gun probably.

"Hey, mister!"

"Hey mister, *what*?"

To Knot's left is a spangling pinball machine. Lots of colored lights with smeary chrome legs.

"Winston Riley say for me to come get him a fifth of Crown—Crown Royal. Say he pay you come tomorrow, you let me have it on a credit."

"You his boy or what?"

"His boy."

"Well, you tell *Mister* Winston Riley I say he's done charged his last in my place of business less he pays up."

"Sho will, now. I tell him what you say." Knot doesn't move from his spot on the filthy but swept concrete floor, a dip in the center, a well for him to stand in, making him shorter, of less importance. That's how he feels.

"He say send him a jug of Strawberry Hill—wine—if you ain't got the Crown."

To the right of the cooler hangs a faded picture, all oranges and browns, of cowboys on horses chasing Indians toward a cliff. Next to the picture is a circle of feathers with bead tails. And farther on, near the corner, a plank of varnished wood displaying arrowheads of various shapes and sizes.

"Strawberry Hill…wine…,huh?" The man laughs, turns away and goes back to his work, bending, standing, placing brown bottles in the cooler. "What yo daddy think this is, a lectioneering picnic?"

Done, he slams the cooler door shut, stale breath ghosting across the room to where Knot is standing. Then he steps along the counter to his right and a wall of shelves containing glass jugs and bottles, reaches up and lifts down a clear jug of pink liquid. It reads "Strawberry Hill" on the label but looks like watered-down Kool-Aid. "Heah," he says and sets it hard on the bar and slides it down in Knot's direction. It stops midway the counter. "Tell him it ain't on the house and I'll be looking for him to settle up first thing tomorrow morning."

Knot steps forward and reaches for the jug, and the man is suddenly standing with his hand clamped over Knot's hand. "Don't, I'm coming after it and the rest of what he's owing. You too, heah?"

"Yessir."

"You people think everything belongs to be handed out to you. Ain't how it works. Least round here it ain't."

"Yessir."

He lets go of the jug and Knot lifts it with both hands from the counter and turns to leave. He is almost to the door when the man calls out, "You drink that up fore it gets to Riley and ain't my fault. It's going right here in my account book with your name by it." He opens a brown book, same color as the counter, takes up a pen and bows low, ready to write

"It's Cee Ray. That's what I go by." Cee Ray, Knot's number one enemy and the neighborhood pest, just naturally pops to mind. Knot's doing good.

"Ain't never heard of no nigger boy name of Cee Ray in my life." He writes the name down anyway. Then looks up. "Hey, you walked up from the old Watson camp road, didn't you?"

Knot bumps open the door, running with the jug. The man would be watching and see Marge's car coming out—he would know her from her having been in so many times before. Knot is not doing so good. He is doomed.

He runs across the highway, without even looking; he runs and runs, listening to the wine slosh in the jug. Sounds like his stomach when he drinks too much water. Why hadn't he just left and told Marge that the man wouldn't give him the liquor, or even the wine? He starts to throw it out in the scrawny pines and trash on the straw floor. But he's afraid she will send him back and he can't go back.

When he gets to the car, Marge is standing at the rear, leaning up with her elbows on the trunk lid and her hips twisted. Her hair blazes in the setting sun. She is facing the other way. She appears to have been watching for him so long that she's grown weary on her feet and now she's mad though relieved, peeping over her right shoulder. Too proud to walk to meet him, though there's a smile fretting at her purplish mouth.

She stands straight, swaying but fighting to steady herself, not to show how eager she is for what Knot has for her, the jug in his hands. He can see the disappointment— she crosses her arms—when he gets close enough for her to see that she's been sent a jug of cheap wine and not a fifth of fine whiskey.

"Old fart!" she says. "Cheapskate."

Knot, out of breath from running, tells her what the man said—that he knows where Knot came from and he'll be watching for the car when they leave the woods road and head up the highway.

Still standing at the rear of the car, she uncaps the jug, drinking from it, long draughts followed by burps and belches and funny faces as if to show Knot that she's not all that pleased with the vinegary sweet liquid. "Piss," she calls it. She would like Knot to believe that this is medicine maybe. She's not drinking this piss for the hell of it, she'll have him know.

At first, she seems willing to do as Knot suggests and wait till dark to ease the noisy old Ford past the "nosy old fart's" beer joint. But then, in the afterlight of sundown, she orders Knot into the car, starts it and revs the engine, backing up and dropping the rear tires into the right ditch, spinning out and u-turning and almost hitting the ditch ahead with the front tires before snatching the car round and straightening up in a cloud of dust, every bottle and can and piece of junk on the floor and seats of the car rolling and clanking and banging, except for the capped jug clutched in Knot's arms. His neck stings from his head being snatched to and fro and sideways. He has barely missed hitting the windshield.

When they are facing the beer joint, lights on inside now and a blue pickup parked out front, she bears down on the horn with the heel of her hand and swerves onto the highway, then heads north without looking either way.

A white semi roars around them, the driver jake-braking and blaring his horn. The wind from the semi blows the car off on the right shoulder and Knot can see the dry grass in the semi's red tail lights, streaming toward him like floodwater.

But Marge is okay, her angel is watching over her. She rights the car and drives on, straddling the white line, but on the highway at least.

Knot is beyond scared and worried about Winston Riley finding out and putting two and two together and coming up with Knot.

He has money at home and if he could get some back to

the beer joint there would be no reason for the man to tell Winston Riley. No doubt he'll want Winston's business, a good customer like him. Knot doesn't know how much Riley owes but one of the bills in the bag at home should cover it. Forget the change, if change is coming, if Winston owes less than one-hundred dollars. It would have been convenient though if the bank had given the robber some tens and twenties and fives.

Marge drinks till she can't stand up and has to lie on her bed next to Knot's, not exactly passed out but oblivious and on her way. Her long arms are outspread, hands palms-up and hanging off the bed like testing for raindrops. Her fingers wiggle every now and then; her eyes bat, open then closed. But if she's seeing anything it is the stars through the holes in the roof or some picture she's conjuring from the spirits at work in her head.

Her ring of keys, to who knows what—other cars she's owned, keys to houses of the white people she cleans for, maybe—except for the old Ford, are on the table under the front window. Knot has no trouble slipping one of the bills from the paper sack between his cot and the wall, and has in mind to take the car and go back to The Line. But it's dark out and he's not sure he can drive well enough to make it there. He's hungry and tired and he still has homework to do. He listens for Winston Riley next door but hears nothing, just racket all around in the quarters: laughing, crying, shouting. Women calling their children in for supper.

Knot sits at the table under the front window to do his homework, and to watch for Winston Riley to come in from work and kill Cee Ray and not him, if he is lucky.

He is just about to begin writing on his essay—"What Did You Do Last Summer?"—when he finds himself writing instead a note to Winston Riley: "Here's the money for the wine I charged to you at The Line. My sister let me have it. Keep change for your trouble. Your neighbor, Marge

He is just about to fold it and head out, to leave it for Winston Riley with the bill in his pocket, when he changes

his mind and sits again, scratching out the "keep change for
your trouble," and writing instead "Don't forget my change."

He feels almost calm, having done that. This way Riley
will avoid Marge to keep from giving her money back. And
of course Marge will be trying to dodge Winston Riley
because she'll think he's found out about her sending Knot
to get the wine and charge it to him.

Chapter 3

First Saturday morning in October, Knot is up and dressed by 8:00. Mad as he is at Marge for pitching another series of drunks and showing up at school, thus making it unbearable, not to mention back-setting his plans to move in with Aunt Willie and them, he is even madder with Cee Ray Collin, who lives on the northeast end of the curve, shack facing Knot's shack. So far Cee Ray has refused to let Knot ride the new blue bicycle paid for with Knot's own money on loan from the First National Bank.

Winston is being Winston and Marge is being Marge and both are hanging low to keep from bumping into each other—that part of Knot's scheme had worked. In time, they would forget it anyway. Some new spat would replace it. The part about Winston maybe bumping Cee Ray off for charging the wine to him hadn't worked. Really it's just as well, to Knot's way of thinking: this armistice between Marge and Winston allowed for a little peacetime; and if Winston had come after Cee Ray, Knot would likely have no chance whatsoever of getting to ride the bike. He might be buried straddled it. Knot couldn't picture him any other way, even dead.

Cee Ray is one more in a string of characters who has suckered Knot—businessman or Santa Claus. Cee Ray's little sister has some kind of crippling disease and has to scoot on her bottom up and down doorsteps, and Knot who is rich could not in good conscience sleep next to an entire sack of money night after night when just possibly five hundred— only half of one banded stack of bills—might buy her a wheelchair or even a cure.

So, Knot had mailed the bundle of money to her mother from the post office. Then mailed one hundred dollars to one of the other women who had dropped by to borrow a couple of dollars from Marge for food—that woman has seven mouths to feed. Then Knot mailed another hundred to one of the old women waiting on one of the porches simply to see if the money would make her jump up and shout. She bought a TV and relocated to the front room. Another time, Knot was just in the mood to give and sent a hundred-dollar bill to some children who cried after their dog got run over and killed by a car. And for a while there, the going got rough for Knot because all about the quarters people got to questioning who was this Santa Claus sending money. When would everybody else get theirs?

Somewhere even Santa Claus has to draw the line.

Truth is, Knot would have given more money—two or three sweet green bills instead of one, as he's been doing. But he is never sure how much is enough or too much—a dollar seems like a lot to him—and he's worried that he might have none left in the sack to return to the bank.

Take Marge, for example. One bill had been *way* too much. Who can ever figure her? His knowing that she is his blood mother doesn't make him feel son-like; he is still Knot and she is Marge—two people living together in the dank shanty that is of a necessity "home" till Marge quits drinking and cavorting and can merge homes with Aunt Willie. Knot hopes, soon. Until then, *knowing* for Knot is not so much a valuable revelation as an inconvenience. He now feels more Santa Clausy and more responsible than ever for Marge's staying sober.

Knot is just about to go out the front door and confront Cee Ray about the bike bought with the money for his little sister's cure when he sees Sammy Bruce, the white pulpwood boss, drive up to Winston Riley's in his green pickup and start blowing the horn. He blows it twice and you better be standing there, if you work for him. If you don't come out by the second BEEP, you will be out of a job come Monday.

Two honks and Bruce is out of the truck, a stocky blonde man with a red face and a neck like a bull.

Sitting in the truck facing the walk space between the

Riley house and Knot's house is Becky Bruce, Knot's enemy number two and next-to-the-quietest person in the seventh grade and daughter of the loudest person in all of Statenville, maybe even in the world. Her hair is white as canned Christmas snow, so white it lights up the inside of the truck. She sits pink-cheeked, still and dumbstruck, staring out the window, while Winston saunters out to the truck and stands, getting talked to by Bruce. A one-sided conversation except for Winston's halting laugh and his "yassuh, yassuh, yassuh." Just happening up, you wouldn't guess that Winston is the same man who beat up Boots, or the same man who broke up housekeeping after she left.

Behind all the blowing and shouting is a backdrop of insect murmuring and tiny sounds of silence, of waiting for winter and for Bruce to go. In the old live oak just inside the schoolyard fence squirrels spiral up the stout trunk, their claws picking at the brittle bark and their plumed tails dragging branch to branch before they leap higher and higher, up in the lacy green branches toward their drowning in the lake of blue sky.

Knot stands in the doorway and eyes Becky Bruce, Marge's accomplice in making his school-life unbearable. Her daddy is laying down the law to Winston about showing up at his house that morning, trying to borrow money from him on a weekend.

Bruce is standing beside his truck door with his whole body cocked like a spring, shaking his finger in Winston's fear-shrunk face. Winston shaking his head and staring down at the ground, at his booted toes and the gray dirt aglitter with broken glass.

"Next time you come messing around my house, on a Saturday morning, I'm gone beat the hell out of you. Hear?"

"Yassah."

"I pay you on Friday and come Saturday there you are again, begging money."

"Yassah, yassah."

The lecture shifts to the entire quarters, the whole Negro

race. "You people drink up your money, and don't make no difference to me, but when you come begging on a weekend, it does."

"Sho' do now."

"Member when I beat Albert Lewis over the head with that straight chair...?"

"Sho' do now." Winston laughs, nodding woodenly, in perfect agreement. "You have to take him up there to the doc to get his head sewed up, sho did."

"Well, ain't nothing up next to what I'll do to you, you show up at my house again and leave word with the wife you need to see me about some money."

Still laughing, pale around the mouth, Winston says, "Ain't wanting none a that, nawsuh. Ain't that right, Miss Becky?" Not really expecting an answer: like Winston, like Knot, she has heard it all before and has nothing to add.

She gazes out her window, that see-nothing look she does so well.

Last thing in the world Knot needs is somebody else to feel sorry for, but he can't help feeling sorry for Becky, who half the time shows up for school looking whipped. No bruises or cuts, just a solemn whipped quietness. Like a kick-shy dog hoping to escape notice.

In fifth and sixth grades, she used to cry a lot. Go home sick. That kind of thing. Now she merely sits pale and meek and doesn't react even when Miss Lillann, their homeroom teacher, comes down hard on her for not doing her homework. Her terrified response to Marge staggering into her desk had been her sole "response to stimuli." Knot could think of only Becky as an example of Pavlov's experiment with dogs during the teacher's lecture on behavioral psychology. What would be her response to, say, a hundred-dollar bill of the sudden kind, he wonders?

Days when Marge helps out Mrs. Bruce, Becky's mother, she tells horror stories about Sammy Bruce beating everybody up, including the dogs. "Something *wrong* with that man!" she says. Once the living room walls got smoked up by a stubborn log on the fireplace and the wind backing down the chimney. Mrs. Bruce was the one who had put on the log for Becky, so Mrs. Bruce was the one who got the blame. Becky had come home from school "sick," and Mrs. Bruce had set her in a chair before the fire with a quilt over her legs. Sammy Bruce had slapped his wife in the face in front of both Becky and Marge. Which, to Knot's way of thinking, might have had something to do with Becky showing up for school more often now days.

Stories like that, from Marge, make him glad there is no man around the house to beat them up and boss them around—not that Marge is all that different sometimes. According to her, the women she works for are commonly "running into doors." Says, looks to her like they could come up with something besides doors to run into when their men take out their meanness on them.

Cee Ray on the blue bicycle pedals along the curve of the road, looks at Winston and Bruce and cruises on by on that bicycle bought with Knot's money.

No more money for bicycles Knot can't ride. No more playing Santa Claus.

As for pitiful Becky Bruce sitting in the truck, Knot figures white people have their own Santa Claus.

Dogs chase Cee Ray on the bicycle, after noon, but Knot just stands in the middle of the horseshoe road while Cee Ray and the blue bicycle zip along the road that hooks around the fenced-in schoolyard. Zip, zing, not even a rattle on the bicycle—yet. "Hey, man, let me ride."

"Get lost, bucktooth." Cee Ray is standing, pedaling, sitting and raising his feet to the handlebars, then steering with no hands. Up the right side of the horseshoe, paisley oak shadows and then full sun. He fades out of sight, then whips back in again. Dogs yapping and weaving behind and ahead. All colors and breeds of dogs, but mostly mixed breeds.

Hard to believe it is fall, it's so hot. And hard to believe the two boys used to go out in the woods and buddy by competing to see who could pee the farthest.

Knot steps out to the gravel road. "Hey, man," he yells, "I give you a quarter, you let me ride."

"I say, get lost." Cee Ray pedals past and takes to the left side, up the road, past the oak where the road divides and the school buses park Monday through Friday.

Knot doesn't have a quarter, just thousands of hundred-dollar bills. In the paper sack that has been handled so much, it's beginning to feel like cloth. The sack waiting for him to reach beneath the bed next time his heart goes soft with the next woman down on her luck.

This time, when Cee Ray approaches on the bicycle, Knot is standing in the middle of the gravel road with his arms outstretched. Dogs moil around him, licking his hands and whipping his legs with their hard tails. "Let me ride that bicycle, man," Knot says.

Cee Ray brakes and the wheels of the bicycle snake right up to Knot's long bare rabbit-like feet. Cee Ray is sweating, his pretty-boy face up close. "Where that quauta?"

Knot fishes in his shorts pocket, feels the bone handle of the jackknife his now-real granddaddy gave him and draws his hand out. "Ain't got no quarter," he says. "But I give you a hundred dollar bill."

Cee Ray laughs, hops high and one-sided and pedals away. "Teeny-weenie have a hunderd dollar but ain't have no quauta." Laughing.

For something to do, while waiting for Marge to get home that afternoon, Knot sits on the grimy kitchen floorboards and transfers the bundled bills from the clothy paper sack to a crisp new one that brought some of the last groceries into the house. Weeks ago. Since then, Marge has been spending her house-cleaning money mostly on whiskey. Placing the last banded stack of hundred dollar bills in the new sack, sitting before the open door to watch Cee Ray whizzing past on the bicycle, following of dogs yipping at the hypnotic spinning of the wheels, and to watch for Marge to drive up, drunk or sober, Knot figures he's about as close to getting to live with his rich kin as he'll ever get.

He has to find a way to break Marge from drinking.

Knot should be used to the sudden appearance of the naked Crazy Lady, he's seen her so many times before. She just stands in the open doorway, looks formed of upended tree roots, knots and scrapes, dark and dry. She doesn't smell and she doesn't speak and her eyes are gone dull and colorless, blank as her brain. He is terrified, always terrified, that she might step up and touch him and somehow her ugliness and oldness will transfer to him. Usually he closes his eyes, trying to wish her away. Usually he pretends she isn't there and she vanishes as quick as she has come, somehow responding to her daughter calling out, "Mama! Mama, you get back here in the house and you with no clothes on. Don't, I'm gone go get the shurf and have him haul you off to Milledgeville."

The naked woman's daughter is calling her now— hooting, shaming, scolding.

Knot holds up a banded stack of dollar bills and waves it. To see if the old lady has seen the money? To see if the one thing she's likely spent a lifetime beating the bushes for will shock her into sanity?

She doesn't move, she doesn't speak.

"Mama! Mama, you get back here in the house and you with no clothes on." Her daughter's voice growing nearer.

Afraid the daughter will see Knot with his money, he stuffs the bills into the paper sack and starts to get up from the floor. When he looks again at the doorway, the Crazy Lady is gone and her daughter's voice is moving away. "I'm gone go get the shurf and have him haul you off to the insane asylum."

Knot continues stacking his money into the fresh sack. Looking out the door.

The fat insurance man, in a turquoise shirt, matching striped tie and straw hat, is driving house to house along the east curve to collect monthly burial insurance premiums. He parks his long white Buick square in front of Cee Ray's house, gets out and goes up on the sloped, junk-strung porch. Cee Ray's sister in a short red dress scoots out the open front door on her bottom to greet him. Creeping before her, her straight wasted legs work like crabs' claws or flippers. The insurance man ignores her. He hugs the porch post with his left arm and digs a white handkerchief from his hip pocket and mops sweat from his jowly red face, waiting for the lady of the house to come out. His turquoise shirt is darker on the back and under his arms where he has sweated.

Heat steeps the hog shit and sour mud of the pens behind the shanties. It is so still that the moss in the spotty scrub trees along the drab gray crescent hangs limp as wet rags. Long shadows flatten like stencils on the sorry dirt, and the only stirrings are the rambling children and grownups, the dogs and chickens. Lone shouts and duets of radio and TV racket load the hot air to a backdrop of crickets and locusts. Even the burbling of birdsong has dried up in the heat.

Finally Cee Ray's mama comes to the door and leans with her arms crossed. She is pouty-faced, thick and wears a blue head rag, no shoes, and a loose-fitting rose print smock. The insurance man will have to collect from her next month—Knot knows the story. Her old man's out of work, and she ain't got a cent to her name.

Still ignoring the little big-eyed crippled girl at his feet, studying his cheap but dressy clothes and roasting face, he begins shaking his fist at her mama. His threats don't faze her; he'll be back. At last, he labors down the porch steps and gets in his white car, backs out and pulls up at the house to the right of Cee Ray's. Heaves his bloated body from the car and goes up on the porch steps.

Next to the steps a flock of chickens are clucking and pecking at a dead white hen, fluttering her feathers as if she's alive. The pack of dogs following Cee Ray's bicycle along the curve of the road spy the chickens and come running, snarling and scattering the live ones underneath the porch, then fight amongst themselves over which gets the dead chicken. A fat brown German Police is the winner. Holding the prize high in his mouth, the dog marches off toward the woods behind the house.

Again and again, the insurance man gets in his car, backs out and pulls up to the next house, when he could have walked the few yards in between and saved energy and gas. Bushed and bothered, he is hell-bent on collecting insurance premiums that insure fancy funerals. He is a cross between necessary menace and messiah. He gives them calendars and hand fans with sun-streamed pastel pictures of shadowy green valleys, angels and Jesus, but his hand is always out for money. On back of the fans and at the bottom of the calendars are funeral home ads and of course bold mention of the insurance company itself, inducement and reminder of why the people in the quarters have to pay up and stay paid up.

Everybody has burial insurance except Marge, who says she'd as soon be buried in a plain pine box. What need will she have for white limousines, a fine casket and flowers and her dead and dumb to the whole affair, her funeral? Give her flowers while she's living, she says. Knot figures that goes for him too. He has been to funerals with white limousines for the family to ride in from their houses to the church to the graveyard and home again, everybody chanting out the dead person's name and crying whether or not they hated that person when he was alive. Dead, a person is celebrated, even if he's never done anything worthwhile. But only if he has the insurance. Truth is, Knot would like such a funeral. By rights, certainly with all his money, all those one-hundred dollar bills, he should be able to afford it. It galls Knot almost as much as Cee Ray riding past this moment on *the* bicycle that he can't hand over just one bill to the insurance man and be assured of a fine funeral himself.

It had come to Knot's attention last summer, during Aunt Willie's daily readings aloud from newspaper obituaries, that white people "passed away" and Negroes "departed this life." Such eloquence—"departed this life." It bespoke of white limousines and flowers that never died. And yet white people were generally the ones with all the money. Except Knot of course, who has money but cannot afford even a white-man's graded-down funeral, much less the insurance.

He scrabbles up from the wide gapped floor boards, picks up the sack of money and carries it to his cot and slides it underneath, then goes to the dinette table under the left front window and takes the last two slices of light bread from its bag and smears some peanut butter on them. The oblong yellow table, an outcast from some white woman's kitchen, is home to an old radio with the guts ripped out, dirty dishes and sour balled dish rags, the peanut butter and bread, and a lazy army of houseflies. They dart, light and crawl on patrol over the slick bubbled surface. When somebody walks past or stops at the table they buzz into action, then land again as if daring anybody to swat them.

Eating his peanut butter sandwich, Knot goes back to the doorway to watch Cee Ray, whose scissoring legs have to be running hot, even if the bicycle wheels are not.

From Knot's front porch, he can view his sorry circumstances, his daily world: the hook of road Cee Ray rides and rides, where the school buses come and go, its paving up to and past the point of the shanty crescent, gray dirt distinguishing poor black life from white; the backsides of the low red-brick added-on school buildings and the gym, and in between the two, the enticing whirl-a-way and tall metal swing set, all a safe distance from the quarters, set apart by the field of weedy grass running to wire fence— KEEP OUT!

Behind the half-circle of shacks, on the edge of the creeping woods, a pistol goes PAP PAP, somebody hollers out. Then laughs. Only way you can tell whether there's been a deliberate shooting or practice, laughter or crying. Generally shooting is reserved for weekends, though Knot has never understood why. A radio is blaring rock and roll. A child is screaming as if he's on fire. A woman scolds him.

He screams louder, fiercer, maintaining monotone, which means he's simply pitching a tantrum.

The insurance man's white car is gone, but Knot spies a little filmy-black car spiriting up the road where the big oak divides the blacktop west of the school. Car of the new preacher. Coming to scare everybody into going to church on Sunday. Not that many of them ever go; if not for Knot and the older sisters of the church, this preacher would be preaching to himself. Of course, him being young and good-looking, he can probably count on attracting a few of the younger women now. Well, maybe not—most are married and their husbands would be jealous of the preacher. Why does Knot go to church when he doesn't have to? To eat.

But he likes this preacher too. Not only because he calls Knot "young man," rather than Knot, like everybody else, but because he's almost famous. His picture has been in the Valdosta newspaper. Knot has never before met anybody whose picture was in a newspaper. Knot hadn't read the whole piece but Aunt Willie had shown them all the preacher's picture and told them how the preacher had been driving home from church, right past her house one night last summer, when he happened up on a car parked on the railroad track on South Troupe Street. Not straddled the track but running with it, facing an oncoming train. The preacher stopped his car and got out and ran to the car on the tracks— they said in the headlights of his car he could see that somebody was sitting behind the steering wheel with his head back on the headrest. Just sitting there. The train was getting closer, its great light beaming down the tracks and glaring off the front of the car. The preacher had yanked open the door, shouting at the man to get out—an old man, who looked addled, in a diabetic coma. Getting no response from the man, the preacher had pulled him from the car and carried him away from the track a safe distance before the train slammed into it, shoving it along the track, shrieking, scraping and clattering, shedding glass, chrome and car parts and sparking the dried grass each side.

Knot waves, the preacher waves, Cee Ray heading up the car, pulls over to the side of the road and stands, one foot on the dirt and the other on a bicycle pedal. After the preacher has passed, Cee Ray pushes the bicycle across the road, to Knot's yard, gets off and leans it against the edge of the porch floor.

Suddenly, all is quiet in the quarters except for the dogs. No more hooting, laughing, crying and people all over leave their porches and head inside or around back. All except for the old ladies, fanning still, who are as responsible for their families making it to heaven as Knot is responsible for Marge making it to Aunt Willie's.

"That preacher come over here," says Cee Ray, panting, "you tell him you ain't *seen* no wheel. Do, I let you ride it anytime you want to."

"For a fact?" says Knot.

Cee Ray wipes his glistening face on the sleeve of his dirty white T-shirt. Looks up. "I ain't kidding you, man."

"How come?"

"Mama say the good Lord send us money for this wheel," says Cee Ray. "And could be, He send the preacher to take it back."

Knot in the lead, Cee Ray follows with the bicycle, walking it at a trot toward the woods behind Knot's house, staring back to see if the preacher has seen, till they are under cover of tall rustling hickories and scrub oaks. A few turning maples. Knot takes the bike from Cee Ray and leans it against the trunk of a tree.

"It safe here," Knot says. He cannot wait to ride it. Anytime he wants. The blue fenders still gleam, though a bit dusty and smudged. Front wheel jacked at an angle, and for once not in motion, the bike looks even smarter. Exactly the kind of bike he'd like for Christmas, if he could have one. So, next best thing is joint partnership with the owner.

Cee Ray is squatting, his bony knees up to his chest. Eyes huge from watching for the preacher through the gaps in the trees and brush. Knot almost laughs—this is one more stupid black boy.

Knot is high on this miracle wrought by the God-sent preacher, so high that after he leaves Cee Ray to guard the bicycle in the woods behind his house, he sets out on foot with a forged note from Marge and a one-hundred dollar bill toward the fourth house from the left on the east curve where the preacher's black car is parked.

Cee Ray's bike bought with Knot's money freshens his yearning for a bike all his own, and his yearning for a bike all his own freshens his yearning to move in with Aunt Willie by Christmas, and his yearning to live with Aunt Willie freshens his efforts to get Marge sober and respectable and keep her that way. One thing works with the other and against the other, it seems. But he can hope, he can try. Who knows? It might work. Beats writing a Christmas list to a broke Santa Claus.

The preacher has now made his way to the shack two houses to the right of the car and is sitting on the porch with one of the old ladies. He sits in a rocker with one muscled-up leg outstretched and the other folded under it. He has on brown penny loafers, his teeth are white as his shirt and he is matte brown and clean looking, the best-looking man Knot has ever seen and he only wishes Marge looked half that good so the preacher would like her. Men always seem to like her and Knot can't figure it.

He walks by the driver's side of the car, reaching inside the open window without stopping, and drops the envelope with the note and the cash on the plush gray car seat. He keeps walking, circling along the yards of the houses with junk he bought—a smashed black plastic phonograph record, a red velvet curtain with a dog sleeping on it, a rubber doll with one leg twisted backwards, a Superman comic book, and a red toy wagon with a warped tongue—then back to his own front porch. And it is there that he is standing when Marge drives up in her celery and rust Ford from working at the Bruce house all day.

She gets out of the car with a paper sack of groceries,

eyes the preacher walking toward his car, and heads quick toward the front porch. She isn't drinking but Knot figures there's a baby brown paper sack inside the larger sack and it has something to drink in it and you can bet it isn't orange juice.

"He come over here yet?" she whispers.

Knot shakes his head no, watching the preacher get into his car, sit there—reading the note probably—looking back, then circling round and pulling up in front of Marge's house.

"Like I ain't have nothing better to do than talk," says Marge and starts through the door. Brushing her feet at the threshold, she's so nervous.

The preacher stops the car, gets out, stuffing the note with the money into a pocket of his blue jeans. "How you, young man?" he says. His hazel eyes look lit from within. His eyes never stray from Knot's eyes to the paper trash, cans and bottles in the yard. He takes no notice of the flies swarming from the house to the porch to greet him. One lands on his depressed brown nose.

He has broad shoulders and a narrow waist. He looks preacherly enough in a white oxford shirt with a button down collar, but the shirt is packed into slim pressed jeans, neat but young and hip.

Knot doesn't know his name. Everybody just calls him preacher. It's as if nobody expects him to stay for long in their crude little church, north of the Statenville crossing, over Troublesome Creek. No other preacher ever has. The flock of sinners refuses to waste time assigning a name to this preacher. Besides, the general consensus is, any preacher this young and good-looking can't be very long-suffering.

At the doorsteps, he sticks out a huge tawny hand to shake. Knot shakes. He steps up on the porch.

"That you, Preacher?" Marge calls sweetly from inside, then comes to the door, arranging the brown leather belt on her brown skirt waist. Even if she doesn't like the preacher, she fears him, like God.

"How you, Sister Marge?" he says.

"Fine," says Marge. "You must be out visiting this fine fall evening." She talks too loud, as if to hide what's inside herself, just as she is hiding the inside of the messy house she doesn't want him to see.

He laughs, a thunderous rumble in his broad chest. "Making the rounds," he says. "Homecoming tomorrow."

"Pull up a chair there," she says and signals to one of the sprung-bottom rockers and sits in the other one herself.

Knot sits on the porch edge at her crossed knees. Across the fence and the sunny expanse of the baseball field, he sees two little Negro girls spinning round on the whirl-away. Safe and free on a Saturday, they have slipped into the school-world of whites. When the whirl-a-way slows, one of the girls hops off and grabs hold of a hooked bar and runs around and around the dirt trench, pushing it. She hops on, riding with one bare foot dragging.

"The Lord works in mysterious ways his wonders to perform," says the preacher.

"That the truth." Marge hum-laughs.

"Wish we had about a dozen more like you, Sister. I've been praying regular for that new piano and somebody willing to play it. Then up out of the blue, you offer."

"*Offer?*"

"Nobody told me you play the piano," he said, shifting in the chair with his hands on the rocker's arms.

"I don't...I used to. I ain't play in a coon's age."

"You play last time you go to church at Aunt Willie's," Knot says and a bony knee bumps the back of his head.

He turns and looks at her dry-hide face, ashy and tight over high cheekbones. Her hair looks wild. Confusion blooms in her stretched yellow eyewhites. Her mouth is gaped, showing horseshoes of white teeth, young teeth, but the overall picture is a disappointment. Yes, she is too old for this young preacher.

"I only hope you haven't disfurnished yourself and this young man here by donating so much money."

"Money."

"Enough that you volunteer to play the piano for us for Homecoming. Why don't you let me give the money back." He stiffens his right leg and slides one hand in his pocket, pulling out the note and the hundred-dollar bill.

"Homecoming." She sounds stuck. Like a scratched record. "Money." Then, "How much money you say I give?"

Knot sucks in and holds his breath. Sure she will take it.

The preacher laughs. "God loves a humble heart." He leans toward her chair and tries to hand her the folded bill. "And a willing spirit. I know you'll do your best on that old piano tomorrow. Need's tuning is all."

Her eyes never leave the bill in his hand. Finally she waves it away. "Go on, keep it. Make up for all them years I ain't tithed."

"On what you make, cleaning, I figure not much is left over after groceries. Remember the widow's mite."

With every round of response, Knot feels sure she will take the money. But she seems spellbound by the preacher, by her new image through his eyes. Either that or she's too proud or maybe too fearful of God's wrath to take back what she hasn't given in the first place. If Knot is any judge, she's doubly tempted by the Blue Horse tablet paper the note is written on—somebody has signed her name to a note she never wrote, somebody with money. As for playing for homecoming, she says, it's the least she can do.

Knot lets his breath go. A small wind in the airlessness. Almost sundown and still it is hot. He can't wait for the preacher to leave so he can ride the bike before dark.

Marge won't be drinking tonight.

One night out of seven, she won't drink. Now for the other six and a chance for Knot to get rid of some money. Marge has to go to church now, so she cannot drink on Sunday. It's a shame really, because Marge plays best when she is drinking.

She would never own up to it, but that Sunday morning last summer when she had come by Aunt Willie's house while the family was getting ready for church, she was red-eyed with an odor of alcohol slop on her breath. Not even bothering to clean herself up, she put in to go to church with them. In a mood to go to church, she said.

Aunt Willie hem-hawed, trying to dissuade her. Made Marge cry like a baby. But at church, under rapture of the music and chanting and amening, Marge had turned happy, woke up and pressed with the urge to take over the piano Aunt Willie was playing.

She set it on fire. Pumping till it rocked while chording to the foot-stomping and clapping of the congregation. Swaying side to side, practically lifting her bony hips from the bench, she shook a small square bottle of clear vodka from her skirt pocket and didn't even notice it skiddling across the wide board floor to the feet of the fat preacher.

He looked down, then up at the vaulted ceiling, still clapping, and began nudging the bottle with one waxed black shoe underneath the podium.

Aunt Willie was so ashamed, she covered her face with her hands. Holy Ghost or alcohol, Marge had no business showing herself at church.

Late evening, while Marge is in a tizzy, stewing hen for rice and making deviled eggs for church the next day, Knot is riding Cee Ray's bicycle along the open-circle road. Till the sun goes down, and then for a spell in the bruised afterglow of sundown, he rides. Warm air pulsing on his face, he stands and pedals fast, high as the trees on his right, so high he is almost level with the door-sized windows of the red brick schoolhouse on his left. Gravel singing under the wheels of the smooth blue bike. Smells of burning leaves and cooking in the quarters, coming up, calming yellow lights of home. Marge is cooking and she's anything but calm.

Through the open front door Knot can see her stomping from the table to the stove. Slamming pots down. From the looks of things, she could be mechaniking on a car; she could be doing piecework in a sewing factory. She starts out measuring rice in a cup, looks at the cup and dumps it into the pot, then shakes more rice from the bag to the pot as if unable to trust a cup to be a cup. The rice boils over, a foamy white cloud, onto the stove; she jumps back, cussing a blue streak, then up to the stove again and slams a lid onto the pot. From where he is sitting astride the bike, near the porch steps, Knot can smell the rice scum scorching on the stove eye—permanent paste for the roaches to feed on.

Whipping the bike around, Knot can see Cee Ray standing on the road. Same spot where Knot had stood that afternoon. Looking just as duped.

"I ain't say you can ride it all night." Cee Ray steps up to stop the bike.

Knot steers around him and on. For one thing, he doesn't want to go inside where Marge is fussing and cussing to the rhythm of banging pots and pans, and for another, he's not tired yet. Three, he's thinking: what Marge needs is more to do. Get her mind off drinking. Make her so respectable and in demand, she'll be ashamed to drink. Then, home to Aunt Willie's!

But sudden as his money in the sack under his bed, Knot is snapped up by the monster truth of nothing changing in this miserable place. He is moving but not moving. Mosquitoes attack; he itches all over. A slow car driven by a cool-cat type roars past, glass-pack mufflers heard for a mile. The young man is slunk low, brown arm stood in the open window to display a shiny gold watch. Sounds of feet shuffling on the floor inside one of the shanties, shouting, children screaming, and random furniture knocked into walls. Even the cats in the quarters strike up fighting, or breeding, eerie yowling that pretty much sums up a day of life in the quarters.

CR • RO

On the way to church in Marge's Ford, with her at the wheel, Knot is a little edgy about the cold pot of hen and rice on his lap and a lot edgy about Marge playing the piano at church. He can smell the gruel, and it smells like it looks— gummy rice, pale chicken blackened with pepper, bed of dark bones. There is a rim of black scum above the rice line that he can't figure. Marge cannot cook, for a fact, and whether she can still play the piano and her sober is anybody's guess. She said she couldn't, Knot said it was like riding a bicycle—once you learn you never forget. The bicycle analogy came naturally. He's been up riding since seven o'clock, because for all he knows, Cee Ray might take back his offer at anytime. Too, he wasn't about to hang around the house and be questioned by Marge. She needed a drink. Said she wasn't going to church. What did Preacher mean about her *offering* to play the piano? And the money— how much? Where did it come from? What if she simply didn't go and Knot had in fact wasted another one-hundred dollar bill like the money he gave to Cee Ray's mother and it ended up being spent for him a bike?

Marge looks down-right respectable in her pressed white blouse and black pleated skirt as she gets out of the Ford and opens the back car door for the platter of deviled eggs. A pasted smile on her bluish lips. But the round egg-yellow platter with shallow holes for the half eggs trembles as she walks across the grassed churchyard to the back door leading to the dining hall. Here, they will leave the food till after singing and preaching for homecoming dinner on the ground.

Knot gets out with the aluminum pot of chicken and rice and follows. Remembering the old days when Marge would take a notion to quit drinking and go to church. The longest time without drinking he can recall. What if the preacher makes a big public fuss over Marge giving money to the church and everybody starts coming to her for money? Or what if Winston Riley puts two and two together and figures she gave Boots the money to leave him on? He has to know that Marge has money, or access to money, since Knot left the hundred-dollar bill to repay him for the whiskey charged to him. The whole business makes him crazy. His face burns. In the forged note from Marge to the preacher, Knot had started to sign it *anonymous.* But he didn't know how to spell it correctly enough to get the message across that the preacher was here and forever to forget it and yet remember it when Marge was close to lapsing back into her old non-church days.

Marge looks out of place at the old splintered-veneer piano in the small frame church north of the stop light in Statenville. Her broomed orange hair and white shirt tucked into the black pleated skirt fanned on the piano bench. Out of place amongst the pious pumped-up women all frocked up in hats and flowered nylon dresses. Knot thinks maybe he's made a mistake in starting Marge on the road to respectability—hence, Aunt Willie's house—with church. Maybe he should have started her off with PTA, his next considered move, though he cannot fathom her there either.

"One Day at a Time"—that's the tune she is playing on the old church piano, what she always plays at Aunt Willie's house. A sort of motto, Knot supposes, because he's read that's how alcoholics have to handle their break with alcohol. One day off from drinking—church. Another day off—PTA.

Built of concrete block, the church is unceiled, so that the rinky piano music patters off the walls like rain. The preacher sits in his chair on the platform behind the altar, handsome brown face lifted and fingers tapping on the chair arms. Marge and the piano are stationed to the right, up front, cattycorner of the white block wall. It is so warm and close inside that the walls seem to sweat—Marge is sweating. Perfume mingles with smells of mold and hot bodies.

This is not the usual church crowd; it's homecoming and even a few men have come with the women. All fanning with their noses in the air, the women, their men sitting cross-armed and some with their legs crossed over their knees, fiddling with their shoelaces. These are not the sort of women to chum with Marge. Not her friends or even her enemies from the quarters southeast of town where she and Knot live, except for a couple of the mum old ladies from the porches. The church ladies for the most part live near the church or across the highway on the orderly camp of the long-abandoned Samson Powder Company, a large operation that dug and hauled pine stumps to be mined into gunpowder and dynamite. These women are Christian and Marge is heathen. She calls them hypocrites and they call her slut. On the sly. They decorate their porches with old pots and coffee cans of geraniums. Marge decorates her porch with old pots and coffee cans. They whisper over fences after hanging out clothes. Marge doesn't have a fence. They don't cuss drink or smoke or hang out with the men at the beer joint on the Georgia/Florida line. Marge doesn't smoke either.

Knot can tell the new preacher knows all about this divide by the way he plays down Marge's abrupt presence at the piano during announcements. He doesn't mention the money she gave to the church and only thanks "Sister Marge" for "agreeing" to play the piano for homecoming. Uh, oh! Knot should have been specific in his note. He'd meant to offer her services forever to hook her into going to church and staying sober every Sunday.

More announcements: Christmas is coming up and the preacher asks for volunteers to help work with the children on a Christmas play. No takers, and no takers for the role of Santa Claus. Nobody volunteers either to help decorate the church for Christmas. Knot would like to volunteer Marge to play for the Christmas program but he figures he'd better wait, take one day at a time, and see how long she will stay sober; besides he's hoping to go to Aunt Willie's for Christmas. He's hoping that come Christmas Marge will have been sober long enough for Aunt Willie to invite her to move back in. That's all he wants really. Well, that and a bike maybe. Even a used one if he can't find a way to slip a little money to Santa Marge for a new one. Too bad that Santa Claus is a sot and will spend it all on liquor. He has to find another way, another Santa.

Following a sermon about casting stones, the women of the church cast their first stone by not even sampling Marge's chicken and rice or deviled eggs. Neither does Knot. His plate is loaded with field peas and butterbeans, creamed corn, fried chicken and corn bread. But the preacher can't seem to get enough of the strange blackened rice and chicken in a pot. He has seconds and thirds till the bones are piled on his plate. Marge sloughs off his compliments and sits at one of the long tables, alone, timidly nibbling a fried chicken back.

The lofty, crude dining hall is abloom with food, flowers and laughter. Everybody talking at once, sampling the many vegetables, meats and desserts. Chocolate layer cake a foot high. Meringue pies—chocolate, lemon, coconut— disappearing like suds on water.

Marge licks her fingers, pushes her chair back and takes her paper plate to the trashcan next to the tea and ice table. Then looking once around at Knot, she heads for the side door, leaving her pot and platter and Knot, and exits as she has entered.

Chapter 4

It's not even Christmas yet. It's just November, two weeks from Thanksgiving. Not late enough in the season for hot fires in the yards and fireplaces of the quarters and leaves in the woods to shed their green and drop. But already fires like blooming yellow-throated red lilies grow in front of the shacks, and the children weave in and out in the dusk on their Christmasey new wheels, tricycles and bicycles and a spanking red wagon, all barefoot and ragged in the sunless cold.

Knot stands on Marge's porch in solitary bleakness, waiting for her old rust-and-celery Ford to show at the start of the paved crescent road, for it to pass the redbrick schoolhouse and the weedy schoolyard. His double-crossing enemy Cee Ray is showing off his new blue bike along the bight of road between the east and west corner posts separating the school grounds from the quarters. Every time Cee Ray gets in front of Knot's stakeout, he brakes and yanks up on the handlebars and the front wheel bucks up spinning. Then he is off again.

It drives Knot crazy: here he has bought his own enemy a bike while he himself remains bikeless. Here he has made a deal with Cee Ray to help hide the bike from the preacher in exchange for riding privileges, anytime Knot wants to (after school one day he came home and Cee Ray was riding the bike and not speaking to Knot). He has bought all these toys for the other children, though not exactly from the heart, and can't even play with them. Has all that money just inside and can't spend it. He would like to tell somebody—Cee Ray, specifically—that he, Knot, is the one responsible for his having the bike. But he can't. What he can do, what he has in mind to do, when he gets to Aunt Willie's in Valdosta for Thanksgiving, is to arrange for Santa Claus to leave a new bike for his cousin Lee, and later Aunt Willie, in one of her generous fits, will pass down Lee's old bike to Knot like the worn-to-frazz Levis and moth-gnawed red ski sweater he is wearing this very minute.

He will take the sack of money with him when he goes for Christmas, leave it in the alley where he found it, and be done with the whole business. After making his whole new family richer playing Santa Claus.

Looking around at all the flashes of color and listening to the high happy squeals of the children, and even the monotonous scolding of the women making supper, Knot feels like God, having made it all possible and wishing he could take it all back.

Two doors down on Knot's right, the smiling woman named Mae is sitting out at her new white wrought iron patio table set with her feet up in one of the dainty white chairs while not two yards away her small brown dog lies dead and bloating. Blow flies buzz over him; the smell is so ripe with rot it is almost sweet. The money for the patio set came from Knot after Mae fell on a broken cola bottle and it gouged a jagged hole in the flesh of her right thigh.

What happened was, a couple of weeks before, one afternoon, a man collecting for her TV set bought on time had showed up at her front door. Not having the money for this month's payment, she had sneaked out the back. Heading for the woods with her head down and her feet ascurry, hands tucked between her thighs to prevent her thin blue skirt from flapping and drawing attention, she had almost made it across the thrash-strung gray dirt when the collection man on his way to his car had spied her and set out running with his tan vinyl zippered moneybag, shouting for her to stop or else.

Or else, would generally mean that he would be picking up the TV set for non-payment. But seeing her slipping across the yard in that sly animal way for some reason set him off, made him *have* to show her that he had spied her and he would get his money if he had to take it out in her hide.

Looking around at the man behind her, still skimming the dirt with her feet and ducking low as if he might shoot her, she stumbled onto a hillock of burnt trash and glass and sprawled face forward. The man stopped running, waving his tan vinyl moneybag in the air—"Serves you right for running." Then he went on to his car.

Just so happened that the preacher was visiting the quarters, had seen the whole thing and ran over and helped May up and took her to the doctor in Valdosta for a tetanus shot and stitches.

It was the blood soaking into the thirsty dirt, that trail of helpless-human blood, from the burn pile to the preacher's car tracks before Mae's shack that had stung Knot into sneaking over and placing the money atop her blaring TV— another one hundred dollars subtracted from his money sack.

Cee Ray at the split in the road and the oak island comes speeding up the road ahead of Marge's Ford, pumping left and right and bearing down on the blue bike's front end with his little-boy ass up in the air. He stays about a car length ahead of her, dodging in and out, left and right, and Knot suspects she's half a-mind to run over him and claim it was an accident.

While she pulls up in front of the shack and gets out, Cee Ray performs his bucking-bike act, then speeds away laughing.

"Be shamed of yo'self," she yells at him and slams the car door with a cocked hip. "Knot let you ride his wheel, he have one."

Knot mentally corrects her heavy Gullah as she stalks mumbling toward the porch. "I swannee to goodness, I wisht whoever be handing out money for all this stuff go broke. Younguns ain't even go to school nomore."

Knot is glad Cee Ray has quit school to ride his bike. He had had a bait of his loping about, hands in his pockets and grinning, face crusted over with sleep and snot, and not a silly thought in his square head that didn't leak out of his mouth. Two years older than Knot, Cee Ray seemed to have lingered in the seventh grade only to make Knot crazy when he got there.

Bruce's green pickup slows on the curve and halts before Marge's porch, center point of the quarters' crescent, and pulpwood hands in tarry dried-sweat clothes hop off or step down and lope off in different directions with their dinner buckets and paper sacks.

Becky Bruce is riding with her daddy again. She looks out the window at Knot, then hangs her head and they drive away.

Becky is in Knot's English and history classes, as well as homeroom. Knot is the one always raising his hand with answers and is hated for it. All except by Becky, who he thinks of as that little white-headed girl who doesn't care one way or the other. She either doodles or pleats notebook paper into fans, waiting for school to be over. But Knot figures she is smart, smarter than him, because unlike Cee Ray she keeps what she knows to herself. She and Knot never speak. And not just because of the fit she had pitched when Marge had showed up drunk at school.

Winston Riley heads for his porch, whistling, not ten feet away, and doesn't even speak. Slams the front door and the TV blares out laughing like lots of family and friends surprising him with some sort of homecoming celebration.

Marge starts through her front doorway, humming a laugh because Winston is alone, maybe lonely, with Boots and the children gone and she is enjoying it. Makes up for the depressing business of her house being overlooked after receiving only $100, as if whoever is sending the money knows how she wasted hers and is punishing her (money given to the church in her name counts only as a curse). Everybody in the quarters knows that some saint is sending money and they all figure that Marge alone has been left off the list. Though she will do anything in the world for anybody, as soon as the neighbors quit needing her they accuse her of butting in. Especially the men. Like Winston Riley.

Just as Knot figured—or hopes—Marge and Winston have forgotten all about the liquor-charging episode. About who owes what to whom. He hopes.

Cee Ray rides past on his bike. Knot turns his back to deprive him of an audience.

"Marge," he says, stepping inside and watching her shed her dull black walked-down shoes near her bed, "you call Aunt Willie and them about Thanksgiving yet?"

"Do it tomorrow," she says, kicking her shoes under the bed with one warped brown foot. "Ain't no time today and all that fussing over Thanksgiving at Miss Dixie's. Got the whole bunch coming in and we been making fruitcake the day long."

"Let's make one for Aunt Willie," he says, knowing better. Marge cooks and cleans where she works each day, so she's not in the mood.

Knot is starving. Is tempted to step out on the porch again to whiff the air loaded with frying. "What's for supper?" he says, sitting in the chair at the yellow dinette under the fly-specked, smeary window to the left side of the room.

"Whatever," she says. Meaning canned soup. There is a cold smell like rancy lard to the shack and Knot would like something fried to warm it.

"Me and you needs to have a little talk before Thanksgiving," she says. She sits in the chair across from him. Arms crossed on the table and looking out.

On the porch, a dog is scratching, knucklebones knocking furiously on the floor. Houseflies buzz in and out the door and light on the table as if listening in.

Does Marge know about the note volunteering her to play for homecoming at church? Worse, does she know where the money she gave to the preacher came from? Even worse, has she seen the sack full of money by his bed? No, she'd be drunk as a skunk right now if she had.

"Sister and them don't know you mine for real yet." A fly lands on Marge's arm. She fans it away to Knot's arm propping up his chin.

He feels stunned, sapped, cold. "But you're gonna tell em?"

"Not yet," she says and rolls her head side to side, loosening her shoulders. "Bad enough they take me for a drunk. You know?"

"Ain't no reason we gotta tell you been drinking again. I was hoping come Christmas we'd been moving in with them."

She eyes him. Her eyewhites are off-white and specked, like freckles. "I know you got your heart set on being a real family with them but you have to wait."

"How long?"

"I don't know. When the mood hits me, I reckon."

Marge's moods control everything, he thinks. Except his money. His money, which seems never to go down in the sack. So far it hasn't helped much to make his life easier or better but it's something. Power maybe, he figures, but through the window he sees Cee Ray riding and riding and that kills that thinking too. Merry Early Christmas!

ርያ • ኤ

On Sunday before Thanksgiving, freezing drizzle, Knot sets his mind to try and convince Marge to go to church with him. After going only a couple of Sundays, she had quit, said she figured she'd played back however much money that busybody gave in her name, she had suffered those hypocrites for free. But Knot has in mind to make her respectable enough that when she does tell Aunt Willie and them that Knot is hers, she will be forgiven. Plus, Knot is hungry. Can almost taste the church ladies' chicken and dumplings and greens and chocolate layer cake. Sister Alva makes the kind with a dozen thin layers, each cemented with hard glazed chocolate that has been poured over the top layers. He can hear the rain pecking on the tin roof; he will need a ride to church.

Marge is sitting on the edge of her bed, hung over and scratching her head. A scrapped-together quilt, hand stitched by her sister, draped over her shoulders and half covering her wasted legs. Knot recognizes a scrap from Aunt Willie's white apron with embroidered yellow daisies and a gray-striping bed-ticking scrap from the old gray granddaddy's flat-topped cap. Other scraps from Judy Beth's homemade dresses, a rose flower square from a curtain that used to hang in the front parlor, he thinks. That's how long Knot has known the family, that's how much he deserves to be one of them for real now.

Marge's gold stiff hair flops like palm fronds in the wind as she scratches at the roots. "Lawd Jesus, it's cold," she says in a burned out voice. Last night, she'd drunk up her earnings for the week. There is not a single thing in the house to eat, and she's feeling guilty.

Knot has built a fire in the wood heater but so far it hasn't warmed the airish room. While the heater walls tick, heating up, he makes her coffee in the blue speckled pot. Rain leaking down the stove flue spits at the fire.

Lately, when Preacher has been by to visit Marge she has been gone, or playing gone. Hence, Knot has really gotten to know the man from spending so much time talking on the porch with him. He knows that his name is Richard Troutman, that he has no hair on his legs between his pants cuffs and socks and that he lives in a house on the old Samson Camp with his elderly grandmother.

Every time Knot thinks maybe the preacher is working up to the newspaper story, he switches subjects, fishing for information about Knot's neighbors: who lives where, what do they do for a living, who is sick and what happened to so and so who lived in that empty house over there?

Knot pours a thick white mug of coffee for Marge and takes it to her. The rich chicory scent makes him crave toasted bread with butter, like at Aunt Willie's. The two seem to go together and with it the memory of easy summer mornings and the soft light raying through the back-porch windows where the cats sun. Light and sunshine and Aunt Willie laughing and good-naturedly baying orders. The old gray granddaddy would sit at the kitchen table, reading his newspaper, and grin. His bare gums—before he snapped in his false teeth—made him look faultless and pure. Teeth get stained with food and drinks, cankered with tar and scum, but gums look healthy red and clean.

Marge's hands shake as she reaches for her old crazed mug. Uses both hands to keep from spilling the steaming black coffee onto her legs. "I wisht I had a nickel for ever time I let you down." Her gold-cast eyes stare up at him as she takes swigging sips from the cup. She smells of cigarette smoke and whiskey. She holds the cup in both hands and lowers it to the quilt on her lap. "What you have for supper last night?" She doesn't look at him now but crosses her scaly dry feet.

"Dab of this and that."

"Hum," she says and sips the coffee. "Didn't know they was any *dabs* in the house." She laughs low. Sounds like rubbing dry corncobs together, her voice and her feet.

"I'll eat at church today."

Dinner is always served at church after preaching, not as much as at homecoming but the loyal old church ladies are Knot's favorite cooks anyway. He goes back to the heater and twists the T-shaped lever on the damper. The stove flue is red as a lit Santa Claus face and radiates a fierce metallic heat.

"That rain I hear?" Marge cocks her head, scratching.

"Yes ma'am, and it's *some* cold."

"I'll take you and let you out but I ain't going to no church no more."

"I prechate it," Knot says and begins going through the hanging clothes and empty clanging wire hangers on the broomstick-rod to his right, cattycorner of the plyboard wall between the kitchen area and the closet-size, rusty bathroom, looking for a shirt to wear. Mostly brown and black skirts and white blouses, belonging to Marge. Like uniforms. The women she works for cannot claim that she's not neat and clean when she goes to their houses to cook and do housework. He finds a thin, short-sleeved brown plaid shirt handed down from his cousin Lee. It feels soft and warm but is missing a couple of buttons. But that's okay because he'll have to wear his silver football jacket over it anyway, another hand-me-down from Lee.

"Reach me a shirt and skirt, will you?" Marge swigs her coffee. "Bad enough I starve you. Can't let you go shame-faced to eat at church and me, a old sot, hiding out here."

Driving along the crescent of the quarters, they pass one of the shanties like their own, but bearing witness to having come into money—a TV glaring from the front porch. A preacher is preaching on the TV but only a tired dog lies watching from its bed of a red velour robe near the doorway. Knot wishes Marge at least owned a hat, maybe a red one. Some color.

A giant Busch beer bottle rolls under his dirty white tennis shoes; he kicks it beneath his seat and it clinks against a nest of beer cans. The car smells of puke and whiskey, is so cold that Knot has to tuck his hands inside his jacket and scrunch his neck into the stretchy knit band of the collar.

Rain taps on the car's hood and sheets down the windshield where the wipers sweep it aside in twin rivulets. The world outside looks gray, wet and frozen, in spite of the smoke curling from the brick chimneys of the facing frame houses along 94.

Marge's long brown fingers grip the steering wheel and she is leaning forward as if leaning forward will get her there and back quicker. Her black wool coat is speckled with lint.

"Look in the glove box there and hand me that bottle," she says. "Just a taste to warm me up and make me play better."

He rams his fist into the rectangular door of the glove compartment on his side of the dash and it drops like a shot. Inside are two half-pint whiskey bottles, one empty, and the other nearly full. Knot recognizes the clinking of the bottles as part of what he'd suspected was the Ford's increasing battle-hymn of engine noise.

He hands her the bottle with the wobbling amber liquid; she unscrews the cap and drinks, sitting at the red light, then hands it back to him almost empty.

Looking out the window at the rain beating like wind on the yellowing vines and exaggerated elephant ears climbing up the steep banks of Troublesome Creek, he searches his jacket pockets for a Life Saver for Marge's incriminating breath, maybe some other candy given to him by one of the church ladies. Sometimes candy will lodge in the inverted tits of his pockets where strange lint grows. But he can feel only the folded one-hundred dollar bill he will place in the collection plate at church this morning.

"They won't be there this morning," he says.

"Who won't?"

"Them ladies treat you like dirt. They don't come when it's cold and rainy. Ain't a bit of heat in the church."

Perked up from the whiskey, she barks, "I ain't studying them hypocrites."

"Got a new piano though."

"Who the hell be giving all this money?" She doesn't ask it so much as say it. "Me? I look like a woman with money?"

He wishes he hadn't said anything, because she is leaning toward him now, preaching to him, not even noticing the mean wet-red semi meeting them. "I have the money for a piano, I get my ownself one. I have the money for a piano, I ain't gone be carting my boy off to church so he can eat."

At the boxy white block church, Sister Alva's small green car is backed up to the side door on the south end. Dressed in black, same as Marge, she and her sister Martha Nell are bundling boxes of food from the trunk to the dining hall. Both old and decrepit and a bit on the stout side, they hobble fast through the drizzle with large purses dangling from their arms and umbrellas low over their heads. Marge parks in front, facing the church house because she has no food, and just sits there—probably of a mind to take another sip of whiskey—while Knot gets out of the car and skips across the dead wet grass to help the ladies carry in their dinner.

Both ladies look stuffed like their pocketbooks. They fuss about spilled pot liquor and sobbing cornbread while Knot smiles, toting boxes into the cold, closed fellowship hall.

When he comes out for the last box of food, he sees a few other loyal ladies hurrying through the drizzle of the churchyard. No sign of the uppity-ups who hate Marge. No sign of Marge either, but her car is parked where it was and the windshield is fogged, meaning she has either just gotten out or is still sitting their drinking and breathing. If she's breathing, she is drinking.

Inside the fellowship hall, Sister Mary Nell with rhinestones of rain on her black felt hat and glasses is hovering over a cardboard box of foil-tented food on the long brown table nearest the door. She picks up a platter and sets it on the table, lifts the foil and takes out a crusty golden biscuit, still warm, and a crisp brown slice of thick lean bacon and hands it to Knot. "Now you eat in a hurry, you hear?" She pats the crown of his springy wet hair. "We got a brand new piano and they waiting on us in there. Good of Sister Marge to come play again." She walks off toward the Sunday school wing, wringing her hands, then tucks them into the opposite sleeves of her black coat to warm them.

Knot sits in one of the chairs, eating. At least, he now knows that Marge is for sure playing this morning, but in what condition? Outside the windows the pecan trees drop soggy speckled leaves to the ground. The sky is gray and swollen and the rain is now falling harder. In the far left corner of the long fellowship hall, the old mahogany-painted piano sits dumb—a few sagging sprung keys bear witness to its heyday in the main part of the church, which now sounds like a jook. Marge at the piano, loosened up and raring to go.

Miserable, cold, wet and worried, as he is, Knot feels satisfied, on the verge of happy. He has never tasted anything at once so perfectly salty and crispy and soft and crusty as the buttermilk biscuit and bacon. He eats fast and longs to sample some more from the platter on the table behind him, but Marge is playing "When the Saints go Marching In," signal for the choir to enter through the door to the right of the pulpit.

Sister Alva and Sister Martha Nell are already in their maroon choir robes, waiting for Knot and two other ladies when he gets to the dim little room directly behind the plaster pulpit wall. He goes over to the mothball-smelling closet on the north wall and yanks his robe down from its wire hanger and slips it on, glad for the warmth, then feels in the pockets of his jacket for the hundred-dollar bill and makes the transfer to his robe pocket unnoticed.

The other two ladies come through the back door with food, put it on the table and go for their robes, all four women clucking like hens through clattering teeth about the new piano. Of course, it was sent by God; to think otherwise would be sacrilege. Knot never has to worry about them questioning where the money comes from—anything connected with the church is a gift from God. They are betting on God sending the gas man before next service. How could Knot let them down? Or poor old drunk Marge, in there playing her heart out. Only problem is, she isn't sober. He'd believed going to church would keep her sober. Now what?

Marge sounds stuck on the marching-saints tune, one foot hammering the floor. The choir of four old ladies and one young boy lines up for the processional into the main part of the church.

"Look like ain't gone be no heat this winter," says Sister Alva. She speaks like a man, looks like a man, all robust and cheery with huge eyes and lips; her hard mannish body fills out the pleats of her robe.

"Have to bundle up," says one of the other women—a late-comer with a cream felt hat and pearl pin.

"The Lord will provide," says sweet Sister Martha Nell. "Just like the new piano and Sister Marge to play it."

"How's her flu?" Sister Alva asks Knot.

"Long as she stay on her cough medicine, she fine. Make her sleepy though."

Please Lord don't let Marge be too drunk; don't let the preacher announce that he suspects it is Marge again who has given the money for heating gas, just let him know.

When they march through the door into the church, they have to pass behind Marge to get to the choir loft to the left of the pulpit. The preacher in a white shirt, red tie and dark suit is standing over Marge, talking to her and trying to interest her in the maroon hymnal in his hand. She snaps her head back and laughs, while still framming her long fingers on the keys, while pumping the pedals with her rundown black work shoes—she has forgotten to wear her good shoes.

"My God!"

To Knot she looks like Jezebel must have looked. The woman behind him, wearing the cream felt hat, is the one who has said My God! he realizes, and believes her outraged cry to the Lord has nothing to do with Jezebel's shoes, but everything to do with her hacking laugh and gold head cocked at the preacher and more than all that the sour-mash smell of alcohol blowing from her mouth and maybe even seeping from her pores.

No sheet music on the pale walnut, spindled stand before her, no hymnal, she is playing by heart. There are five women in the congregation with children, but not a single man and none of the snooty church ladies from homecoming. Children coughing, being shushed. White vapors of their warm breath rise like smoke from the pews each side of the main aisle. Gray light from outside fills the many metal-framed windows along two walls, and rain sliding down on the north side.

The choir is standing with their maroon hymnals opened to the first song of the service—a Christmas song—waiting for Marge to quit playing the song she is stuck on. Finally she stops, giving the preacher and his hymnal full attention, and the choir and congregation are so still they can hear the rain pecking at the window panes and the preacher whispering to her.

Finally she takes the hymnal and places it on the stand, open to the page where he has left it. Then like anybody sober playing piano at church, she plays the prelude to "We Three Kings." Knot is sweating now, feels like the sun is on his face. The preacher in his chair, between the choir loft and the piano, waits for the choir to finish singing, then stands and asks everybody to bow for a word of prayer.

All is well till he drops to one knee and begins earnestly beseeching the Lord. Thanking Him for the rain and other dubious blessings including these good ladies braving the cold and wet to gather and worship as the bible commands.

At first, nimble creeping sounds like a night possum on the prowl can be heard from the corner where the new piano stands. Then the solid flat clap of a hymnal sounds on the wood floor and the piano bench slides back a foot or so, followed by a series of *glug-glugs*.

The preacher continues praying, using up about half his planned sermon to give Marge time to cap and put away the bottle under the lid of the bench, which closes with a *whoosh* like the lid of a coffin as the preacher ends with an amen.

Everybody joins in on the next hymn. And the next.

While Marge plays the piano, Knot sidles out of the choir loft, to take up the collection, careful not to step on the ladies' toes. The only time he feels loveable and cute, which generally results in a reflexive springing gait, is when he's around the sweet church ladies, but Marge is the focus today. He shouldn't have made her come. He should have walked in the rain, let her stay home and drink instead of coming to church to drink. His plan isn't working anyway. As for her and the preacher falling for each other, Knot cannot believe he even considered it. He goes to the altar and takes the red-felt bedded pewter collection plate and begins walking up the center aisle, sidling again between pews left and right for the scattered women to place their donations in the plate. Up front he starts to bypass Marge but instead goes over and holds out the plate before her. She looks at it, quits playing and takes it in her right hand and places it on top of the piano, and begins playing again. She doesn't even look at him while he slips from his choir robe pocket the one-hundred dollar bill and places it on top of the nickels and dimes and a single dollar bill while picking up the plate. Then he strolls over to the pine altar platform and hands it around the podium to the preacher in his chair with his hands folded in a steeple, praying.

After the next song, Marge seems to close down, dozing with her straight stiff back to the preacher and the choir.

During announcements, the preacher stands. His cream brown face suffuses in the cheap hanging light over the podium. The whites of his eyes are so clear and bright they look glassy, tears like lodged specks of crystal in the corners of each eye. He seems to be on the verge of crying but he is smiling, lips drawn back exposing those perfect white teeth.

He asks prayer for the sick, the sad and suffering, naming names. His old grandmother is growing weaker, but praise the Lord she's not in pain. He pauses, his chest appears to swell. "I know you'll all be glad to hear that there's an angel among us." His head turns toward Marge at the piano, still sitting stiffly, on hold. "She has just donated another hundred dollar bill, so looks like we'll have gas for heat come Thanksgiving Sunday."

Suddenly, it seems to register with Marge that he is looking at her, that he is speaking of her. Slowly, stiffly, she turns on the bench, eyeing him back. Then she points to her chest and begins shaking her head. Not me, mister. Not me.

The women in the choir are shaking their heads too, bearing down on Marge with spite-quickened eyes. Everybody starts hissing. The woman who earlier said "My God!" when the choir had filed in says, "Money made flat of her back, you can bet on that."

Marge is foot-stomping mad on the way home. "I been tricked," she says to Knot. While Knot was eating in the dining hall, she'd been drinking black coffee and is sober as any of the few and random drivers behind the wheels of cars out for a Sunday afternoon drive. "Where I gonna get no hunderd dollars? How anybody gone lay it to me and me a cleaning woman? I ask you, how?"

Knot tries for a frozen face, is too cold to look otherwise. But he is full, so full his stomach aches and sweet tart lemon-cheese cake feels tanked in his throat.

"Tell you what I think"—she slaps the steering wheel with the flat of one hand. "What I think is that preacher be the one with the money and acting like it me to keep me coming back to play that new piano he buy. For that matter, where that money come from I get in the mail a while back if it wadn't from him? Tell me that. And that TV there on that porch..."

They are almost home, passing the cold bleak shack with the TV on the porch. The rain has slacked off and a raw damp cold is taking its place.

But she doesn't really seem to be asking, just spouting off. Because, for a fact, who would suspect Knot, poor lil ole thrown-away Knot? Who would suspect Knot when up ahead his double-crossing enemy Cee Ray is taunting him with a new bicycle?

Done with accusing the preacher, for the moment, Marge begins naming everybody she knows who could be the cause of her own ruination. Problem is, not a one of them has any money. Not as far as she knows, and she would know, because as she says, money shows, sudden money most of all. It's something a man or woman either one can't help but show off and it's why the Bible says a rich man has as much trouble going to heaven as a camel through the eye of a needle. Something like that.

Now knot has to get rid of the money or wind up in hell. But hell or not he's going to hang on to it till after Christmas when he's betting on getting Lee's handed-down bicycle. That's his plan—to get money to Aunt Willie to buy a new bike for Lee and pass his old one down to Knot.

ය • ෙ

Boots comes back the day before Thanksgiving, loaded down with bellering children and about as bedraggled and shock-eyed as when she left.

It is Wednesday and when Knot gets home from school Marge is standing out on her porch mouthing off at Winston Riley. He cusses at her, yanks his fist at her as if pulling a chain on a train whistle. That kind of thing. Then both, mumbling to get in the last word, go inside.

The quarters are alive with children home from school for the two-day holiday, and the old women are out cropping Thanksgiving collards in the patches next to their shanties. Cee Ray is keeping the road hot with his bicycle. Now and then an old car with its tailpipe dragging or a flatbed truck passes, packed with women, children and men who are greeted by the quarters' dogs—kinfolk coming for Thanksgiving.

But only Winston Riley is home from the pulpwoods, and the entire quarters is about to learn why.

Bruce's green pickup motors up the road and stops at its usual central spot before the house where Marge and Knot are inside, listening to Boots and Winston next door quarrelling over where she has been, who she took up with while she was gone. He says he has a good notion where she got the money to leave on.

The weather has warmed up to rain for Thanksgiving and the front doors are open and the squirrels are barking in the live oaks just over the fence separating the school grounds from the quarters. Had the oak grown the other side of the fence or had the fence been strung on this side of the oak, the Negroes in the quarters still would have been borrowing shade from somebody white who Knot doesn't know but knows he would look like the short quick-speaking man who can cut off their water and kick them out of their house if Marge doesn't pay, first of the month; or the man loaning them shade would look like this stocky muscled-up pulpwooder striding across the yard toward Winston Riley's house, leaving his little timid white-headed girl in the truck, looking out. So mad he is red-faced, the pulpwooder, belching up cuss words like they'd been stuck to the point of choking him.

All gets quiet next door. Boots steps out on the porch, barefoot, children clinging to her long red gathered skirt. She has on an oversized gray T-shirt with a silver star on front and some faded maybe-political writing that means nothing to her anyway.

Bruce stands before her, a few feet out from the gnawed-wood doorsteps, one work boot forward and his hip cocked in heavy blue jeans with rolled cuffs. "I come to get what Winston Riley's owing me for cutting that truck tire."

"He ain't here," Boots says.

"Uh oh," says Marge and gets up from her watch at the table and goes to the doorway, holding to the doorjamb each side.

"Ain't, huh?" the pulpwooder says to Boots.

The little boy who had slept with Knot the night Winston beat Boots up is bare-chested and pop-bellied in dirty white drawers down to his knees. He ducks underneath her roomy skirt. She pushes him away. The other children dart inside as the neighbor children and dogs gather to see what's up. Not another grownup in sight. The women cropping collards and the visitors have vanished.

Even Cee Ray and his bicycle are nowhere to be seen.

"Well, in about a minute from now," says Bruce in a level tone, "I'm gone find out if he's gone or not."

Marge sashays out on her porch with her arms crossed and leans into the porch post over the doorsteps, hip-slung and sassy like she gets with Winston Riley. Or the new preacher if he catches her on off-days. "She say he ain't home, he ain't home."

"I was you," says the pulpwooder, "I'd be heading out the back door bout now. Course, for all I know that SB could be laid up in there. Ain't that right?"

"He ain't but if he was, it be my own business. Besides, ain't got no back door no more." True. Marge had long ago boarded up the back door and piled clothes and junk in front of it. Why, she cannot recall precisely—could be she needed more space for the old rags and knickknacks palmed off on her by the women she worked for. Too, with only one door, she finds it easier to monitor the goings-on in the quarters and mind off the monkeys when she is drunk.

"He go off riding with some man," Boots says to Bruce and peels off another child grafted to her leg beneath the frivolous red skirt.

Marge holds her post and casually sticks out a slim foot with the walked-down black shoe dangling. "You go on now," she says to Bruce. "Don't, we gone have to call on the law."

"The law! Hah!" Bruce laughs, head thrown back and hands on his waist and that thick brown belt that serves both as weapon and device for holding up his pants. "Tell you what, gal," he says, no longer laughing, "seeing as how you so sassy, don't look for no work at my place no more."

"I ain't never work for you *no how*. The missus who I work for. Ain't that right, Miss Becky?"

The little white-headed girl in the truck locks eyes with Knot in the doorway of his shanty. Finally they have spoken after their homeroom teacher put them both on a committee for the Needy Children's Christmas Fund (Knot had long since forgiven her outburst the day Marge showed up drunk at school). "Where are they, you reckon?" Becky had asked Knot as if asking herself. "Who? The needy children?" Knot said. "Yes. I don't know of any needy children hereabouts, do you?" Knot had had to think about that. "You mean *hungry*, right?" "Whatever." Becky shrugged her shoulders and turned to see if anybody in the classroom had seen or heard her talking to Knot and went back to doodling—big-headed fish formed of cursive S's, enough fish to feed the multitudes.

"You better get on out here this minute, you S.B. I'm gone have your ass for cutting my truck tire." Done with Marge, Bruce is now shouting louder at the hidden Riley, shaking his fist, then flattening his hand and making chopping motions to demonstrate. "I seen the axe mark right after you headed out. I give you a job and what do you do? Pay me back by cutting a new truck tire."

Blond arms cocked and elbows pumping he walks fast across the foot-tracked gray dirt of the run-together yards to his truck, kicking aside an Orange Crush bottle in his way. His head is swinging and his bull neck is red. Not a man to be messed with.

Boots and the crying children in the doorway back into her house. The neighbor children scatter but the dogs waggle around Bruce's truck. One pisses on his left front tire. Becky Bruce only sits there, staring straight ahead—not at Knot now, but at nothing. Just staring because she doesn't know what else to do, staring because she has eyes. Sammy Bruce says something to her as he yanks open the door on the driver's side, he says "nigger," he says "son of a bitch" but she doesn't even flinch. It's as if his deafening voice has no effect, or maybe she's lost interest like she lost interest in the needy children she'd asked Knot about at school.

"Go out the back way. Get the shurff," Marge says in a sucked in breath. She doesn't look behind at Knot but he knows she is talking to him.

Last thing he sees before he goes is Sammy Bruce crouching behind his open truck door aiming a rifle or shotgun at Winston Riley's shack and Becky Bruce's pale blue gaze fixed ahead.

Knot is about half way to the open window over his cot when Marge dodges inside, standing big-eyed with her back pressed to the narrow wall space between the left front window and the open door. Arms down by her side and not moving. Her hair looks lightening struck. Knot tramps across his unmade cot and with his right foot shoves free the tacked, wood-framed window screen, rigged for quick escape. It pops loose from its tacks and slides along the brittle gray wall to the ground. Knot sticks his foot through, straddling the sill, one leg out the window and head ducking to keep from hitting the double framed glass panes above. He has to work the other leg through the opening, that's how much his legs have grown since last he used the window during a crisis—Winston Riley trying to gut Marge for interfering again. Knot drops to the ground, on his knees, then springs up running across the yard toward the woods. The short distance from the bare dirt yard to the woods seems like miles. He can smell the sour rooty hog pen on his left and hear the hogs snorting and snuffling, grunting. Green of the woods coming up, welcome sight and smell. His heart is drumming and he can taste fear like chewed tinfoil on his tongue.

He has to cut across Boot's back yard, grown up in rusty metal drums, logging chains, old tires, burned wood and paper either blown up or already there, to get to the tromped-down shortcut path that will take him to the sheriff's office in the courthouse at the crossing. Mostly the path is used for going to the store across 129, facing the courthouse, because people need groceries even if the law isn't of much use to them. He doesn't expect to report the pulpwooder to the law—he's not stupid—and if Marge thinks the pulpwooder was stupid enough to believe her she is a fool. But Marge's sending Knot for the law is just part of the game of survival—what women, white and Negro, say—because sending for the law is the only weapon they have, even if saying it is like a butcher knife with a broken point and a blade that won't hold an edge.

Knot has just reached the footpath between hedges of briars and mulberry when he hears the shots, one followed by the other, one scream followed by the other, the pulpwooder shouting for Riley; and Knot hears—sees—men, women and children, everybody but Marge, flushing like rats from the shacks; some scrabbling under houses, some ducking and running toward the woods. Shots going off like firecrackers, up, down and around. But no Marge.

Knot stands behind a pine and watches for her to climb through the back window of her shack, sees Boots and the children ragtag and clumped heading out the back. If the pulpwooder had wanted to shoot Boots he'd have had plenty of time. But he is inside her shack and shooting up at the ceiling and the tin roof pings with every shot.

Knot hates himself for not going back to check on Marge but he is terrified, and around the north side of Boot's shack Knot's eyes again are locked on Becky Bruce now sobbing openly in the truck. And that seems the biggest cruelty of all to him—not Winston Riley, not Boots, not Marge, not the old ladies fleeing their houses with grandbabies on their hips, not even Cee Ray's mother lugging his crippled screaming sister like a rag doll who has lost its stuffing—but the little white-headed girl who has to ride home in the truck with a mad man and sleep in the same house she can't leave.

As it turns out, Marge has shot a few times herself, up in the air to scare the pulpwooder, and he has turned the shotgun on her. "You a crazy bitch, you know it?" he said.

"That right," she said, "and don't you forget it."

"Somebody's gone cut your throat in your sleep, one of these days."

"I don't sleep in the day. Now, get on out there, you bout scared your little girl to death, showing out."

Chapter 5

That's how Marge told it to Knot on the way to Thanksgiving at Aunt Willie's. Knot doesn't know if he believes her or not—for a truth, Marge is as loose with her tongue and gun as the pulpwooder and never cares one bit if she scares Knot to death. But he can't get over the helpless look on the little white-headed girl's face and knows Marge never gets to him like her daddy gets to her. Marge is a flea and Sammy Bruce is a bulldog.

It is trying to rain and the sky is bloated with low gray clouds. The tall pines each side of the highway stand still and straight. The car smells of burnt motor oil and stale upholstery. Engine like a factory generating racket from refuse.

"You gonna tell em today?" Knot asks.

"What that?"

"That I'm their real kin."

"Why you wanta go messing up with me thi'smorning?"

Marge is a bulldog too, Knot decides.

Getting out of the car at the curb, before Aunt Willie's house on Troupe Street, Knot can tell he has grown by the way his eyes graze level across the tongue-and-groove boards on the porch floor rather than the brick pillars and dusty openness under the house.

The big padded cushioned rockers they had sat in all summer before are tipped to the wall and the screen of morning glories on the north end is woody vines and white twine. The old granddaddy in his gray starched and ironed twills is no longer sitting in the green metal settee on the south end. No pigeons cooing and swirling and the sun overhead is gone.

"Reckon they home?" Knot asks Marge.

She gets out of the Ford without answering with her keys hooked on her pointer finger, jangling them as she goes up the grass-knitted old bricks to the porch.

Knot follows, thinking how much has happened since last summer when he found the money, and nothing much seems to have happened compared to this emptiness, this sudden dilapidation of his rich kin's house. He figures it's because, here he is truly kin now and nobody even knows, not a one of them *can* know, so nothing has changed but just looks different.

Marge eases open the screen door and knocks on the huge paint-scaly brown door then turns the rusted oval metal knob.

Whiffs of food cooking overlaid with menthol and alcohol odors drift on the warm air. The dusky rose wallpaper on the high walls looks dingy and drab and the fringed parchment shades are drawn against the outside light.

A spoon clanks on a pot in the kitchen, breaking the quiet, and they walk on into the hall and then the kitchen toward a yellow light and the yellow walls Knot had so loved.

Aunt Willie is standing over the stove, back turned to them, stirring in one of the big pots. The smell of stewing chicken overpowers the menthol or alcohol in the hall.

Marge tiptoes over and covers Aunt Willie's eyes from behind and Knot laughs, waiting for Aunt Willie to start shrieking and the two women to begin carrying on and kissing and rocking each other with alternating feet clearing the floor like they used to do.

"Tears," Marge says and turns Aunt Willie with both hands on her shoulders.

They hug, rocking—no kissing, no laughing—only shushing and whispering.

Knot sits at the kitchen table. A big white bowl with a cooked turkey neck, liver, heart and two boiled eggs is sitting before him.

"How you, Knot, honey?" Aunt Willie says, letting go of Marge, crying too now, and walks over and hugs him. The legs of her glasses are attached to the main frame with safety pins. "My how you growing!" she says, laughing. "Stand up so I can see you."

He stands, hands by his side and useless.

She says, "Goodness gracious! If you ain't about to outgrow Lee." She stifles crying; he can feel it. "Next thing you know, you be handing down clothes to him."

Knot hasn't grown that much, not in inches. It's just something to say. Like, how is school?

She says that too, then goes back to the stove where Marge is peeping into the oven, trying to be useful, but getting in Aunt Willie's way.

"Let me get to those dishes," Marge says, in her town voice. "Something I know for sure how to do." Marge can talk as good as anybody when she wants to.

The counter to the right of the stove is stacked high and close with dirty dishes, pots and pans; two white metal dishpans of greasy water hold more. She unloads the dishes from the left pan, picks it up, and pads across the kitchen in her good black ballerinas. When she opens the back door a tabby cat slides through. Meow.

Water dashes out to the yard with a practiced solid sheeting splash.

Starting over with fresh water and soapsuds, Marge begins washing dishes, standing next to Aunt Willie at the stove.

Both backs turned on Knot.

Marge looks trim and scrubbed—the cleaning type—in her black skirt and white blouse. Aunt Willie looks soft and sweet—the cooking type—in her faded floral shirtwaist dress and white bib apron. The large mullioned windows over the counter and stove show the broad, gabled terra cotta roof of the house next door and above it pouty gray skies. The wall of windows overlooking the back porch where the sun usually shines through are blank, as if dirty bed sheets have been hung to cover them from the outside.

"I believe I'll just sit over there with Knot for a spell." Aunt Willie turns from the stove and ambles over and sits on the far end of the small rectangular table, right side slid to the yellow wall. She takes off her glasses and wipes the lens on her apron, puts them back on. One leg easy behind the ear and then the other.

"You just sit there," says Marge. "I'm gonna show you I can cook."

"Yaa Lordy," says Aunt Willie and laughs weakly. "That'll be the day."

Marge and Knot learn that the old gray granddaddy, in the back bedroom, is dying of cancer—his colon, they say; that Lee is running with the wrong kind—a gang of good-boys gone bad, who harass and taunt white teachers, policemen and students; that Judy Beth has quit school and has been working at the dime store uptown to help make ends meet.

"What little savings I had at the First National Bank is long gone," Aunt Willie says. "And all these bills, I declare."

Knot's scalp tingles, burns. Has he stolen Aunt Willie's money from the bank robber who stole it from the First National Bank?

Aunt Willie's big brag, as far as cornbread dressing goes, is that she uses only fresh chicken—backs will do—to make the broth. No sage and don't stint on the onion. It pains her to have to reveal her secret to Marge, who would as soon douse the combined celery, toasted white bread and cornbread crumbs with water, and skip the onion, but under such circumstances what else can Aunt Willie do?

She really cries when Marge scorches the cornbread dressing. Marge scrapes off the scabby black top of the dressing and puts the long waiter back in the oven on broil to re-brown the top, then cries herself when at last they go into the dim back bedroom to see the old gray granddaddy, who is more yellow now than gray.

He is dozing but rallies long enough to go on and on about how Knot has grown. Tells Marge she needs to put a brick on his head to make him quit growing. He laughs and closes his waxy eyelids and looks dead already.

Knot steps away from the bed. The room is almost bright, seemingly lit by sun beyond the drawn brownish shades, though it is raining slow and steady outside. Wide boards painted white take on the same shade—sickroom light. Sickroom smells concocted from the various medicines in the blue and brown bottles on the small table next to his bed, but it's the bed and the shell of a man that are the vessels and essence of the tinctured dankness.

"I just give him his shot about an hour ago," whispers Aunt Willie.

"Morphine?" Marge steps closer to his bed, peering down at her daddy, what's left of him.

The rain tapping on the roof sounds cozy, oddly comforting, as if all life is gathered in this one room and everything else is on hold.

"Doctor keeps upping the dose." Aunt Willie looks at the electric alarm clock with its neon green hands on the table next to the bottles. "Don't last long though."

Earlier in the kitchen Knot had seen the brown bottle and hypodermic syringe and needle in the refrigerator when Aunt Willie had gone searching for butter.

"They say colon cancer's the worst kind." Marge smoothes the sheet over his shrunken body, a tube of waste under the covers.

A slow car passes out front, a train is rumbling south along Troupe Street. No birds singing, no children playing. The clock sounds like blood shishing through the chambers of the heart

"Nighttime, don't neither one of us sleep." Aunt Willie turns toward the door. Her graying hair is done up in a bun with tight oddly girlish curls around her square face and on her nape.

Marge shakes her head, following.

Knot longs for life beyond the door.

They are leaving the room just as Judy Beth in only her blue panties, with titties now, flits from the bathroom down the hall into her bedroom across the way, slamming the door.

Not even speaking.

Aunt Willie doesn't say a word!

Knot feels displaced and light-headed, full to bursting in the end-of-the-world gloom of the house. He thinks it is mostly from Aunt Willie's crying and the sick-room smell and light of the house. But over dinner—he, Aunt Willie and Marge alone in the cold closed-off dining room—he realizes that his displacement and light-headedness is because he now knows they are poor. Were they always poor and he hadn't known it? Had he thought they were rich because they were happy? Were they happy or had he only thought it?

The dining room that had seemed so elegant and finely furnished last summer looks shabby and smells dusty to Knot. The source of the dust, the wine wool rug with its withering cabbage roses and green leaves that he used to tiptoe over to keep from tracking. The heavy dark buffet, along the wall at Knot's back, looks clunky, its many drawers with keyholes no longer promising treasure, only receptacles for old pictures and yellowed papers proving the family's members have been born, been baptized, served in war, vaccinated, graduated from school maybe and died certainly. The buffet looks ancient as the black and white smiling family pictures propped against the no-color wall— catch-all for the family's past lives: Aunt Willie's summer embroidery project, her muslin-covered hoop and skeins of colored thread; the flat tweed cap belonging to the granddaddy; Mailbox Club correspondence leaflets, Judy Beth's Bible studies; and Lee's sandwiched blue and orange yo-yo.

Lee doesn't show up for dinner, and Judy Beth shows up about halfway through. She eats fast, barely speaking to Knot on her right, except to ask how he's been doing.

He can tell she doesn't really care—he's no kin to her anyway, as far as she knows, and besides he's ugly, runty, poor. He listens to Aunt Willie saying it's gonna be a poor Christmas at her house, and knows he will send her money regardless. Enough to repay the savings he has stolen from her and probably some extra. And enough for a new bicycle for Lee, of course, so Knot can have his old one.

There is food aplenty; Aunt Willie could feed all of Troupe Street on the put-up tiny green peas in butter sauce, mush of yellow squash, candied yams with orange wedges, cornbread dressing and a golden crusty turkey with one leg sticking out. The other is on Knot's rose flowered plate. As Marge says to Knot, it's either feast or famine. He's learned to fill up on the feast and forget the famine coming up. Or tries to. But his brain always gigs him with the fact that, come morning, he'll be hungry again. And he wonders, if Aunt Willie is so broke, how she can come up with all this food. Biting into the crisp, juicy turkey leg, he watches the sisters across the table. How different they are. Aunt Willie likes to eat and Marge likes to drink; no matter how broke, each finds a way to get what she craves most.

Judy Beth is really pretty now, cream-brown and short with a sucked in waist. Pretty in a cheap red pullover sweater and straight red-and-navy plaid skirt. Actually, under the sweater, her breasts are mere risings, but now that Knot knows how they round out on her bare chest they seem larger.

While they eat, for the sake of conversation, Marge fills them in on what's going on in Statenville. Judy Beth perks up when Marge starts talking about the mysterious person who is sending money to everybody, says she wishes he would send some her way. Aunt Willie says the Lord will provide, hanging her head and eating. To perk her up, Marge says she's now playing the piano at church, a new piano bought with money given by the mystery money man (she of course doesn't tell about the one hundred dollars she got through the mail and how she squandered it, or under what conditions she was last playing the piano at church). Aunt Willie cries with her face in both hands and Marge shakes one of her arms, saying, "Hush, now. Hush."

In a wheezy wet voice, Aunt Willie says, "I'm just so happy, that's all."

"*Happy?*" says Judy Beth, holding her tea glass to her painted lips in mid-swallow.

"Happy," Aunt Willie cries. "Marge is back in church now, that's why."

She and Marge lean into each other, hugging and crying like people do the just saved. Then they eat again while Marge, safe on the subject, lies about how the church in Statenville is growing, how the new preacher has the worst sinners going to church. Somehow—Knot is hardly listening—they make the connection between the young man in the newspaper last summer who saved the old man on the railroad tracks and the preacher at Marge's church. This connection makes for much squealing and hugging and Aunt Willie agrees with Marge that the preacher, good-hearted as he is, is likely the mystery money man.

"Money *man?*" Judy Beth, reaches across the table for the scallop-rimmed pink bowl of peas floating in butter sauce. "Maybe it's a woman."

Nobody responds because they know a woman wouldn't have that kind of money. Silly child.

Corrected and shamed, Judy Beth pipes up again, "Then how come him to be preaching in that dump if he's so rich?"

"Men of God go where they are called to go." Aunt Willie sits straight, fork in the air scented with spice and chicken and menthol.

"But where did he get his money from?" Judy Beth wants to know.

"You can't out-give the Lord," says Aunt Willie.

"Amen to that." Marge kisses her sister on her teary drooped cheek.

"Hey," says Judy Beth, "maybe the preacher's the one robbed the bank last summer."

Knot feels flushed, sinking into his chair.

Aunt Willie and Marge both shame Judy Beth for saying such.

"They ever catch who did it?" asks Marge.

Knot has to say something, has to change the subject

with something shocking.

"Never did," says Aunt Willie, primping up to cry again. "Seems like people just gets sorrier and sorrier in this old world."

Judy Beth sucks in her breath. "Not *that* again."

"I belong to Marge," Knot says.

Nobody speaks. Forks quit clinking on plates.

Aunt Willie and Judy Beth eye him as if he's retarded. Marge gives him a cold daring glare.

"I do," he says. "Tell them, Marge."

Marge doesn't speak.

"Like we don't know it, after her fishing you out of a dumpster and doing without to take care of you all these years," says Judy Beth with venom.

"Judy Beth!" says Aunt Willie. "Knot's been a blessing on this earth if ever there was one. Hasn't he Marge?"

"He has." Marge looks amused, incredulous, but undone—Knot, her focus. "See, that dressing turned out okay after all."

On the way home that evening, Knot presses a palm to the filmy window of the Ford and the glass feels like ice, but beyond the glass looks hot with the pumpkin sun set bright and low, the rim of the world blue-violet and the pines green as summer grass.

Heading up the straightaway, home, past the cold closed red brick school, to the curve of the quarters, everything looks too still, too cold. Chimney smoke chuffing and laying over the tin roofs and settling out over the woods. No children out playing, nor old women on the porches. It is as if they have all moved, and on a holiday. Generally, on holidays, even when it's cold, everybody in the quarters is out drinking, whooping and laughing, roiling around yard fires.

"Something's wrong," Marge says. All the way home she hasn't spoken.

Though Knot knows what she means, or thinks he does, he thinks a lot is wrong. He's still fuming at his family for dismissing his announcement that he is Marge's boy.

Except for something red on the porch, only Marge's shack is without color—a dead give-away that the money-sender has overlooked her.

She is sitting forward, driving, staring straight ahead, speeding up and braking at their front porch.

Clothes and pillows and sheets and trash are scattered from the doorway and across the porch. Marge's blue-speckled cook pot is upside down in the yard. Knot's red sweater is spread across the back of a chair, one sleeve hanging down to the arm, as if a ghost is waiting.

She opens the car door and sails out into the frigid air, bounding up the doorsteps and eyeballing the mess on the porch, then stepping into the doorway. "What the...!" She just stands there.

When Knot gets to where she is standing, he has to peep around her to see inside. He smells raw vomited whiskey, and sees Winston Riley sprawled on Marge's bed, boot toes pointed out and him snoring. His scattered beard looks like pills of mud.

"He do all this? " Knot whispers, looking about the room at the overturned chairs and table, pots and pans on the floor and clothes in heaps as if he's gone through each piece searching for something.

"Well," Marge says, turning and rubbing her lined forehead, "looks like it, don't it?"

She seems calm but isn't and to prove it she begins slinging things from the porch through the door, threatening to drag Riley's ass out in the cold.

He sleeps on, still, except on occasion when he punches at his large flat nose.

With each item slung from the porch into the house, Marge gets louder, shouting, shrieking, threatening to cut Winston's throat, to send for the law, to make him pay.

Teeth chattering from cold and fear, Knot goes out to the bed of bark and firewood on the left side of the house and gathers in his arms what remains of the fat splinters and split

pine. The cold smells of cooking, of frozen hog mud and
sulfur. Marge, on a roll, is stomping on the floor inside;
accidentally or on purpose she kicks what sounds like a pot
and the shanty vibrates as the pot strikes a wall.

Cee Ray steps out on his porch, hands in his pockets,
looks Knot's way, then appearing stiff, bored and casual
goes back inside. The woman, in a heavy dark coat and red
headscarf, at the house to the right of Cee Ray's, is gathering
wood. Bending, standing, she glances at Marge's cabin, then
hurries inside too. A big black dog in her yard is gnawing
what looks like one of Marge's walked-down everyday
shoes. It's like a war zone, all over the quarters—everybody
keeping to their houses to avoid stray shots.

Surely they know about Winston Riley ransacking
Marge's cabin, and knowing Marge, Knot figures, they are
expecting she will kill him, and that's why nobody is out and
about on Thanksgiving evening. Either that or they are afraid
that Marge will think they took part in the ransacking too.

On the porch, Knot has to step over the remaining
clothes and junk, to get through the open door and Marge
standing over a pile of clothes in the middle of the room,
metallic orange hair aglow from the bare hanging bulb
overhead, shouting at Winston Riley, who sleeps on. It is still
light out, but barely, and when Knot looks again it is dark.
That sudden. Like his money. Which he is scared to death to
check on, so sure is he that it is gone. So sure that any
minute Marge will uncover it from the heap of clothes she's
now sorting through and tossing on top of Winston Riley
sleeping on her bed.

Knot opens the door of the black barrel-shaped wood
heater and lights a splinter with a kitchen match from the box
she has tossed to him. He eases the smoking reddish splinter
inside the sooty dark cave of the heater and ricks more
splinters on top. He doesn't turn around, only watches as the
feathering soot along the heater walls moves in the breeze
off the fire, smoke twisting up to the round dark hole of the
stove flue. Finally, when Marge says nothing about money,

only cussing at Winston Riley, Knot lays two pieces of split pine on top of his lighterd fire and turns around. The pile of clothes she's been sorting through is now low enough that he can see to the floor—no money.

He breathes deep and rises and steps around her and then Riley's booted feet at the very foot of Marge's bed, goes over to his own space, a pitiful dim cold strip between his cot and the wall and almost laughs with relief to see the sack as he has left it, block-shaped with double rows of paperback books showing at the mouth of the sack. Huck Finn and Grimm's Fairy Tales, library books never returned, so long past due that the library has given up dunning for them. Knot doesn't feel guilty about not returning the books. Who else but him would have read them so many times? Nobody, and the untouched sack is proof.

Neighbors are always bringing letters and articles for him to read for them and sum up in a single sentence they can understand. Not because they can't read, at least most of them, but because they *don't* read or *won't* read.

When he looks around, Marge is tugging at Winston's left leg, trying to drag him from her bed. "Come get the other one," she yells to Knot.

Winston throws one arm over his eyes, sleeps on.

Knot takes hold of his right boot at the ankle and tugs as Marge tugs. Winston rolls onto his left side, ready to curl with his legs bent at the knees and overlapped.

"Move out of the way," Marge orders Knot.

He steps back to the wall at the foot of the bed as Marge grabs Winston's right arm and snatches him to the floor. The shack trembles like a shook box.

Winston leaps to his feet, facing the other way, then turns with his fists balled, ready for a fight. He looks around to get his bearings, during which time Marge takes advantage and steps up and socks him under his bearded chin like a man.

Blood seeps from his mouth, he lets out a yelp, and Knot figures he has bitten his tongue, otherwise he would be beating Marge to a pulp.

Drunk and confused and in great pain, he stumbles over the clothes in the doorway and steps out to the porch and doesn't even opt for the doorsteps but tumbles off the left edge, landing on the strip of dirt between his own shack and Marge's. She is after him like a setting hen, cackling, clucking from the edge of her porch.

He begins circling the yard, trying to talk with his bit tongue hanging out, sobering up in the cold. Sounds like he is speaking a foreign language.

The fire is roaring in the heater and the chimney is ablaze, but the cold from outside keeps the heat banked in the kitchen corner of the room, to Knot's right. Knot, standing in line with the open door, where he'd earlier backed to the wall, can feel the cold air from several feet away. He doesn't go to the door, only listens to Marge and Winston shouting, in case he has to climb out the window next to his bed to go for help. Any minute now, Winston will be back to his old self and beat Marge to death.

The lit-red heater flue begins roaring louder, smoking— its inner lining of creosote crystals caught good now. Sounds like a tornado, and if Knot doesn't temper it by closing the damper, the house and his money might catch fire.

Afraid to move, but more afraid not to, he steps quick and high over the clothes on the floor, picking up one of Marge's white shirts and wrapping it around his right hand to keep from getting burned. With his wrapped hand, he twists the damper lever, about a quarter of the way up the flue. The flue seems to blaze hotter, redder, blistering his face. But gradually, as he backs away, smoke burning his eyes, the roaring fades out and the stove flue dims and begins to tick like a clock.

At some point, Marge and Winston outside have started talking, still loud and mad but making more sense. Back to normal.

Best Knot can tell, the gist of it is: Boots is gone. It is Thanksgiving and Boots is gone and Winston Riley has pitched a drunken tantrum because before she left she told him about the money somebody had sent through the mail and it has to be Marge or some man and either way Marge would know.

"Which is it?" Winston wants to know. Sounds like he's said "Whidizit?" because of his bit tongue.

Knot doesn't look out, but instead goes over and sits on the edge of his bed facing the dark window. He can picture Winston Riley with his strong killer arms crossed, puffing air through his shaped-fudge nose.

He is on his porch and Marge is on hers, sounds like, and her arms are probably crossed likewise, not aping him exactly and she doesn't even sound scared. But Knot, inside the house is, is scared enough for both of them. Sitting on his cot with his dirty white canvas shoe on his cash sack and the packed side by side library paperbacks: Huck Finn, Hans Christian Anderson, Narnia.

"*Which is it?*" she repeats. Loud. "I look like a woman wid money to spare?"

"No, but what I hear yo kinfolk do." Nobudwhadiheayokinfokdo.

"Where you hear that *trash?*"

"Yo boy say his auntie gone get him a wheel for Christmas."

Knot has no trouble translating that. Next thing, he expects to hear Winston Riley bring up the hundred-dollar bill she sent to pay him back for the charged wine.

"Knot ain't say no such," Marge shouts.

"He say it sure as I standing here. Wid my own two ears I hear him say it to Cee Ray."

"Well, she ain't. Sister bout down and out as the rest of us."

Here it comes, Knot thinks, the part about the money she got from her sister.

"Okay. It be a man then. A man send Boots that money."

"I doubt it."

"How come?"

"I get a hunderd dollars in the mail same day and ain't no man I know of gone send me none." She stamps across the porch and steps inside, slams the door. Opens it again to let out the heat and smoke and leaves it open.

Okay, Knot thinks, they have forgotten all about the charged wine and pay-back. Either that or they are afraid to bring it up. Also thinking that he has sent too little to Boots and too much to Marge. He has two more people to send to now, then he will hide the cash elsewhere till he can give it back to the bank.

"Why you tell that lie bout Sister giving you a bike for Christmas?" she asks, picking up plates from the floor, practically juggling them.

Knot turns his back to her, facing the window again and her reflection. Her orange hair flashes like fool's gold. "I figure Lee might get a new bike and Aunt Willie be handing his down to me."

"Well, you figure wrong then. Not down and out as Sister and them be. Can't hardly afford Daddy's pain medicine she say."

He takes his foot off the sack, lies back on the cot.

That night he sleeps with one hand on the sack, feeling the words between the covers of the books bumping up like Braille. Dreaming that the money under the books is an illusion, a dream, and glad to wake up though still asleep and dreaming. Over and over, dreaming he is dreaming and waking, dreaming and waking, forming a whorl that sucks him down with a piercing surge in his chest, falling into blackness.

જી • ৪৩

The preacher comes on Saturday morning, bringing with him hammer and nails, a never-bounced genuine pigskin basketball and a bright orange hoop with a green virgin net. The weather has warmed up, so he is wearing cutoff navy sweatpants, white T-shirt and a red kerchief covering his head and knotted in back. No hair on his legs, as Knot had noticed before, but muscles like swirled chocolate in a cookpot. His shoulders are broad and true, his neck is thick, and his sculpted chest swells above a flat stomach. White socks bag on his ankles and run down into navy and gray athletic shoes. But what sets him off, what makes him shine, is that perfectly matched set of pearly teeth, his ever-smiling.

Four tough tall boys, who the preacher has enlisted to help hang the basket ball goal, jaunt out one by one from their houses. They are wearing shorts and ragged T-shirts, gray, white and green. Knot can name two of them who play first-string on the basketball team at school; sole reason they go to school is to play basketball. By night, they glow like stars. They are glorified, valued players, at the games, in high-standing with the white boys, their families and teachers. By day, in the classroom, they are damned princes, defrocked priests, dull as dirt.

Long-legged and loose-limbed, the boys gather in the wind-swept clearing, middle of the crescent, where the dirt is like concrete, half-way between Knot's station on his porch and Cee Ray's station on his own.

Cee Ray steps out first. The big boys and the preacher aren't six yards away, but Cee Ray stands his bike from where it's been left by the doorsteps (he no longer bothers to lean it against the porch) straddles it and pedals out, dismounts after checking to be sure Knot is still on his porch, and drops it again. Wheels spinning and making pinwheel shadows on the hard dirt.

Two of the taller boys, standing side by side before a power pole, spread their stilt-like legs and hoist the preacher up to their shoulders with the hoop in both hands and the hammer in his pocket. Feet planted and barely teetering on each of their shoulders, and nails between his strong teeth, he places the base of the hoop to the pole, bracing it with one arm underneath.

"Ho now! Ho now!" the other boys shout and laugh. They back, squinting up at the young preacher with sun-glinting nails like spiked teeth.

Dumb Cee Ray races around the pyramid, slapping his scrawny legs and hawing, maybe hoping the preacher will fall and break his neck for the fun of it.

But with deft motions, the preacher hammers one nail and then the other through the hoop's base to the pole, then squats and drops to the ground. Springing from his knees, grinning and staring up at the sun and blue sky through the orange and green hoop, he brushes his hands together.

Knot steps from his porch to the yard, watching as the boys begin dribbling the new brown basketball on the packed dirt, traveling and passing it, leaping and shouting—"Ho now! Ho now!" Cee Ray is circling, shouting for the boys to get the ball. The dogs have gathered now, barking, circling the ball team with Cee Ray. The preacher gets the ball and driving hard between them toward the goal, dribbling all the while, jumps up level with the hoop and slam-dunks the ball.

The net squeezes the ball, holds it for an instant, then lets go.

The boys slap his shoulder, one shakes his hand. And they are off again, dribbling, passing, shooting at the goal. But the preacher, shorter by a head, dodges and lunges and steals the ball and rings the goal again. Suddenly he throws the ball, long-shot, to Cee Ray, who catches it, drops it, has to run after it where it has rolled and stopped almost at Knot's feet.

"Let's play ball!" the preacher shouts to Cee Ray.

He joins in, mostly dodging among the long legs and huge feet in midair, gawking, hawing. The preacher gets the ball and passes to Cee Ray again and he dribbles—walking!—loses the ball, retrieves it, while one of the first-string players from school scratches in his square hair, his strong features registering impatience.

The old ladies on their porches are fanning, watching, grinning without their teeth. Others out watching, moving closer, some of the men joining in the game. Cee Ray's little crippled sister wearing only white drawers with a filthy seat, scoots down the doorsteps on her mop bottom and crawls into the crowd of spectators.

The preacher has the ball. Dribbling, driving straight through the mix of men and boys and dogs, he shoots it Knot's way. "Let's play ball!" he calls through a megaphone of hands.

Knot is holding the ball, the pebbled pigskin ball that smells new. All eyes are on him—the runt with buckteeth, no bigger than a knot on a log. Hands on their waists and watching, the basket ball boys on the first-string in school yell, "Let's play ball!" Some of the others groan, kicking at the dirt and wandering with hands on their waists.

Knot has to play now. He has no choice.

But for the moment, he almost hates the preacher, everything all turned around. Because before he had seemed to be the only one in the quarters who liked the preacher, who stood up for him, and now everybody seems to like him.

He is petting an old pesky mangy mammy dog, whose pink-pied tits are practically dragging the ground, her entire litter of six brown puppies suctioned by their mouths, draining the life from her.

Knot bounces the ball, dribbling into the mangle of giant players. None tries to take the ball from him, but make a big show of whooping and waving their arms, running around him. Their arms are almost as long as their legs. Knot is facing the goal, sizing it up and getting ready to shoot, when up pops the preacher, sweating and smelling no less of sweat than the other mortals, and easily steals the ball from Knot. It slips from the preacher's fine brown hands and like lightning striking glides up and down through the hoop.

Which really kind of ticks Knot off. Out of the corner of his eye, he sees Cee Ray, a blur of Cee Ray, straddled his bicycle, laughing with his tonsils showing, as Knot ducks low and dodges through the mass of grown men, following the preacher dribbling the ball to the edge of the crowd and circling back toward the goal for a shot. Knot heads him off by tricking his way through the men also trying to cut the preacher off. But Knot is smaller, faster, madder, and before he can even think about it, he dashes for the ball and catches it mid-dribble. This time he doesn't try to shoot but throws the ball to one of the first-string players whose mouth is wide open with wonder, maybe even awe. Everybody whooping, "Yo Knot!"

The preacher, taking a break, walks over and slaps Knot on the shoulder. He doesn't say a word. The slap on the shoulder says it all. Knot wants to die right there while he is a hero. He wants to die right there while at last everybody likes him.

Except of course Cee Ray.

All take a break and drink water, passing a glass gallon jug. Pouring it on each other's heads and heading for the pitcher pump in Cee Ray's side yard for more water.

Cee Ray, still straddled his bicycle, walks it over to the edge of the ferny mimosa shadow where Knot has wound up standing, glowing with his heart pounding his ribs. "Man, yo old lady got a nerve, going to church drunk," says Cee Ray. "Them ladies bout ready to whup up on her, money or no money. Say she can't play that piano less she be drunk."

Cee Ray ducks his head, seeing that the preacher, dripping wet, a few feet away in the crowd, has overheard and is glaring at him. Not smiling for once.

Then the preacher places both hands on his knees, stooping, shaking his head and breathing hard. One of the boys who had earlier helped hoist him up to nail the hoop to the power pole, rushes over with a jug of water and empties it on the preacher's head and shoulders. The preacher laughs out loud and chases after the boy, who outruns him backward to show the preacher he's no match.

"Who tell you that trash?" The glow is gone but Knot's heart is still thumping.

"Everybody talking bout it." Cee Ray slings his head, motioning to the crowd, now thinning out. Going back to their houses for the noon meal. Little crippled girl trailing them, leaving drag marks on the dirt and erasing footprints.

The preacher is standing next to the open door of his car,

parked in the lacy shade of a chinaberry tree between Cee Ray's house and the house next door. He takes out a white towel and drapes it around his neck, head up and smiling, walking back over to where Cee Ray and Knot are standing. Cee Ray shoves off on his bicycle, and takes to the road running half way round the schoolhouse. Standing on the spinning pedals with his little-boy behind in the air.

Knot knows that the preacher has heard Cee Ray talking about Marge. Last thing in the world Knot wants now is pity replacing his glory. He can still feel the warm rays, but "Yo Knot!" is fading. He starts to walk away, toward his house, but he stops, facing the preacher.

"Nobody is going to *whup-up* on Sister Marge." He strips the knotted wet red kerchief from his head and rolls it round and round in his hands. "But I do need to go over there and have a little talk with her."

He walks off, turning, adding, "She is home, I guess?"

Knot nods and steps underneath the spread branches of the mimosa. As always, he is hungry, hoping Marge is awake and fixing something for him to eat. But he doesn't want to go over there and hear her cuss out the preacher. Too, he doubts she is awake and finding her asleep would be too embarrassing with the preacher there. Knot has left the front door open and the preacher will see her bed from the porch. Worse, if she is awake, she is slouching around in her man's white T-shirt with her bony legs sticking out and the orange crown of her hair sticking up like a bad wig above the dark new-growth of hair underneath.

On the dirt under the broad green fronds of the mimosa, pink blossoms with soft spiked petals like tiny pompoms have shed, withered and turned brown. But looking up at the blue sky through the green branches Knot spies more pink. He can smell the tang of green mingled with starbursts of chicken droppings and the cool rich dirt, and he'd like to stay forever or at least till the preacher leaves.

Peering out through the swags of low branches, he sees the preacher standing on the porch, knocking at the open door. Knot closes his eyes tight, so tight he can see red spangles. When he opens them the preacher is peeping through the door. Knot can hear him calling. He can hear the sproinging of Cee Ray's bicycle coming up the west side of the road toward the curve. Suddenly Marge pops through the door, dressed in a dark skirt and white blouse, her uniform, as if she hasn't heard him knocking and calling but is glad to see him. They sit on the left side of the porch, Preacher on her right with his elbows on his knees, rolling his hands inside the knotted red kerchief, while leaning toward Marge, talking to Marge, listening, shaking his head. Her rocking, rocking, aloof-looking, her smile switching to a grimace that shows her many teeth.

Cee Ray is now taking the curve on his bicycle, looking at the preacher and Marge, and misses Knot under the tree who doesn't even breathe. Listening to the bicycle rattle past and Cee Ray stomping down on the pedals along the east side of the school grounds. Knot can't hear a single word Marge and the preacher are saying, but takes it as a sign that her rocking and smiling again means that she's not going to sock him under the chin like she did Winston Riley, Thanksgiving night.

Then the visit is over. For better or worse what the preacher had come to say has been said, and he is standing in front of Marge in her chair, taking her right hand in his. Not shaking it but holding it like the hand of somebody ailing, or a queen.

Loping down the doorsteps, he strides toward his car, glancing at the mimosa but not seeing Knot there. Or maybe the preacher does and he's decided not to bother with the coward. As he gets into his car and backs out, Knot says, "Yo Knot!" low and beneath hearing.

He shrinks behind the cover of branches, sure he isn't visible. But as the preacher drives past the mimosa, he lifts one hand and smiles.

Marge is still rocking, arms on the chair arms and staring out.

The boys come out again and start playing ball, quarreling and cursing, with the preacher out of earshot.

It's all for naught.

Knot slips out from his hiding place and walks slow with his head down toward his own house. At the porch, he backs and hoists himself up on the edge, at Marge's feet, hearing her shoes paddling and slapping on the floor. He wipes sweat from his face with the back of his arm. "You don't want to go to church no more," he says, "I don't blame you."

He waits, watching the boys dribbling, passing, stealing the ball and leaping at the goal. The quarters vibrate with their laughing and shouting. Cee Ray rides up and sits straddled his bicycle, fanning gnats. Dogs surrounding them all.

Winston Riley is gone but his front door is open and clothes and trash have spilled out to the porch. A tabby cat is sleeping curled on a pink-checked shirt.

Knot can smell the stale and fetid odors of his own house inside. Nothing cooking and he hadn't expected it. "Say something, Marge."

"I'm thinking."

It is then and only then, when she speaks, that he smells fumes of alcohol on her. Had she fortified herself with whiskey in order to meet with the preacher? Knot tries to recall having seen her speak to the preacher at all, but he can only recall her grimacing and smiling. He has to face up to the fact that she may never be free of the need for fortification; they may never get to the point of being able to move in with Aunt Willie.

He turns and looks at her and he cannot believe how queenly and serene she is—not at all her usual wild and over-friendly, or mean, self when she is drinking. Her hands are folded on her lap. Her face looks bright as her hair and her eyes are wide, staring over his head. She could be anybody but Marge. "Thinking what?" he asks.

"Thinking bout that lowdown backwoods trash badmouthing me. *Me*, granddaughter of a preacherman and daughter of a deacon own his own shoe-repair shop fore he sell out and retire."

Her voice is tight but low and calm, spiteful.

"I ever tell you yo granmama be a saint? Rose of Sharon, they call her. Play the piano at the Troupe Street Baptist church for some 30 odd year. Take in boys home from the war, feed and get em on they feet. Little younguns throwed away—I can't tell you how many she take in.

"Sister—let me tell you bout yo Aunt Willie: she be Valedictorian of her class, marry a railroad man who up and die on her. Leave her with two younguns to raise. She ever once step out with another man? Never.

"Fine upstanding old family we come from," she adds.

On and on she goes—uncles, aunties, cousins who fought in The War and came home heroes—till her recitation turns to reminiscing and then she is reminded of who she is and where she came from and the shame of her wasted life. She is the only bulb blown in a string of lights.

"I'm going back to church, and I ain't gone be drinking when I go. I'll show that bunch of backwoods hypocrites. Wadn't for me, for all they know, they wouldn't have no new piano. Wouldn't have no gas to warm their ripe behinds by, wadn't for me."

Knot nods, staring down at his fingers locked between his knees. He cannot believe that she has included him— *your granmama, your Aunt Willie, we.* Yo Knot!

"Course me and you both knows, it the preacher what got the money. All anybody have to do be to look out there where that new goal shining—two and two make fo'."

Knot can see out of the corner of his eye her finger pointing, which means she's had more to drink than just a sip.

"Look out there at that bad boy on that new wheel; look out there at that new television on the porch." Preaching now, Marge takes stock of all that is new and colorful within her range of vision, like counting blessings of her own, not with bitterness or even envy but enlightened amazement. She's like a blind person having just received the gift of sight.

Done preaching she leans forward, speaking low to Knot. "Know how come us not to get no mo' money after that hunderd come in the mail?"

"How come?"

"Cause he know I drink it up." She taps Knot on the shoulder.

He stares into those newly-opened eyes.

"He knows ain't nobody else fitting to play his new piano," she whispers madly, stabbing at her bony chest with her preaching finger. "Nobody but me."

Chapter 6

Knot is on his knees in the north end of the Bruce's two-acre pecan orchard, picking up pecans. He can see Becky Bruce on her knees, south end of the orchard. There's an undrawn line about halfway between the eight shedding trees and Knot knows where it is without being told. So does Becky.

Frost from last night melts on the white humps of grass, but the westward-leaning shadows of the trees are still stenciled in white.

It is the brightest cold Knot can recall, or maybe this Saturday morning just seems brightest because of Becky Bruce's sheet-white hair. Or the white glaring against her puffed pink cheeks. The southward-arcing sun is white and has withdrawn its heat from overhead. The cloudless sky is coldest blue, and the air smells of cold, like block ice fooling you into believing it smells cold when it's only cold-feeling. The dead grass, weeds and leaves smell toasted, cured, but feel soggy to the touch. Oblong pecans shine like polished wood eggs peeping through, tiny treasures that never cease to surprise even those who hate picking up the brown streaked nuts in the cold for a mean man like Sammy Bruce.

Marge is back at the Bruce house because none of the other women in the quarters would come (they are either down in the back or laid up with "old colds" when Bruce comes after them). So it's Marge or nobody but she's not taking anymore of his shit, she tells Knot. Besides, she needs the little dab of money; otherwise she'll have to go on welfare like the rest of those lazy good-for-nothings in the quarters. And too she needs the money for Christmas, or drink, whichever she deems more urgent, whichever overcomes her first, the craving or the Christmas spirit. All week before, following Sunday and church, she has gone without a drink and it's beginning to wear on her. How much is it wearing? When Sammy Bruce came by to ask her to help his wife butcher chickens this morning, she said yes sir, not even hinting at their recent shoot-out. Neither had he. "Your boy there can pick up pecans for me and I'll pay him," Bruce had added in proud monotone. It's a record that has been played over and again, the refrain: Marge sasses, Bruce cusses her out, he comes for her and she goes because she needs the money. But they have never before shot at each other.

Knot crawls forward a few feet toward a cluster of nuts. The knees and hems of his brown jeans are wet. So far, he has picked up about enough pecans to cover only the bottom of the croaker sack he is dragging. The sack smells of cottonseed meal, corndust and rats. His lips are chapped and he longs to lick them. His nose is running and he longs to wipe it. He starts to lick his lips and wipe his nose on his plaid flannel shirt sleeve but remembers that Marge has warned him not to, not to lick his lips, not to wipe his nose on his shirt but to use the handkerchief she has given him. Why? Licking chapped lips will only make them chap worse. Wiping his nose on his shirtsleeve will prove Sammy Bruce right—nasty, snotty-nosed colored children always wipe their noses on their shirtsleeves. Becky, on the other end of the orchard, is wiping her nose on her sleeve. Then her eyes.

Is she crying?

Sitting back on her heels in the frost-glinting grass and leaves, when she should be picking up nuts, she resembles a white Easter rabbit with pink eyes that some child has dressed in blue. Knot imagines her nibbling grass like a rabbit, paws together before her then one going up to her mouth, but he decides she's probably hulling and eating a pecan. Wonders what would happen if he were to eat one— just one. For breakfast, Marge had had her usual coffee, and Knot had had the last slice of white bread smeared with the last of the peanut butter. His stomach is gnawing, feels raw. His heart burns. When Marge eats peppers, she says she gets heartburn. Since Knot has eaten no peppers and little else besides, he lays the flaring, stinging pain in his chest to feelings of sorrow for Becky Bruce.

A frantic chicken squawks in the back yard of the Bruce's small white frame house, north of the pecan orchard and over a hogwire fence. Knot turns and sees Marge wringing its neck. She slings the white hen's fat body in a circle, neck in one hand, and wings flapping. The hen's wings sound like a kite shredding in March wind. When she lets the chicken go, it flutters off a few feet and settles at the wood gate set midway in the fence between the yard and the pecan grove.

The women are killing the laid-out hens for the freezer today. Mrs. Bruce, in blue jeans and a red flannel shirt, is inside the chicken yard, pointing out to Marge which hen is bound for the freezer. She is a pretty woman with a tanned tapered face and curly brown hair. She is wearing brown loafers like the ones Becky Bruce wears to school. Together the two women shoo the selected hen into the corner of the chicken yard, holding their arms out like basketball guards and easing forward with their shadows following. The white hen cackles and steps, pecking at the dirt, but as the women close in she begins fluttering her wings and flying up to the diamond wire fence, clinging by her claws and clucking faster, louder, as Marge's spread hands reach out and grab the hen.

As Marge leaves the pen with the hen held fast in both hands, mutely clucking, mop head tucked into her neck feathers, the other chickens peck and step and yank their heads as if hoping to look useful or escape notice. All except for the strutting red and black iridescent rooster with a red cone like a king's crown on his head and spurs on his feet like a cowboy's. Nobody kills the rooster.

If Sammy Bruce shows up before she gets done, Marge has told Knot, remember not to look him in the eye and say yes sir no matter what. That morning Knot had begged her not to make him go, but she'd made him anyway. Time he started earning a little money. To buy Christmas presents for the family she won't let him claim yet.

Light traffic passes on the highway out front, slowing for the city limits sign if headed into town, speeding up if headed toward the Florida line. Blue-black crows above the trees are cawing, cawing alarm signals to the other crows, warning that humans are below. Woodsmoke is on the chill air. But all is still as if time has been gelled, won't quiver till shook.

Hens cackle, cluck and squawk in the yard. And Marge snaps their necks, blood on the white bib apron she is wearing over her black coat. She seems to be enjoying herself, standing in that one spot and slinging hens by the neck like some kind of game.

At church last Sunday, wearing a silky royal blue dress Knot had never seen before, she had played the piano sober like she said she would. But not with gusto, no feeling, no soul. Which probably worked out best all round, because the church was packed with the regulars and those who usually came only for special occasions. Come to vote that Marge be ousted probably, had she been drinking, although she'd never even joined their church. She'd been saved when she was a girl, she told Knot, at the Troupe Street Baptist church in Valdosta, during revival, but after revival she got unsaved before she could be baptized. So, if she is of a mind to, she can "move her letter" to the church in Statenville. Much as Knot wants her to quit drinking, so they can get on to Aunt Willie's before he gets too old to live with the family, he hopes Marge won't move her letter to the church in Statenville, he hopes she won't get baptized. Because then she might become a little too saved and sanctified and never want to leave the good young preacher and his church.

Knot will have to hold back now from giving more money to the church—Marge is hooked on revenge like some people get hooked on religion, or like she is hooked on strong drink, as the Bible calls it. *Showing them* is a fever now. But Knot yearns, even itches, to dump the sack of money at the preacher's feet, tomorrow morning. Not even sending some of the money to Aunt Willie to take care of the—his—granddaddy. Knot's notion of Lee and Judy Beth as better than him has been squashed by Thanksgiving revelations. Being a knot, being a nothing, Knot needs them superior as a gauge, a reference, representative of who he is by belonging to them, one of them by blood. If Aunt Willie can hire help for the dying granddaddy, she can take up her switch again and reshape Lee and Judy Beth from their squashed state. Of even less importance, in light of the preacher's revelation last Sunday, is sending money to Aunt Willie to buy Lee a new bicycle and hand down the old one to Knot, to pay her back the money he accidentally stole from the robber, who deliberately stole it from the bank and broke her.

The preacher had revealed from the pulpit that because of the gift from the church's special angel—he looked right at Marge, sober and softened up at the piano, smug in her knowledge of who really is giving the money but humbly accepting credit—he has paid up the church's long-standing gas bill and bought new basketball equipment, and anybody else so moved to give will be contributing to his youth group fund: "It's up to the church to give the wayward-seeking young people in the community something to do and keep them out of trouble." A concrete basketball court in the quarters; later, a decent baseball field for them to play on. Field trips, special visiting youth ministers, a youth choir with a trained music director.

Knot can see clear how such money in the hands of the preacher would buy him that bicycle he's been hankering for. Plus, more church functions mean he will never go hungry.

When Knot's sack has just enough pecans in it to feel slightly weighty, Becky Bruce rises from her knees, brushing grass from her faded cuffed denim jeans and matching jacket. Then she starts toward him, dragging what looks like an empty croaker sack, crossing that undrawn line in the orchard on her way to the house. But she cuts wide to keep from walking into Knot's space, eyes down like she's been taught.

Knot is starving and behind him he can smell the oily sulphurous odor of chickens scalding and hear Marge talking to Mrs. Bruce in the kitchen. They laugh like old friends. The back door squeaks open and shut as Becky passes through and Knot is alone with his pecans. Free to eat all he wants. He knows Marge will be bringing him a baloney sandwich soon, same way she does when he rakes yards for some of the other women she works for.

While he waits, he sits behind a pecan tree, back to the road and resting against the tree trunk, and begins cracking two pecans together in his fists, hulling and eating them. He gets a green one—bitter—and throws it out on his left, into the melting frost of shrinking tree shadows. Dead-still, he watches as a squirrel runs and stops, and runs and stops. Twitching and kinking its long furry tail, it finally snatches up the pecan and sits back on its haunches, nibbling the nutmeat held human-like between two front paws.

He tosses another one to the squirrel and it scampers away, then comes back, sitting, posing, eating, flicking its button eyes at Knot the Master. Knot eats one, then tosses another nut, and soon another squirrel with a plume tail joins the first. Eyeballing each other, eyeballing Knot.

He cracks two nuts at the same time and picks away the hulls and gouges out the thin woody divider between the halves, eats one and tosses the other to the squirrels.

At the house the women are no longer talking or laughing. Light footsteps sound on the floor. There is a rapid *clink clink clink* like a metal spoon raking food from a bowl. Whoosh and clap of a refrigerator door—baloney and mayonnaise maybe being taken out for Knot's sandwich. Maybe. On the highway at his back he hears a truck slowing at the city limits sign.

Knot has a gathering of about a half dozen squirrels and the crows are calling the all-clear, ricocheting tree to tree and filching pecans. He begins tossing nuts up in the air to chase off the crows but doesn't come close to winging one. They are blacker than black and swift as water.

"Hey! Boy!" a man shouts. "What the hell you mean throwing my pecans away like that?"

The squirrels scamper up the trees, claws pick, pick picking at the bark, and spiral among the branches.

Knot peers around the tree trunk to see Sammy Bruce standing not fifteen feet away. His face is red and his arms are cocked and you could hear him clear across Statenville to the quarters. It's like he has some special loud-speaking device in his throat.

Knot stands, feeling weak and light, spangles before his eyes.

"I say, boy, what the hell you think you doing?"

Marge is on the narrow back porch, watching with her hands on her hips. No coat now but she is still wearing the bloody apron.

"Yessir," Knot says, not meeting Sammy Bruce's eyes as he starts closer. So close Knot can make out the ribbed knit of his white undershirt beneath the green twill outer shirt.

"YESSIR, what?"

"I was taking a break. Eating some pecans."

"You getting paid to eat, boy?"

"Yessir. I mean nosir."

"You not all that bright, are you, boy?"

"Yes sir."

"Smart, huh?" His green eyes are like comic book lasers.

"Yes sir."

"Well, I tell you what, I bet I can take you down a notch or two."

"Not long as I'm living." Marge is there, bare-armed and tall, behind Sammy Bruce so suddenly it's as if she has flown. Becky and her mother are standing on the back porch where Marge had stood as if keeping her spot for her.

All eyes are fixed on Marge.

The squirrels bark. The crows caw. The winter sun

slides overhead and melts the remaining frost and all shadows shed into heaps.

"Hey, Doris!" Sammy Bruce calls to his wife. "I hope you're listening to all this backtalk out here. I hope next time you want a little help you'll call on that lazy gal of yours. Not send me after some nigger bitch with a boy don't know his head from a hole in the ground." Then to Marge with her hands on her hips and blanched yellow almost, "Get your boy here and get him off my place, you hear." He digs in his right jeans pocket, pulls out some change and hands her a quarter. "More than you worth, either one of y'all."

On the way home, Marge driving the Ford and fuming, reaches over and hands Knot the quarter. "Keep it forever," she says. "Keep it to remember by."

Marge had stopped off at the store across from the courthouse and bought a half-pound of sliced baloney wrapped in white paper with the corners taped fast. She bought a sample-size jar of fresh mayonnaise—the mayonnaise in the mildewed white refrigerator at home was almost gone, the bottom of the jar smeared a runny white and yellow and tasting like rancid oil—and a loaf of fluffy white Wonder bread.

At home, she stoked the dying coals in the wood heater with the split pine and sticks brought in by Knot. They would need more wood soon, which meant they either had to call the man who cut, hauled and sold firewood to the quarters, or Knot would have to do it himself.

Fire burning high now, Marge and Knot sit silently, listening to the black heater tick, snap and sing, staring out the window above the crumb-strewn, tacky-topped table, and watch the preacher and his rag-tag team playing basketball.

White package of baloney opened before them, Marge, on Knot's right, makes a sandwich for him, carefully, thoughtfully, peeling the red rinds from two slices of meat, grainy gray as brains but delicious smelling.

While he eats the sandwich she nibbles a slice folded in half and drinks from a mug of steaming black coffee.

Knot wants to talk but he is afraid to. Afraid he might break her calm and spoil his sandwich. But strangely she doesn't look mad, simply deflated, scrunched up and squinching her eyes as she sips the coffee.

When Knot has only a couple of bites left, she begins making him another sandwich, her hands shaking as she dips a spoon into the tiny jar of mayonnaise and rattles it against the glass lip.

She hands him the sandwich, gets up and goes over to the roaring-hot heater, twists the damper lever, pours more coffee from the speckled pot on the stove between the heater and the plyboard bathroom wall, then comes back and sits at the table with Knot.

Outside the preacher has just slam-dunked the ball and one of the first string players from school has the ball, dribbling and dancing on the wind-swept dirt. On the school playground, between the low redbrick building additions and the gym, the swings are flying higher than the top metal support; standing out against the blue sky are the small dark legs and heads of forbidden children, at school on Saturday only because they don't have to go to school.

"Run on out and play," Marge says. "I got things to do here." She gets up and sets her crazed white mug on the cookstove, turns right and takes six steps into the bathroom, and closes the door.

Like last time, Knot, with the keepsake quarter in his right jeans pocket, has to warm up before joining the players. And again the preacher has to induct him by throwing him the ball. But this time, for the most part, Knot only dodges and steps about like the hens at the Bruce's that morning, trying to look useful.

His mind is elsewhere: replaying all that had happened that morning, and on a full stomach, then rushing ahead to the heat-ticking silence over lunch.

He fully expects that Marge will be drinking by now. Will she go to church drinking tomorrow or say, "To hell with it!" and stay home? Is it over, is it starting? Why her sudden concern over Knot's eating after starving him all these years?

Twice while he plays ball, she comes out with a bundle of clothes and puts them in the Ford. Second time, she gets in the car, backs up, pulls out and is gone. Smoke shooting from the tailpipe, fogging the trailing dogs. She almost runs over Cee Ray on his bicycle, meeting her head on; he dodges the front end of the car, the bike jackknifes and he lands broadside in the frost-burned weeds off the left side of the road.

The dogs give up the car for Cee Ray and the spinning wheels of the toppled bike. He stands, kicks at the dogs twitching around him, watching the car fade out in the pure golden light. Then he picks up the bicycle and pushes it back onto the road, straddles it and pumps, weaving among the dogs hypnotized by the turning of the wheels.

Knot is glad Marge is gone, but having taken her clothes, she probably won't be coming back. He has always dreaded her leaving, feared that she would go, and now she is gone. He can breathe now. He can play. Really, he's always been alone. It comes to him that he is old enough to be on his own and the dread and fear of her leaving is an emotion clung to from his past. Like sucking his thumb and suddenly realizing that he's sucking when he no longer needs to, that it's only a habit. The preacher throws the ball to him and he catches it, dribbles toward the goal, shoots and misses.

"Where yo mind at, boy?" the first string player barks. Yo Knot! is only a rumor in his head.

But fifteen minutes later, the old Ford rattles up the road, blocking the setting sun for an instant. Marge parks before her porch and gets out with a small brown paper sack hugged close inside of her coat. Knot knows that trick. Inside he is a bit relieved—okay, a lot relieved. Though he'd just been daydreaming about how he would get the preacher to take him to Aunt Willie's in Valdosta, tell her the truth about his being her own blood kin. Without Marge cutting the fool,

Knot would be welcome as the flowers in May. He would help out with his granddaddy and leave Aunt Willie to her cooking and bringing back in her lost children.

A few minutes later the rusty black heater flue rising out of the dull tin roof of Marge's shack begins pumping out black smoke. White steamy smoke, at intervals, means Marge has had to pour water on the fire to keep from burning down the house. The fire flares and dies and flares and dies. At times no more productive than smoke from an old man's pipe.

"Play ball!"

Knot plays to keep from going back inside and because moving about, hopping about, distracts him from the blossoming sunless cold and watching Marge putting stuff in the car, Marge on the porch, Marge in the yard—Marge, coatless, stealing into and stealing out of Winston Riley's house! Something hidden inside her old white sweater.

What is she up to?

Has she stolen whiskey? What?

One of the worst fights she and Winston ever had was over her sneaking into his house while he was at work and stealing his half-gallon jug of corn whiskey—moonshine, he called it. When he came asking, later that evening, Marge swore up and down she hadn't set foot in his nasty old house; as for that rot-gut whiskey, she wouldn't be caught dead drinking it. Her eyelids were at half-mast and her words were slurred. She lay limp on her bed, toes pointed out. Winston grabbed her by her flaming hair and slapped her flat-handed and backhanded on each cheek—an economizing flapping motion. She bit his hand and wouldn't let go, even as he yanked up on her hair. Finally Knot, standing frozen in the corner of the bathroom wall and the nailed up back door, stumbled forward over the heap of old sheets, blankets, bedspreads and curtains the women Marge worked for had supplemented her wages with.

What Knot had in mind was to make it to the door and run for help. But Winston, balling one fist and nursing the other freed one to his chest beneath his unbuttoned shirt, blood soaking the front of his tarry khaki pants, mistook Knot's shooting out from the corner as an attack and stuck out his big booted foot and tripped Knot. He sprawled face-first to the floor, feeling the bone in his nose smash into his forehead and cheekbones. Blood in his mouth, Knot tried to crawl toward the door, but Winston planted his foot on the small of Knot's back as if he were stomping a cockroach. Knot had to play dead, listening as Winston rared and cussed and rooted among his and Marge's belongings. Finally, finding his jug and stepping over Knot in the doorway, he was gone. Knot alone with Marge, passed out or dead on the bed, brought his arms up to rest his head on them and stared down at the patch of wood on the floor that had caused such pain. Afraid to get up and go to the bathroom and look in the mirror. Afraid to check on Marge, figuring she was dead. His face still felt like it was slamming into the floor and he could see a red puddle of his own blood, his nose dripping, dripping, dimpling the puddle. Had he stayed there all night? Had he gotten up and checked on Marge? He couldn't remember. What he did remember was learning not to take every one of Marge's near-death encounters to heart. He learned to separate himself, to go beyond what was going on. Because, always, always, the sun came up the next morning.

Winston isn't home now, but he'll be back. He has a new woman and now when glass breaks at the house next door, it is usually from a dropped dish or whiskey glass. They love and laugh and make merry throughout the night.

Marge comes out on the porch again, a little later, looking bushed, or drunk, orange hair covered with a white headrag. In both hands she is carrying a white dishpan of water. Teetering to the edge of the porch, near the woodpile, she dashes it to the yard.

Somebody is frying ham, smells like. And though Knot is still packed with baloney and Wonder bread he thinks it smells good. He smells biscuits baking, the tangy buttermilk kind that one of the older church ladies makes for dinners at church.

Cee Ray rides his bicycle up to the spot where the game is going on, stops and sits astride. Dogs panting in the breathing cold.

The preacher shoots the ball his way. Cee Ray ducks and it flies over his head and rolls to the fence near the big oak on the school grounds. One of the players has to chase after it. Dogs yapping at his heels. He looks mean at Cee Ray who doesn't care.

Off and on all evening, the people in the quarters in coats and hats or head rags have built up fires and stood around warming and watching the game. Gradually they have gone inside their houses, and the yard fires have burned down to hot white ash, and the chimneys blaze with fresh fire. Smoke layering over the gathering dusk of the quarters.

When finally the sun gutters out behind the west line of pines, Marge steps through the door and stands on the porch wearing her royal blue church dress with a wide bow at the throat and buttons down the front. The strange slinky dress Knot had never seen before and which he thinks would look better on a man. She steps over to the doorsteps and holds to the right post, one foot out before her, sporting a best black shoe.

Is she leaving? Is she drunk? Has she found his money, took some and hid the rest for later? Will she drink herself into oblivion with no shortage of cash now?

The game is over, but the boys and the preacher are walking off an imaginary boundary for the concrete basketball court which Knot's money, courtesy of the bank, is paying for, but which everybody either thinks is paid for by the preacher or Marge, who knows better, or at least believes that the other is paying for.

Dizzy already from the long cold day, his terror of Sammy Bruce, and trying to keep up with Marge while keeping up with the ball, Knot's mind buzzes from sorting and recalling all that has happened since he came into money. The jumble of the blessed and the cursed, from Cee

Ray on the blue bike he has just cast aside on the ground by his doorsteps, to the preacher staking out the court, to Winston Riley probably on his way home to make merry with his girlfriend now that Boots is gone, to Marge standing on the porch, likely freezing, in the silky blue dress. Knot, himself, cursed—unable to spend a dime for a Moonpie—a breathing lump, a knot on a log, yet Lord of it all.

Nights before falling asleep, having said his prayers in case he died before he woke, he used to try to figure time and space, where he was before he was born, where the world begins and ends, geographically and historically, the point of it all—living. Going the limit, as deep into logic and science as he was capable, to the core of his mind, and spinning into a numb state with weariness and no answers. Piercing heat surging, radiating from his chest to his head, causing a tumbling, swooning sensation, followed by dreamless sleep. And that's how his thinking about the money makes him feel.

"Knot!" Marge calls, waving. "Hey, Knot!"

He leaves the fellows to their staking off the concrete court and runs over to where Marge is hugging the porch post. He stops quick before her, breathing hard, and stoops with his hands on his knees, bracing himself and praying for her mercy.

"Knot, go tell the preacher I said to come eat before he leaves." She turns in her good black shoes, clicking the heels going inside, closing the door and leaving Knot with his hands on his knees staring at the clean swept porch. Smelling an after-draft of moss-scented bath soap, smelling the bleach water dashed to the yard, and if he's not crazy, smelling the fried ham and buttermilk biscuits at his own house.

She has to be drunk. She has to be. Either that or she has found his money and is pacified by the fact that she can drink as much as she likes, when she likes. So, she doesn't have to worry where the money will come from and consequently can take a break from drinking without feeling threatened that tomorrow she won't be able to afford another drink.

Going through the door first, preacher behind him, taking off his white cap and brushing his navy and gray athletic shoes on a rag mat, Knot is struck like a blow with an iron pipe across the head by the warmth and light, the fried ham and the raw but inviting clean-house smells.

Dazed, he takes in the room: the oblong dinette table is facing the doorway, center of the room. It is covered with a white cloth, and in the middle stands a clay tar pot full of green holly boughs with red berries. The two beds, her larger one and Knot's cot, are slid together to make space for the table and packed tight with white chenille bedspreads. Something glaring—the window where the table used to sit and the one to the left of the wood heater are so polished that the contents of the room smacks in reflection and bounces back. White plates stacked and gleaming on the shelf above the stove. Flatware standing in a polished fruit jar. Big bowls, little bowls, grouped on the ends.

Everything is neat. The old blankets and sheets and curtains are gone from the corner formed by a wall of the bathroom and the back door (must have been the two bundles she put in the Ford that Knot had thought were her finally-leaving clothes). Something else missing—the sack of mummified rotted hulls of potatoes by the door. So strange how they'd quit stinking at a certain stage of rot. But strangest of all is Marge standing over the stove with a stirring spoon in hand. Turning, smiling, speaking in a sweet tone that even Aunt Willie has never before heard.

"Knot, move yourself out of the doorway, please," Marge says, "and let the preacher in." Gone is the self-conscious exaggerated speech. When she laughs, as she is now doing, it is warm and natural, not turned in on herself and mean-spirited.

Knot had absolutely forgotten the preacher, shivering behind him. The cold rushing into the warm room.

For the first time ever, the old heater is behaving. Usually it is too cold or too hot, is belching fire and raging or smothering the fire out, but now it peacefully crackles and purrs as if filled with milk-fed kittens.

"Sister Marge," the preacher says, taking off his brown leather flight jacket. "Don't know when I've smelled such good food."

She sets a lid on a pot, softly, and walks over to take his jacket and hangs it on the rod in the corner between the stove and one wall of the bathroom. "Now, now. I know that grandmother of yours is the best cook in this county. How's she doing?"

Knot cannot figure where to sit, what to do. The room is too light and neat and clean and he feels disoriented. He stares at his cot shoved to the wall and pictures the banded stacks of hundred dollar bills scattered like rocks from a landslide underneath. He hopes. But better sense warns him that Marge has found the money. The house looks and smells too clean and he has seen her cleaning other women's houses and her big boast was always dusting and mopping underneath beds and it is a mystery to her, she says, why people stick all their junk under their beds for her to have to get down on her knees and pull out and put back. Half her time is spent pulling out and putting back.

She's too happy; the fried ham is too cooked to perfection and Knot cannot believe that the fluffy brown-topped biscuits are her own. Somebody else must have baked them. Who?

Talking in a toned-down mealtime voice, the preacher sits with his back to the door, at the long side of the table, Marge on his left and Knot on his right. Marge answering, sitting up straight and passing the tomato gravy and white rice. She never cooks rice. Hates rice because it boils over and is difficult to time.

Knot longs to drop to his knees and dive beneath the chenille fringe hanging down from Marge's bedspread on his right. To look for his money.

Marge asks the preacher about the man he saved on the railroad tracks in Valdosta last summer, and briefly summarizing he tells what happened, much the same as the newspaper's account of events. Then at her prompting he tells about growing up in Detroit with his mother and two sisters, then "coming home to the South" to preach and care for his grandmother. Nothing much new in what he tells, but the way he sums up his life makes it seem easy, makes it seem he didn't exist till he got to Statenville and that nothing had ever happened to him except what he has told and that is just filler, not facts.

The preacher looks even less like a preacher inside Knot's shanty than he had, minus his white shirt and tie, on the basketball court. His brown leather jacket mocks Knot and Marge's sorry clothes hanging in the midst of them on the rod. Knot tries to find something familiar about his face, something to place him in memory. His ears are neat and close and a bit smaller than Knot recalls. Ears of a stranger, up close.

"Sister Marge," he says, "I believe I'll have another of your good biscuits."

She passes the bone platter of biscuits Knot has never seen before.

The preacher takes a biscuit and holds the platter out to Knot, who only looks at it as if taking stock.

"Knot," Marge says.

"Yes ma'am. No ma'am."

The preacher passes the platter back to Marge; she sets it on top of the bowl of tomato gravy.

"Knot's kind of stunned, Preacher Troutman." She folds her hands under her chin, eyes gleaming like her halo of washed and combed hair.

The preacher sips his coffee, staring at her, listening, though not looking at Knot for fear of embarrassing him maybe.

"Knot's not used to a good meal and me dressed up like somebody."

"I understand." The preacher sets his cup down, slides back his plate and crosses his arms before it.

"No sir, you don't," she says. "There's more to it."

Knot sits up straight, squares his shoulders, back aching with strain. Now she is going to tell about the money—that's what she's up to. She has figured it out—the bank robber and all. She's put two and two together and baited a trap with her cooking and cleaning and lured the preacher over to attest to her innocence and Knot's guilt before turning him over to the law. Maybe finding the money and figuring where it came from and the mystery of money sent and spent has shocked her into respectability—her own boy, a bank robber!

Knot is just before confessing, has his mouth open to explain happening up on the robber and the money in the alley last summer; getting stuck with the money and all that owning money involves, when Marge begins speaking in a tired, shamed tone.

"Knot's had a bad morning." Going on she gives a blow by blow account of their going to the Bruce's to work and Sammy Bruce's threat, ending with the slap across the cheek—she says that—when Bruce pays them a quarter between them.

The heater purrs. Knot gets up and goes out the door without his coat. Stands in the cold on the porch. "Thank you, Lord, thank you." The moon is full, glinting on the tin roofs and glowing on the packed dirt. The air smells of smoke and cold.

When he comes back inside, toting firewood, the preacher stands and goes over and opens the heater door on front, then takes piece by piece from Knot's arms, stacking it on the pulsing kittens of coals.

Knot just stands there. The preacher stands there. Facing each other. Marge at the table is sitting sideways with her right arm crooked over her chair back.

The preacher slaps Knot on the shoulder. "It's a hard and valuable lesson. Worth more than the money you should have been paid, had you been paid fair after working all morning."

He crosses over to the broomstick rod in the corner

between the stove and the bathroom wall, takes his coat from the wire hanger and slides one arm through and then the other, lining up the front and snapping it. "A fine young man like you, just don't let it get to you."

He walks past Knot to the door, looking back as he opens it. Blast of cold. "If it's any consolation, the price for picking up pecans has gone up since I was a boy." Lump in his throat riding up and down, teary dark eyes cutting Marge's way, he adds, "I don't think I've ever felt so full."

While Marge washes the dishes, still in her blue dress, Knot takes off the tablecloth, goes out the door and shakes it off the edge of the porch, like he's seen Aunt Willie do. The white cloth looks palest blue in the moonlight. He comes back inside folding it.

"Needs washing," Marge says. "Just put it in the basket under the sink."

He goes into the bathroom. Rusty water streaks have been scoured from the old white lavatory and toilet. The floor is still soft with patches of rot but bleached white as Styrofoam. And sure enough under the lavatory there is a brown wicker basket for dirty clothes.

"You can put the table back where it was"—Marge is drying dishes—"so we can slide the beds out."

Walking one end and then the other to the window, centering the table, he lifts the clay pot of holly from the floor where he has set it and places it in the middle, centering, delaying looking for the money he fears she has found.

He slides her bed out, forming a walk space between it and his cot. But he leaves the cot butted to the wall with the polished window over it and watches himself in reflection, folding back the spread to old but clean white sheets with pressed folds meaning they have been lying in the stack gone from the foot of his bed, a clean corner now.

He lies waiting for Marge, now putting dishrags in a bleach soak in the dishpan. Waiting while she puts a pine log in the heater and sets the damper for the wood to burn slow.

Scorched wall behind, a reminder of her long years of sloth.

He lies still with his eyes closed as she pulls the string on the dangling bare bulb in the middle of the room. Standing a minute, watching him, sliding off her shoes and nudging them under her bed. Then tiptoeing in bare feet to the bathroom, closing the door and leaving a seam of white light like the seam of red around the heater door. All windows glow with moonlight.

While she is running water, he jumps up and kneels on the floor between their beds, looking, feeling underneath the narrow cot. Nothing. Not even a dandelion of dust. He pulls out his cot—maybe he has missed the sack near the head of his bed.

He is lying on his stomach on the bed with his head between the wall and the cot when Marge steps out of the bathroom and stops, watching him.

He rises to his knees, staring at her. She is wearing a striped pink flannel granny gown. She fans the skirt self-consciously.

"Burnt that old T-shirt," she says low. "Burnt a lot of stuff didn't add up to no good."

"My books? Did you burn my books?"

She walks over to her bed, folds back the covers, sits, yawning and brushing the bottoms of her feet, then lies back, snuggling and turning face-away. "Now what kind of mama would I be, burning your books? There're in the car, to take back to the library. You want em, go get em. I'm about mama-ed out." Then to herself in a sleepy voice, humming a laugh, "That boy, he do love his books."

Knot gets up and goes into the bathroom and when he comes out she is snoring. The heater is purring, red seams defining its shape, and moonlight streaming through the spanking windows, whitewashing the clean room.

He steps out into the cold and stands on the porch, in the cleft eave and post shadows of the sliding moon's light. Dogs are barking way off, oak smoke on the air. Then he goes to the Ford and opens the door. The yellow light inside comes on and Knot's eyes pick up immediately the brown paper sack of money with the books on top sitting unmolested in the backseat.

In the house again, he pulls his cot closer to Marge's and makes room at the head of his bed for the blocky sack, then lies down just as Winston and his girlfriend get home. Laughing, talking, knocking about the room as usual. Then all is quiet. The iron bedstead begins slamming the wall nearest the wall where Marge and Knot are resting their heads with a primitive rhythmic drumming, him moaning and her shrieking.

"Ole cats mating," Marge mumbles.

Chapter 7

The little white-headed girl, one seat up and a row over from Knot, has her head down on her desk, sniffling. Maybe crying, though when the teacher asks Becky says she is sick. Her hair is thick and tends toward curls but not really curly. More humped up below her nape, and the teacher says for her to go to the principal's office.

It is morning.

Just before history class is over and Knot and the others have suffered through note-taking on Magellan, Becky returns. The red sweater she is wearing makes her hair look whiter, her face pinker. She closes the heavy wood door easy and creeps around the back of the room, up the aisle by the window and sits in her desk, head down and sniffling again.

"Blimp!" shouts a lanky boy with freckles in the front desk, window-side, who has been placed there for throwing spitballs.

Desks skitter and books slap the floor and pencils roll. Everybody scrambles to the tall paned windows, peering out at the massive gray blimp floating past like a mean storm cloud.

The teacher threatens and cajoles. "Back in your seats, children! Back in your seats, or else!

GOODYEAR is written on the side of the blimp like a God-sent clue on a spelling test. The room grows dim as it covers the sun at eleven o'clock.

Only Becky has remained in her desk, frozen, sobbing, tears rolling down her pink cheeks. Hair whiter in the sunlight, as the blimp passes, heated air busy with disturbed dust specks, lead and chalk smells.

After everybody has returned to their seats, picking up dropped books and pencils, Becky bawls with her head on her desk.

Wise to the order of her class having collapsed with the

appearance of the airy gray balloon, the boxy looking teacher—thirty or forty years old, depending on whether her glazed moon-colored hair is fixed or not—switches to the subject of "non-rigid, buoyant aircraft." She asks for hands to go up if anybody can explain what fuels and propels blimps.

Knot starts to raise his hand, but the little white-headed girl's low sobbing and sniffling distracts him more than her bawling had. He feels so sorry for her that the peach fuzz on his bony arms prickles. His scalp tingles. His heart stings.

Everybody in the room is watching her.

Finally the teacher walks down the aisle between rows one and two, stops at the white-headed girl, bends and asks low what the school nurse had to say. No fever.

The gray blocky heater bracketed over the green chalkboard they call black chuffs a baked-dust smell, which Knot thinks could be the cause of the girl's sniffles.

No. Now she is mewling like a cat, and the smart-ass white boy ahead of Knot starts sniggering. He is the tallest boy in the class, wears a flattop haircut, and Knot is witness to his spurting growth—daily his head rises on his long neck, squaring shoulders blocking Knot's view of the teacher and the blackboard. He wears pressed plaid shirts everyday that smell of starch.

The bell clangs for changing classes. Thrill and alarm, nobody gets used to.

The little white-headed girl stands and wipes her nose on her red sweater sleeve, and files in with the other students on their way out to break. No recess now that they are in seventh grade and if you have no friends like Knot and the little white-headed girl, you don't care. Fifteen minutes is about the right amount of time to go to the restroom and get some water and not have to linger in the halls looking hopeful that somebody might speak and make you look popular.

Out of maybe 300 students in the all-grade school, only twenty-five or thirty are Negro. Most over sixteen years old have quit rather than move from the Negro school near the Sampson Camp after the government-enforced integration. When the lower grades line up along the sidewalks to go to lunchroom, it is easy to see how segregated the school still is by the gradations of white to black faces from front to end of the line—tagging snotty-nose bawling black babies, the token generation, forced to go to the white school and serve always as example.

Knot finds it interesting that the three Negroes—all boys—in his class have nothing to do with each other. According to Aunt Willie, at the big school in Valdosta, where Lee and Judy Beth go, the Negroes sit together in the classroom and gang up in the halls, strengthened by an undiluted alliance. Hate festers and breaks out in fight. But at Knot's school, in his class, it's as if the Negro boys are afraid the other students and teachers will think they are in cahoots, or as if their blackness will stand out combined. Their aim is to escape notice. Knot, having never belonged to anybody anyway, feels exempt from the entire process of integration, which he hears about second-hand or reads about as exotic history in the making. Like slavery before his time, integration, Civil Rights, and all pertaining have nothing to do with him personally. Before integration, at the all-Negro school across Troublesome Creek, he'd never belonged, never *needed* to belong. Only to Aunt Willie's family did he need to belong. Except for Sammy Bruce, he has never been mistreated or treated at all by whites. They don't even see him. Still, during break, he makes it a point not to go into the restroom while another Negro boy is in there. The restroom seems a particularly dangerous place with no teachers on patrol.

Opening the huge gray door, coming out of the damp restroom with the fake lemon smell and the wild laughing and dirty talking of the boys inside, Knot sees Becky Bruce standing by the door across the hall from where their last class took place. She is now crying with her scrubbed red face turned to one side and away from the other students shuffling along the hall.

Knot starts to walk over and say something—no, he doesn't start, he never would, but his heart is in the right place—when he is saved by the history teacher stepping up to the white-headed girl and placing her right hand on the girl's forehead. She shakes her head—no fever.

So much racket in the hall now that Knot has to change sides, looking off while eavesdropping on what the little girl is mumbling to the teacher.

"Tornado...Mama...Daddy...broke arm."

Knot wishes she would speak clearer and quit sniffling and everybody would get the hell out of the hall.

Next class, after the bell, and the girl is gone, either sick or suffering from fear of tornadoes or Mama and Daddy or a broken arm which must be the mother's because it's for sure not hers.

CR • ZO

Marge has to go to church now, but she doesn't have to like it. Sort of like the white-headed girl has to go to school.

Life is like that.

And too in South Georgia, in the winter, you can look for two days of cold followed by two days of rain. Today, Sunday, it is rainy and mild. Soppy mud holes in the road to and from church and straight-down rain across the blond dead grass yard and field behind the church. The humped pale grass reminds Knot of that little white-headed girl and he would like to tell her that tornadoes hardly ever crop up in South Georgia during winter. But he figures that wouldn't help her fear because her fear is like his of Winston Riley now, who rags Marge every chance he gets about her giving Boots the money to leave on.

Fear is like that.

Besides Knot is what's coming to be called "Black," like that's some improvement over "Negro," and the girl is white and if anybody at school saw them talking they would make something out of it. Talk about ragging!

Marge is testifying, on her feet next to the piano,

testifying. "That money give to the church before Thanksgiving…"

"Praise the Lord, Sister!" somebody butts in shouting.

"Amen. Thank you, sister!"

"I ain't lying when I tell you…," she tries again. She holds out both hands for them to shut up, to listen.

"Say it like it is, sister."

Inside the church is bathed in fake moonlight from the new slender florescent lights overhead. Outside is steel gray and the rain falls slow and regular as if it might rain forever.

Dressed in a navy suit and blood-of-Christ tie, same red as the new carpet, the preacher behind the podium motions for silence in the packed church. "Let Sister Marge speak."

"Amen," a man says and raises his right hand. But the mumbling grows to a rumble and the chant goes on. Marge opens and closes her mouth, nods to the preacher, even sticks her pointer fingers in her ears to show she can't hear herself think.

"Thank you, Sister Marge. Thank you." The preacher sets off a chant: "We all thank you. Jesus thanks you. Wadn't for you, wouldn't be no heat this chill morning in God's house. Wadn't for you our young folk be out scouting for trouble stead of playing basketball on a Saturday."

The preacher shakes his head, biting back laughing, Marge speaking anyway, toneless it seems. She is wearing a furry pink jacket over a white blouse, maybe *borrowed* like the blue dress from Winston Riley's girlfriend. Pay, Marge explained to Knot, for all the racket she has to put up with at night. And for Boots, she added to excuse her stealing, for all that she had to put up with.

She stands again, blurting the truth—"I ain't have no money, hear me! My sister ain't have no money. I ain't know nothing bout no money!"—while they chant and hum and fan the hot gaseous air.

Their humming vibrates the new slick pale pine pew Knot is sitting on in the choir loft, snug between two oversized holy-ghost enchanted sisters of the church in new wine robes stung with fresh dye.

Marge: "Don't come to me for no more money; I be just as poor as the least of y'all."

Knot thinks he sees an exchange of puzzled looks pass over the potted red poinsettias on the altar table between Marge and the preacher. Almost accusing each other of not taking credit or blame.

"Wouldn't be no new piano," somebody shouts, working up another chant. "Wouldn't be no fine new choir robes, wouldn't be no..."

Somehow the preacher leads off into the story of Joseph's cloak of many colors, and Marge takes her seat at the piano, fuming with her arms crossed.

Knot doesn't know what has come over her to suddenly want to take up that cross again. Confession is good for the soul, they say. But his guess is, she has changed her tune because everybody and their kin are after her for money for themselves. Knot sighs and breathes easy and sinks back into daydreaming about how to get some money to that little white-headed girl so she and her mother can leave the pulpwooder who broke the mother's arm—it has to be her. Knot can picture it. He's been witness to one of Mrs. Bruce's breakings, and it was among the cruelest of persecutions he'd ever seen.

Knot had found himself, unbelievably—on a Saturday!—sitting in Marge's car out front of the Bruce's two-room wide, white frame house, at the city limits sign on the southernmost edge of Statenville. This was before Winston's run-in with the boss over his Saturday mission to borrow money, but after Bruce had broken a chair over the head of that other hired hand for having committed the exact same crime. Everybody in the quarters had been talking about it and now here Knot was, waiting on a gray Saturday morning for Marge inside to try to borrow "a little ahead" on her next house-cleaning job.

Before they had stopped, Knot had tried to reason with Marge, reminding her of what happened to the last person to show up at the pulpwooder's house on a Saturday. But made brave by Bruce's green pickup being gone, on her way to the Line for liquor, she had stopped anyway. And now all Knot could do was watch and pray that Bruce wouldn't drive up before Marge got back.

His neck ached from turning his head, watching; his prayer was like a wad of hardened gum in his mouth.

"Come on, Marge," he whispered to himself.

She had left the car idling, full choke, and with every beat of his heart, the engine galloped in synchrony, the car shaking as if his own shaking had triggered it. Smells of gas and burnt oil, and gusts of exhaust smoke chuffing from the tail pipe like the car was on fire. Clouds pressing the smoke low, layering it across the highway and circling round to the fresh-painted front porch of the Bruce house.

Knot's eyes were burning, his lungs filling with smoke as it sailed through the open window on his side of the car.

Suddenly, from inside the house, near the back, came the sounds of screaming, high-pitched woman-screaming.

Then, "Knot, help! Help! Get on in here." Marge.

Sounded like a chair overturned—*wham*! Feet pounding on the floor.

"House on fire," Knot said and yanked up on the door handle, hopping out and running up the concrete walk, up the doorsteps, across the porch, and through the left-open door— Marge left the door open, he thought, remembered later thinking, not about how he alone would save everybody, not how he alone would put out the fire, only about Bruce coming up and finding the front door wide open and Marge there to borrow money. On a Saturday! Lord help!

He was in the forbidden green living room with its sheer criss-cross curtains on many windows, when he heard, "Snake!" and more screaming and then he was in the kitchen, where the screams were coming from, peering down at the clean yellow linoleum rug—no snake—and then up at Marge standing in a kitchen chair about halfway between the white kitchen counter and cabinets and the back door. She was pointing at the bead-board wall on Knot's left, shrieking, "Snake! Help!" and dancing on the chair bottom, one shoe on and the other gone, and her in running gear with nowhere to go.

Becky and her mother were standing stiff in the bedroom doorway on his right, other side of the square white kitchen table, clutching each other and looking dumb-struck while at the same time shouting, "Snake!"

"There, Knot," Marge said. "There, wropped up in them cords."

"Cords?"

"There. Catch him! Catch him!"

Snarled black electric cords leading from a table with a percolator and toaster on it trailed up the wall to a socket-type receptacle with one cord, red-checked, braided around the others. It moved.

"Lil ole ratsnake," said Knot, relieved that the house was not on fire, though exhaust smoke from the car was billowing through the open front door to the kitchen. Choking gray smoke.

The women renewed their screaming, all three in hideous harmony, as he walked over and caught the slender, foot-long snake behind the head and lifted it wriggling from the twist of cords and winding its body and tail around his hand and wrist like a bright bracelet. "Lil ole rat snake," he said again and held it out for the three of them to see.

Again, Marge danced, lifting one foot and then the other from the chair bottom and hollering, "Hooooo! Get that nasty thing out ahere," as if filth was the main thing and not her fear. "I mean *now!*"

Becky and her mother had vanished into the bedroom, carrying on as if Knot were chasing them with the snake.

The kitchen was swirling with the oily exhaust fumes and smoke from the idling car out front as Knot started toward the back door with the wiggly red snake, holding it still behind the head but in both hands like a tiny bird fallen from its nest.

His ears were cringing from their combined screams, Marge on his left latching both hands to the top slat of the chair as if to keep it from tipping over if Knot started her way and she had to leap down and make a dash in the opposite direction.

"Ooooo, Lordy! Don't let em loose, Knot. Get a good holt." Marge, with her gold hair bushed out, was laughing a little now that Knot had saved them all from the snake.

Mrs. Bruce and Becky had crept back into the doorway to watch, laughing a little bit too, but still hugging one another—saved and seeming to feel sort of silly, but after all they were women with a God-given right to fear snakes.

Almost to the back door, Knot stopped, facing Sammy Bruce, lumber-jack large in blue jeans and a red-plaid flannel shirt, just standing there, exhaust smoke from Marge's car sucking around him and out the door to the narrow porch.

"What the hell's all that hollering about? Thought the house was on fire."

"That ole rat snake," Knot said and started to hand it to him as proof of his innocence, in explanation for being inside the white man's house, or as if the snake was Bruce's property and he had been caught in the act of stealing it.

Bruce backed up, stopped. Dodging round as if Knot had tried to put the snake on him. Clearly mad now for having shown fear and been made a fool of. "Don't give him to me," he said, getting his fear in check, "give him to the wife." He laughed mocking and low, looking only at Knot as if to deny his wife those wild green eyes. "She's the one making a nigger-jook out of my house, so take it to her."

"I just take him on out, now sir." Knot inched toward the door, the snake's tail curling around his forearm, up to his elbow, though its head was still clamped between his forefinger and thumb.

Bruce boomed: "I SAY, TAKE IT TO THE WIFE."

"No! No!" all screamed, including Marge, who added, "What I tell you, boy. Get that thing out ahere. *This minute!*"

"I can't do that, sir." Knot couldn't take his eyes off of

Bruce, he felt charmed, though the exhaust smoke was making them tear and blink. "Miss Bruce, she be scared…scared to death of this here snake."

Speaking to his wife, though still eyeing Knot and the snake, Bruce said, "Then that good-for-nothing girl yonder. You don't want to take it, Nell, she's gone have to."

Becky began crying, or maybe she'd been crying and Knot couldn't hear for all the screaming stopping up his ears. He didn't turn to look; all he wanted was to make it out the back door with snake, and hit the woods running till he got to the quarters. Home.

Nell Bruce stepped away from Becky. "You stay where you are, hear?" Her voice was firm but feeble.

Behind him, Knot heard her bump into the table, then step around, stopping a few feet behind him.

"Be shamed of yo self," Marge yelled at Bruce. "She ain't wanting to hole no ole snake, nasty thing."

"What about you, Marge? You wanting to hold it?

"I wrap it round yo sorry neck, you mess with me."

"So. What'll it be, Nell? You or Becky."

"Me." She sounded frozen. Not even a squeak in her voice for all of her screaming before.

"No. Mama, no." Becky began a muted, seething crying.

Bruce hooked his thumbs in his belt loops, enjoying himself now. "Y'all make up your mind now."

"I take it on outside, sir."

"You do what I tell you. Do it now."

"Knot, no," Marge shouted. "You ain't gone hand that po woman no snake. Do, I wear you out good fashion."

Finally the wife crept up alongside Knot and gingerly took the snake, thumb and forefinger pinching the head as Knot had done but holding it out, away from her body. Its tail whipping at the smoky air and trying to attach to her arm, to anything it could wrap around. She closed her eyes, sucking in.

"Ma-maa!" Becky screamed.

Nell Bruce looked like a statue of a woman presenting a

snake. Her brown hair was neatly curled, and she was wearing a belted red-striped nylon shirtwaist with buttons from the collar to the hem. Her flat black shoes were planted on the yellow floor. Her eyes remained shut and if she was breathing Knot couldn't hear her.

"I take it back now," Knot said, and reached for the snake as if they were passing it around and it was his turn.

"Like hell, you will," shouted Bruce.

Fearing she might be next, Marge stomped down from the chair, sending it skiddering to the wall next to Bruce, and gimped out the front in that one worn-out black shoe. "Get yo self in the car, boy. Now!"

"Yeah, you go get in the car, boy." Bruce shook a finger at him. "And next time you come at me with a snake, I'm gone stomp you in the ground, you hear?"

☙ • ❧

After church, everybody is hugging Marge, patting her back, while the preacher stands aside smiling because the spirit of love is at last being extended to this generous woman. Knot can vouch that it's been weeks since her last drink. He only hopes that now that revenge is no longer a fever she won't start drinking again. But really he is growing numb to the new sober, dependable Marge. She's still cleaning the shack, mopping around his money sack; she's still cooking, not all the time but often. And since he is no longer perpetually hungry, he's beginning to take her for granted. If not for worrying over the little white-headed girl, who is on the verge of becoming "Becky" to him, Knot would be resting easy for the first time in his life.

☙ • ❧

The girl doesn't come to school on Monday but she is there on Tuesday. Her navy book satchel is on the floor between her desk row and Knot's.

He has a hundred dollar bill folded in his pocket and has to figure how to slip it in the satchel when nobody is looking. It has to happen soon, before history class is over. He may not get another chance.

The door-size windows feature crayon pictures of Christmas trees and silver bells and a red Santa with a black sack over one shoulder, boots to match. Like in grade school. Which makes Knot feel as if he is moving backwards instead of ahead. And he's not sure that he has come all that far, actually, except for the fact that he is now a thousand-aire, a rich boy, for all the good it does him. Santa Claus!

The teacher is writing on the green chalkboard. Chalk *snick snicking* and the students are taking notes. Now or never.

Knot stretches in his desk and digs out the bill and wads it in his left hand, then starts writing, bearing down till the point of his pencil snaps free. He stands and starts up the aisle and kicks over the girl's satchel. She looks down at the satchel as he sets it upright, then down at the composition book on her desk and starts writing again.

At the pencil sharpener next to the green board and the teacher, he pokes the blunted pencil point in the hole of the sharpener and begins turning the small metal crank with the smooth wood knob on the end. Making it clear to the teacher that he has no intention of disturbing her class—see how he has tiptoed to the front of the room, see how he turns the crank slow and easy. She stops writing and looks at him with those slanted green eyes, smiles and writes again. Her moon-glazed hair is fixed today, the sides pinned up high above her neat ears and the back flipped, giving her a perky look, a girlish look. He tries to gauge her absorption in the neat snappy printing on the chalk-swirled board: Names of United States presidents and the periods of their respective reigns.

Sometimes when she talks about President John F. Kennedy, her look seems to bear down as if she's stuck. Then she tells where she was that grim November day the year before when HE was assassinated and has each of them tell where they were—where were you when you heard that *the president* of the United States had been shot? Knot lies and says he was doing his homework, some such, when really he'd been out wandering the quarters, looking for

Marge on one of her long drunks, fearing she might lie down somewhere, pass out and freeze to death. He had heard about the assassination on a neighbor's TV. Marge hadn't sobered up till Thanksgiving morning, so was the last person on the planet earth to hear the news. Then to Knot she pretended she had known all along—*where were you when you heard that the president of the United States...?* To Aunt Willie she made out like she was sick and tired of hearing about it.

Knot has the hundred dollar bill still clutched in his left fist.

The teacher looks at him again, this time more of a side-long glance, writing. "Knot, all you're doing is grinding down the point and re-sharpening that pencil. Why? Drop that paper in your other fist in the wastebasket on the way back to your seat."

"Ma'am? No, ma'am. It's a dollar brung from home for the Needy Children's Christmas Fund." He waits for her to speak, expecting her to tell him to give it to her.

"Put it back in your pocket then. Isn't a dollar a lot of money for a boy your age to be giving away?"

He knows she means that it's a lot of money for a poor boy like him. "Marge give it to me."

"Marge *gave* it to you and you *brought* it from home." She pecks the board with the chalk, stooping to write the last president's name on the bottom above the chalk and eraser tray. "Think about it."

Does she mean that he should think about his grammar or giving so much money? He turns to go to his seat, watching the rows of faces to see if anybody is looking. Except for Becky Bruce nobody has even noticed and she doesn't matter to anybody either except to her daddy and only for showing off to and scaring to death. She makes Knot glad he matters to nobody.

After lunch, the committee for the Needy Children's Christmas Fund meets at the long table in back of the room to discuss money-making projects.

Next to Knot is the smart-ass white boy, who sits in

front of Knot in history, then next to him is Becky Bruce in a short-sleeved white shirt and blue jeans. No jacket on and everybody else is wearing theirs because they've just come back in from the lunchroom and it's cold in the breezeway between buildings.

Knot looks over at the coat rack in the corner on his left, next to the world globe on its high stand, and sees the girl's navy parka.

While the smart-ass white boy puts down in writing the ideas from the two white girls across the table, and Becky Bruce works her humble art on a poster at the end of the table—her hair is a sheer silk curtain over her face—Knot goes over to the coat rack and takes off his cousin Lee's old silver metallic football jacket and hangs it. Smoothing down the sleeves and body of the jacket, he makes a quick pass over the navy parka, finds a pocket and slips the bill inside.

CR • EO

Every day, Tuesday through Friday, after slipping the money into Becky Bruce's pocket, Knot expects her to be gone. To not show up for class ever again or if she does to at least show some sign that she has found the money and will be moving away, she and her mother. But she works on her poster for the Needy Children's Christmas Fund, silently, timidly, spellbound. Like a crazy person in a nuthouse finally with something to do.

It is all he can do not to ask when she is leaving, she and her mother.

On Friday the boxy teacher with limp jaggled hair tacks the girl's poster on the main bulletin board in the high school hall: a caricature of grinning children riding rainbow shades of tricycles, bicycles, and tossing yellow beach balls up to a yellow sun.

Knot can tell this teacher is surprised that un-miraculous Becky Bruce has created such a miraculous, vivid poster. Before taking the poster out into the hall to hang, she had held it up for all the class to view. Mum, so as not to distract from the impact of the art, she had turned it this way and that. Becky hung her head and smirked, right corner of her mouth tugging down—It's nothing. But she knew it was good.

Her finale, Knot figures. She won't be back on Monday.

But she does come back.

She is back with her head held high for the teacher's announcement that somebody has anonymously donated one hundred dollars to the Needy Children's Christmas Fund. Becky almost twinkles but doesn't say a word and doesn't smile and Knot would like to lam her over the head with the history book he is holding. He has to cross his feet under his desk to keep from twitching them. He crosses his arms and squeezes his bony upper arms till his fingers tingle.

Word is out in the quarters and at school that Marge has given Knot $100 to donate anonymously to the Needy Children's Christmas fund.

Knot, walking home from school, hears Cee Ray on his bike behind him. The front fender is gone and the thin black tires look naked.

"She still gone get you that new wheel for Christmas?"

"Who?" Knot keeps walking.

"Yo rich auntie."

"That's for me to know and you to find out."

"I was you, I'd ax for a *car*, man!"

"I might," Knot says.

"Hey, man, you wanta ride my wheel?"

"No."

"Be that way then." Cee Ray shoots off on the bike, standing, round head bobbing left and right.

How to say to anybody that he'd rather have a bike than a car? Sounds crazy even to him. But of course if he did get a car—yeah, *if!*—he couldn't drive it. He could trade it in for a bike though, that is, if Marge didn't hog it for herself.

Lined up on the west side of the school, the yellow buses begin rolling toward the quarters to make their circle to the highway, children laughing, squealing, calling out to one another. Burned oil smells mixed with pencil lead and sweat. A special winding up roar of the engines, leveling out as they pass the east curve and take the straightaway to 94.

At his house, Knot goes inside and puts his school books on the foot of his cot, lifts the paperback books, one by one, from his money sack, takes two one-hundred dollar bills and rolls them and stuffs them in his jeans pocket.

Without the paperback library books on top he can now see that the stacked money has gone down. The sack is getting soft and beginning to tear where the sharp corners of the books and the bundles of money have gouged. Marge is at work, but she has left the house smelling of pine oil, chlorine bleach and fresh air. Not a thing out of place and both beds are made up like iced cakes. The wide velvety floorboards of leached wood stir with patches of sunlight and shadows from the open doors, both doors, and windows. White dotted Swiss curtains billow, sucking in and out, in the mild breeze. The room is gauzy and dim but not bleak. The ticking clock on the small table between Marge and Knot's beds lends to the order, comfort and cleanliness she has manipulated from filth and junk. Even the sack of books and money has been squared in the corner below the window at the top of Knot's cot.

So, he has to move the money to a different place now because of Marge's cleaning. Who knows? She might even take a notion to start reading.

Outside, he can hear the rattle of Cee Ray's bike chain sprocketing and reeling. He waits till the sound fades then wraps the sack of money in his silver football jacket and slips out the back door, heading across the packed dirt yard to the shortcut through the woods. Keeping to the path between dead brown vines and bushy green myrtle bushes, he angles through the block of woods, hearing the sounds of the children in the quarters wane into silence, then the roar and hum of traffic stopping and starting at the crossing downtown.

Stepping from the woods to the paved school bus shortcut, only minutes later, about halfway between the school and the courtyard, he sees Cee Ray pedaling along the hooked horseshoe to the quarters, prowling, hoping to locate and buddy with Knot in case he gets a car for Christmas.

Quickly, hoping Cee Ray has missed him, Knot walks on. When he gets to the courtyard, he steps over the white metal railing, just east of the small red brick jail joined by sidewalk to the courthouse. He walks diagonally under the huge live oaks and through the courthouse breezeway. Checking behind him and west along the sidewalk running from the school to the crossing, Knot crosses 94, parallel to the school bus road, and takes to the dead-grass shoulder of 129.

At Troublesome Creek, traveling north toward the church, he re-bundles the money sack in his jacket and keeps walking, down the dip and up the dip. Right side of the highway, a narrow stream of black water is embedded in blond frost-burned watergrass. High up on the sharp clay embankment a small yellow house sits tucked into dead vines and wintering trees, smoke from a smoldering leaf fire rising from its yard. Left side of the road, Troublesome Creek meanders through the green pines and bony shed gum trees on its way to the Alapaha River, west of Statenville.

Two semis in tandem rock out of the haze up the highway, heading south to Florida. Knot makes a fist and yanks up and down and the first toots a greeting and hisses air brakes. Hot wind of the semis farts loose gravel and burnt diesel smells. Knot wishes he hadn't done that. He checks behind him for Cee Ray. No Cee Ray.

At the church, across from the empty-looking old Sampson Camp, he crosses the yard and goes through the side door. What if the preacher is inside? He listens for sounds in the sanctuary from the hollow cool tomblike room, strange ticking silence and smells of burned wax and book-mold. Only the scuffing of his own feet on the new white tile floor as he walks past the rows of long dining tables to the old black splintering veneer piano in the northeast corner. Placing the bundle of money and books on the piano bench, he steps up beside it and lifts the lid of the old upright, then steps down and unwraps the sack of money, and holding to the bottom stands on the bench again and lifts up the sack and sets it down easy into the guts of the piano till it rests flat inside. The piano's breath, rising from the open lid, smells of musty felt and copper. No danger of anybody playing the old piano, now that they have the new one, so no worry about the money being discovered.

Coming out the door, he hears, then sees, Cee Ray highlighted by the low sun across the stunted dusty palms— symbol of the old Sampson Powder Company's attempt to pass themselves off as a class establishment. No palms grow naturally in South Georgia, or even in northernmost Florida, but Knot knows that palms are a sign of true Florida paradise to be found just over the state line. He's never been there, but in Valdosta he has seen the Palms Court Motel and the clustered runty palms in front of restaurants he might go to one day. When he gets some money.

He has to hurry now to make it to the post office before it closes. He doesn't know what time it is, but the sun has dropped behind the small frame camp houses and pinewoods background. In his head he is still operating on daylight saving time and the longer days of summer, so has only a notion of what time it is: late.

Jacket tied about his waist, Knot walks fast along the gravel edge of 129. Cee Ray, up the highway behind Knot, wheels around and spies Knot and begins pedaling full speed, then slows as he gets closer, but maintains still some distance.

"Hey, Ray," Knot calls out, walking backward, "let me borry that bike and I'll give you a ride in that Vette I'm getting for Christmas."

"*A*wright!"

Knot has Aunt Willie's address written down on a scrap of paper and is copying it onto the white letter-size stamped envelope just bought from the postmistress. Standing with his back to the door on his right and the wall of black mailboxes on his left. Ahead, on the counter where he is writing stands a Rolodex of black and white snapshots of men and women wanted by the law. He feels like one of them as he slips the two bills from his pocket and starts to stuff the envelope, hearing the postmistress filing mail into the hive of boxes, the front door whisk open and somebody coming in.

He bows over the envelope, working, end of one bill showing above the flap, the numerals "100" and that fetching dollar-bill green. Licking the flap, he turns, eye to eye with that dumb little white-headed girl. She doesn't even blink. Her pupils stretch so that they cover the irises of her small sad eyes. She is wearing a red-checked shirt with short puffed sleeves and blue jeans. He has never seen her in a dress like most of the other girls at school and he has wondered why.

"You," she says.

Maybe she's just being friendly. "What?" He feels blood rushing to his face.

"I saw you put it in my parka pocket."

"I gotta go." He walks off toward the mailing window on the west end of the dim cool room.

When he comes back, she is gone. His first thought is that she has gone for the sheriff, somebody, whoever a white girl might go for when a black boy has given her money. He has to get home. But outside the door he finds her standing, waiting, in the late sun. Her hair is the color of the sidewalk, which is the color of the lingering sunset now blazing a path down the center of the concrete river bridge and east along highway 94. The traffic light at the crossing looks red, yellow and green at once with the sun shining behind it. A pickup truck and two cars stop at the undecided light, then motor on, left, right and straight.

"Why?" She cocks her head.

"I don't know what you talking about." He takes the leaning bike from the red brick wall and swings round, straddling it.

No use playing now. She knows. He plants both feet on the eerie-colored concrete, cold in the going sun, and stares off at the Methodist Church with its glowing amber stained glass windows and white steeple pointing attention to peeps of first stars. The sky is a grainy blue-gray, gathering dusk.

"Okay," he says, holding to the worn rubber handlebar grips. "But why did you give it to the Needy Christian Children's Fund?"

No answer. She just stands there.

"Why didn't you use it yourself, what I mean you to do?"

"For what?" She shrugs her shoulders and smirks, right corner of her mouth tugging down.

"You one dumb white girl," he says, gazing out at a passing car as if to say, What white girl? I ain't *seen* no white girl. "To leave your old man on, you and your mama, that's what for."

"And go where? *How?*"

Knot is mad now, no longer too concerned about somebody seeing him talking to her, this white girl. "Take the Trailway, thumb a ride. Walk."

"It's not that easy...where do I say the money came from?"

"Marge," he says, pushing off up the sidewalk and pumping hard. "What everbody else say—Marge's rich kin."

Marge is standing on the porch flocked with neighborhood women and children, when Knot pedals up on Cee Ray's bicycle. No sign of the bike's owner.

The sky is void of light, milky dusk in the quarters with bands of smoke from the control burns in the surrounding timberland and the frantic chimney and yard fires in the quarters. With the sun down, the air is growing colder, the dirt chilling and blossoming into essence of frying food, foul toilets, rust, must, roots and hog.

On the porch, everybody is talking at once. Children in and out of the house, passing through the open front door with Marge scolding them. She is wearing a red pleated skirt and a white turtleneck sweater that looks new. The other women, for the most part, are wearing old drab clothes. They are seated in chairs and all along the edge of the porch; no longer neat, the porch, but littered with their rags of clothing. Marge does look kind of rich. But she'll look poor if Winston Riley's girlfriend happens up and catches her wearing her clothes.

Finally, the sheriff has come and hauled off the naked Crazy Lady. And the women on the porch are in a frenzy of judgment on the daughter—some stoning her with words, others blocking the stones and redeeming her.

Marge, lording over them, by virtue of being loudest, points out that the daughter had no choice. "What she s'posed to do, let her own mama wonder round nekkid and it wintertime?"

Half for and half against, and all at once, they rail at Marge.

"It break my heart seeing Miss Mavis drug off like some old *dog* or other."

"That gal of hers what break my *heart*. The way she stand there at the car and beg the sheriff not to be mean to her mama."

"And he say, 'Won't nobody lay a hand on yo mama, I give you my word.'"

"Huh! He liable just to drop her off longside the road and be done with her, what I say."

"She be good to me, all I know. Miss Mavis be *mighty* good to me."

"I hope somebody go on and knock me in the head, I get in that shape. Don't haul me off to no *in*-sane asylum."

Knot's ears ring from their back-and-forth, such rabid shouting. He feels shaky from his encounter with Becky Bruce at the post office—she knows he has slipped her the money, no doubt about it. But he eases his mind by assuring himself that she will never leak a word, never speak unless spoken to, at school anyway. At home around the raging pulpwooder, she'll be even less likely to tell about the money. Knot absolutely cannot imagine her blurting that a black boy has slipped her a hundred dollars without getting in trouble herself. Why were you messing around with a nigger boy? And for what did he give you a hundred dollars? Of course, Knot still seems the least likely in all of Echols County to be the one with the money who is handing it out like the pecans to the squirrels.

Marge is the one. Marge with the rich family. Marge standing on the porch, arms folded and shaking her head. That her house is the only one in the quarters minus color and new plastic seems not a clue.

Crazy Lady on hold, the women drift on into other more pertinent matters.

"Look like ain't gone be no Santy Claus this Christmas, don't it, baby?" A thick hatchet faced woman speaks to Marge through a tiny doll-like girl with button eyes.

"It gone be a poor Christmas at our house," another one says and scratches in her short rowed braids.

Just as Knot un-straddles the bike and starts to kick the stand in place, Cee Ray darts up from his left and takes it. "Don't forget about me driving that Vette soon as you get it now," he yells and pedals off.

"What Vette?" Marge steps on the top doorstep ignoring the baiting conversation at her back.

Knot shakes his head as if he doesn't know, but it's too late. The woman with the tiny girl is eyeing him, eyeing Marge.

Marge seems to feel her eyes like ice picks in his back. She swings round. "Ain't gone be no Vette. We ain't got no money. Did, you think I be driving round in that old rattletrap." She points at her old rust and celery Ford, its engine still ticking down from the short drive just past the schoolhouse where she has worked this day.

The day before she had raked the dirt yard and the tine marks are still fresh, neat but for the shoe and foot prints of the women and children and the paw-pad depressions of a single dog. No scraps thrown out of doors now, so no dogs.

If one wanders up on her porch, Marge sweeps them off with her broom. She likes dogs even less than these beggars on her porch, and that's saying something.

"They say, them that's got money don't act like it." The heavy-set woman seated on the left edge of the porch by the doorsteps is wearing dirty fuzzy blue bedroom shoes shaped like bunnies.

"Well, *I'd* act like it, let me tell you," Marge says.

Knot eases through the throng of women, goes inside the shack, and the little girl with black button eyes stands in the doorway watching. He finds a pack of Ritz crackers on the table and sits, eating. He reaches one to the little girl and she backs from the doorway. They're still quarreling on the porch; somebody mentions his name.

The men are coming in from work, unloading from Bruce's green pickup bed at the central point before Marge's porch. One whistles at the women gathered there.

"You hear bout the sheriff coming to haul Miss Mavis off thi'safternoon?" the woman on the doorsteps shouts out to one of the men.

"You don't mean it."

"Knot, get out here," Marge shouts, ignoring the men in tarry caps and work clothes sauntering toward their own houses.

Knot gets up and goes to the doorway. The little girl steps to one side watching him while gnawing on a finger.

"You got any money on you, Knot?"

"Yes ma'am."

She wrinkles her eyes at him. "Turn them pockets out then. Show us." She shakes a finger at him. "You be stealing and I'm gone have yo hide, heah?"

"Yes ma'am." He turns his jacket pockets out, dingy white flaps warmed by his body.

"Britches too."

He digs into his pockets and plucks up the seams in the bottoms and a quarter falls to the floor and rolls to Marge's feet. She steps on it with one of her good black shoes, worn for everyday now.

"I'm sorry, son," she says to him. Then to them, waving her hands, "Y'all git on out away from here now. Ain't nobody here with no money." Mumbling as she goes inside, "Somebody give money at the school, ain't no never-mind to me."

She had called Knot "son." He's never before been called that.

She takes the screen-wire fly flap hanging on a nail by the right side of the door and begins walking, swatting madly at flies threatening her clean house. Then loud, she says, "Ain't the preacher. Ain't you." Swat. "Ain't me—rich kinfolk my foot! So *who* the hell is it?"

⍐ • ⍗

It comes to Knot like a dead bulb overhead suddenly coming on that the money is more trouble than it's worth. Actually, the money is of no value—one hundred pennies in a dollar, one hundred ones in a hundred dollar bill and it's all the same. He can give and give till he gives it all away but he cannot control Marge or Boots or any of the other women in the quarters who have spent all he has given them on whiskey, toys and junk. He cannot control the church or the preacher or Becky Bruce. He can't control the fate of the little crippled girl or the granddaddy with colon cancer. He can't control Cee Ray, abusing the bicycle that rightfully belongs to Knot, and he can't control the big boys hogging the basket ball court. He cannot control even himself—he just gives and gives and they take and take and soon the money will all be gone and everybody will be just as sorry and doomed as ever: Marge will be Marge and Boots will come back and the preacher will move on and Becky Bruce and her mother will stay till they can go and any other way would be too easy, too unlifelike. People have to do for themselves. They have to do the best they can till they can do better.

He is standing beneath the cooped ferny branches of the mimosa, not hiding exactly but hoping not to be seen and not to see up close two of the big boys fighting on the packed dirt of the basketball court. They tangle like dogs, like lean greyhounds, long bare legs in shorts twining while they sock each other crazy. They curse and shout and breathe out the heat of hate. People come out on their porches, shaking their heads, a woman hollers for the boys to cut it out. They don't hear. They are deaf and blind to all about them, attuned to and aware of each other only. The two first-string basketball players egg them on, the taller boy who had said "Yo Knot!" is hugging the ball and stepping up to the jumble of bodies and back. One of the boys fighting has blood leaking from his nose, like a spigot half on; the other boy is one-eyed, his right eye having been punched shut.

The preacher's black car speeds up from the road, cuts hard across the run-together dirt yards in front of the row shacks and stops just short of the mimosa. He doesn't even see Knot when he steps out in his navy cut-off shorts and walks fast over to where the boys are standing now, hugging like they love each other but really trying to break free, to duck and dodge and gain enough distance to deliver more swift deadly punches. Winded, whipped, they let go, step back, dancing and boxing about the ears, head and shoulders. Then they lock up again, heads together and shoving like two bulls.

In his haste, the preacher has left the door of his car open and there is a keen steady dinging signal; doors slamming as the neighbors pop out to the porches to watch the fight. But the thick grunts and curses lay waste to other sounds.

The preacher tries to pry the boys apart by wedging between them. They separate, panting, cursing. Then— always the way of it—the boy with the punched out eye begins calling the other boy's mother a whore. The whore's son calls the other boy's mother a mother----ing whore. Which makes no sense.

"Okay, okay, that does it," the preacher shouts. "Trouble, you and Muck, break it up." He looks puffed up, eyes blazing and not-smiling now. "Leave the mothers out of this, I mean it! I don't know what started this, but it's over now."

"Yeah." The boy with the ball, nicknamed Rackem, begins dribbling around the threesome. "That ole girl ain't studying neither one of y'all."

"So," says the preacher with his arms crossed on his chest, "this fight started over a girl."

Rackem says, "Way I hear it, Trouble, she been making eyes at old preach here."

"I don't even know her," says the preacher. "I don't know who you're talking about."

"Girl go by the name of Wonder," says Shooter. "Live over yonder with her granny." He points to the shack smack center of the row. "Big-eyed gal."

The neat unpainted shack is set apart by its dotted shrubs and staked flowers, its clean-swept yard. No sign of Wonder or her grandmother.

"I know Wonder," says the preacher, speaking to Trouble and Muck. "A fine girl. Too fine for either one of you."

"But not too fine for you, huh?" Trouble shouts.

"She comes to my church, that's all."

Muck pipes up, speaking around the preacher to Trouble. "Wonder my girl! Ask her."

Trouble with the leaking nose tries to get at Muck with the socked-shut eye.

The preacher shoves them apart.

True, the young women have been filling up the front pews at church—Wonder among them—hoping to make time with the handsome young preacher, Knot can attest to that. But the preacher treats them no different from the young married women and older ladies, offering only a smile, a greeting and a handshake.

The one-eyed boy called Muck, says, "Mother----ing!" and spits at his fuming opponent, misses and spits in the preacher's face. Foam of spit turns to liquid and drips from his right cheek, a cheek too clean to be spat on, cheek of Jesus.

"Yo mama's a ho sho nuf."

"No more and I mean it," says the preacher, wiping spit with his shirt sleeve and holding his ground between them while they sock at and over and around the preacher, trying to get at one another, though barely able to stand. Sweat on their faces, arms and legs like rain. Their clothes are soaked through, clinging to their hot bothered bodies.

Trouble turns full attention on the preacher. "What you know bout nothing—you a preacher and ain't never have it rough."

"So, you know me? Think you got me all figured out for soft, huh?" Speaking up, the preacher seems to grow taller, broader, fiercer. "Well, I grew up on the meanest side of Detroit with boys would make you look like sissies. Yeah, I know the word you'd use for sissy. *I've* used it; I learned the streets and the gangs same way I learned basketball, the rough way, watching, playing, mixing and hearing my own mother called worse than whore. My mother was a long way from a whore—she raised me and my two sisters all by herself. She worked two jobs, from can to can't, to put food on the table and clothes on our backs. My daddy...my daddy, he was gone. Just gone." His face takes on a lean, drawn look. "We didn't even know she had breast cancer till two or three months before she died."

"What yo point, man?" Rackem stands before the preacher, holding the ball in both hands, shooting position.

Knot steps from beneath the mimosa canopy to the front of the black car. He knows these boys. Any minute now, he figures, they will gang up on the preacher and beat him into the dirt. Who will help save him?

The preacher sucks in, a long breath, as if aiming for control. "My point is, these mothers you're calling filthy names are the ones who brought you into the world, and likely all that has stood between you and starvation. And how do you repay them?"

"That just talk, man. Don't mean nothing." Trouble has his white T-shirt off and is scrubbing his busted nose, lower face and chest with it.

"Yeah. Talk," says Muck. "Don't mean nothing."

"Yes it does. It reflects your lack of respect. It says to me you'll lean on your mothers till you can find another woman to lean on and curse for a whore. I've seen it all my life—I've been there. But I had better sense than to stay there. I grew up, which is more than I can say for the likes of you."

"Tell em, preach." The shorter of the first-string players, Shooter, swipes the ball from Rackem and makes a dash for the goal, leaping up and hauling the ball over and inside.

"You too." The preacher shakes his fist at Shooter and places both hands on his hips. "You think you can get by in life on nothing but your playing. Not so. We haven't played a game that you didn't try to cheat your way through."

"Whoa!" Shooter grins, dribbling round the preacher, muscled-up legs like a wrestler's.

Trouble and Muck stand off, breathing hard and mentally nursing their wounds, eyes cutting toward the preacher.

Knot leans against the low sleek hood of the car, foot on the bumper. The preacher can handle himself. Knot might never think of him the same; now that he knows the preacher's tough side, he may never think of him as tender again.

"Throw me that ball," the preacher shouts.

Shooter pitches underhanded and steps back and stoops with his hands on his knees. He looks mad but curious.

The preacher throws the ball to Trouble on his left, whose nose is still dripping blood. "Now, play ball. Or maybe y'all want to go home first and have your insulted mothers bandage you up. Maybe y'all want to step off over there to your houses and heap a bunch of meanness on those mothers who brought you into the world. Fuss a little, blow off some steam, then out a-there. All over and forgotten, except for those women left to sort it all through and worry whether next time you get in a fight you'll be brought home in a box."

Trouble tosses the ball back to the preacher and the preacher tosses it to one-eyed Muck and so forth, till there is a circle of heated pitching and catching and frowns turn to smiles.

 CR • ৪১

Knot doesn't expect anything, come Christmas at Aunt Willie's, and is so surprised that he plans the rest of his life, till he's as old as the old gray granddaddy, to keep on never expecting. Not to lay his hopes out there to be wrecked but just to muddle through life and let things happen. That's how good it is, that's how rich.

The sun is bright as ice melting into air on Troupe Street. Frost on the azaleas and children in colorful stocking caps on skateboards and tricycles; big kids on bicycles. It's like the poster that Becky Bruce had created, plus the sounds of squealing and shouting and the smells of orange and pine, and Knot forgives her the squandered money.

That Christmas is on a Sunday makes it even brighter and finer and gives order to the week.

Lee is home, Judy Beth is home, and Aunt Willie is humming in her kitchen where she belongs. The old gray granddaddy is parked in his black motorized chair before the living room fireplace. The chair looks like an executioner's electric chair in pictures Knot has seen—high-backed, straight and square, with flat armrests. Nothing missing but the arm and body straps. Even the dual plates for the feet to rest on are square pebbled plastic panels. His feet in the brown-plaid flannel slippers are long and blue-veined with lighter soles. He looks nothing like himself dressed in brown flannel pajamas and a wooly brown robe instead of his uniform of starched and ironed gray twill. When he wants to say something, he motions you over and you have to place your ear to his mouth; he seems to breathe words rather than speak from the voice box. "Tell Marge I say put a brick on your head." That toothless grin.

He is going through what's called a period of remission, according to Aunt Willie, but it won't last. "At least it's a letup from the pain," she says and her sagged face lifts with a smile. "Marge, you have to go to church with us tonight; you won't believe who's coming and I can't tell you yet. It's too dangerous if word should leak out."

The Christmas tree, a tall cedar, is drooped, but the rainbow lights give the tree a cone shape. Underneath the tree are tidy-wrapped presents with different names on each; the paper with Santa faces and holly sprigs is old but the bows look new. Last Christmas the family had drawn names from the granddaddy's peach-fur gray felt hat bedded in satin. Aunt Willie had drawn Knot's name; he had drawn Judy Beth's.

Marge had really gone all out on wrapping her and Knot's gifts—large frilly bows covering the neat foil-papered boxes containing her soft pink bed jacket for Aunt Willie and Knot's prim white blouse for Judy Beth. Both bought by Marge from the Smart and Thrifty downtown. Everybody exclaims over how beautiful her gifts are wrapped and Aunt Willie proudly tells about Marge having worked at Belk-Hudson's as a gift-wrap girl during Christmas vacations when she was in high school. Marge corrects her—that was after she quit school. She's had a dozen-dozen jobs since then, some it won't do to tell about, she says. Aunt Willie laughs and tells her to hush, as if she's joking. But she's not.

During the gift opening, paper ripping and bows flying, except for Marge's gifts, Aunt Willie flutters her hands and smoothes her white apron and apologizes for such a poor Christmas. She gathers up the paper, folding and pressing it with her hands; the bows she places in one of the large boxes to keep them from being crushed during the unpredictable events of her household between this and next Christmas.

For Knot, she has bought a big, thick blue cloth-bound Webster's dictionary, which he loves, but not half as much as he would have loved Lee's hand-me-down bicycle had Santa Claus brought him a new one.

While everybody hugs necks and says Merry Christmas and thank you for their gifts, Knot looks up the word "family": A group of persons sharing a common ancestry.

In the kitchen again Aunt Willie tells Marge about the money she got in the mail—$200! Marge goes to pacing the bruised yellow linoleum, pounding her brain for answers. But she's no longer unhappy about it now that Aunt Willie has been what she calls a "recipient." Marge does wonder aloud though why she got $100 right off the bat and then never another cent. She says the mystery money man must be from Valdosta. She bets he's been giving to the poor all over Valdosta as well as Statenville. Some Robin Hood maybe, who steals from the rich to give to the poor. She tells about somebody giving $100 to the Needy Children's Christmas Fund and her getting credit for it. About all the neighbors coming to her for money.

Aunt Willie can't stay on the subject; she can't stay on any subject except her secret surprise for Marge—whoever is going to be at her church tonight. All she does is hint and Marge finally guesses it's one of her old boyfriends, Freddy Newsome, who went in the Navy, and she's not interested. Maybe Knot's daddy, he thinks. But why would saying his name be *dangerous*? He knows Marge's sore spots and this is one of them and Aunt Willie would know that as well, though she doesn't know that Knot belongs to Marge, which means he has to have a daddy somewhere. He's never asked who for fear of ticking Marge off and besides it doesn't matter. Mothers are what matters, Knot has learned from the quarters, daddies come and go.

Knot slips out the back and straddles Lee's bicycle and pedals between the northeast corner of the house and the old open frame car shed with the cut-out arched entrance, along the bumpy dirt and rock drive leading to the street, then pumping hard and fast up the smooth paved straightaway of Troupe Street. Cold air snapping at his ears, he zips past the close-set roof-heavy houses facing one another along the street. Smoke rising from the tall red brick chimneys loads the air with smells of burning oak and pine.

No new bicycle for Lee. Aunt Willie is using what she has to have, saving the rest of the money for future emergencies, she said. For what they need, not what they want. And Lee is now working too, done with that bad crowd of boys harassing white people and the law.

The ticking of the haywire hooked to a front wheel spoke measures off Knot's time, his yardage, and he is just moving, glad to be moving, glad to be out. Who needs a new bike anyway? He should have expected that Aunt Willie wouldn't throw her money away on such like everybody else.

The urge to cry is stuck in his throat, liquid sorrow on the verge of strangling him. Some leaks from his eyes. He wipes it away with his jacket sleeve, riding on. He really wanted this bike. Such a little thing, such a big thing, to wish for.

He rides and rides, standing, then sitting, high up on the seat. He rides to the corner of Troupe and Gordon, to the closed poster-plastered one-room store where the old men sit out on the benches in summer. Today, they are standing on the corner of the lot near the street, warming their hands and backsides by a fire in a fifty-five gallon oil drum, turning like hogs being barbecued. A few younger men in the mix, wearing smoky drab clothes and stocking caps. The sycamore shade to the right of the drum has dropped its leaves and the white peeling bark of the trunk is scorched brown.

Down the street again, right past Aunt Willie's house and the other big dilapidated houses, Knot marvels at his own recent ignorance, at his ever thinking that the people in these great old houses were rich. Chipped paint and leaning porches, withered shrubs and flowers gone to thistle, trash in the yards like at home in the quarters. Is he getting smarter or dumber? Knot wonders. Does he care anymore about belonging here?

At the railroad tracks he stops, gazing up and down to where the twin rails vee out at the ends of the earth. Smells of creosote from the split-grain crossties. He imagines the car in which the old man had straddled the tracks and the light of the coming train and the preacher pulling him from the car and saving him. Knot thinks he would have probably driven around the car and pretended he hadn't seen it. What he cannot imagine is putting somebody else, somebody he doesn't know, ahead of his own safety. Even the family he doesn't truly belong to. The old granddaddy is a special disappointment in his flannel pajamas and robe. Aunt Willie with her dangerous secret seems as silly and undependable as Marge.

Knot turns the bike, riding up Troupe Street again. Birds warble and titter in the brittle bare crepe myrtles along the cracked and root-buckling sidewalks where a few younger children are riding bright new tricycles, chasing and calling out to one another about what Santa Claus has brung them.

A couple of the bigger boys, who Knot had tried to hang with last summer, are springing south along the street curb in glaring new white shoes. They look older, taller than Knot recalled. Talking and smoking, they cross paths with Knot riding north but don't speak. No doubt they recognize Lee's bike but not the rider.

The boy and his two little sisters, who Knot had seen with their puppies the day he found the money in the alley, are peddling the mangy, wormy, leggy dogs up and down the street in a red wagon. "You want one of dese dogs, boy?" the brother calls out to Knot.

"What I want with no ole dogs?" It makes Knot mad that now that the dogs are no longer cute puppies the boy is willing to give him one for nothing. Just his luck.

Nobody recognizes Knot and nobody else speaks and he feels lonesome and glad to be. Nothing is expected of or from him and he is free.

At the store where the men are gathered to warm, one

turns, eyeing him—a large blocky man with a blocky head, eyes white as his teeth, big as Winston Riley back home. Knot brakes about five yards away, feet planted on the pavement, eyeing the man back.

It can't be.

"Hey," the man shouts. "Where you from, boy?"

"Nowheres," Knot says, casually walking the bike around, aiming south.

The man calls again. "What yo name, boy? I know you?"

Knot goes numb, hot with shock. He just stands there as if to prove he's not afraid, though he has never been so afraid in his life. First thought: the worst thing he can do is to show how scared he is by leaving. Second thought: the worst thing he can do is to sit here and give the man time to catch him or at least see where he is bound for, where he lives. Then a rush of adrenaline sends him flying, flying, not looking behind, not looking back even when he gets to the driveway at Aunt Willie's and the bicycle bucks over the ruts and slues around the corner of the house to the wooded-in backyard.

It was him. It was the bank robber.

Knot's heart is beating so he can hardly breathe. He goes up the high steps to the wide back porch, then through the shabby door to the warm kitchen smelling of roasting chicken and allspice.

"Ain't cold, are you?" Aunt Willie is peeling oranges at the counter under the north window. Light glares on the filmy lens of her glasses as she looks sidelong at him.

"Where yo hat, boy?" says Marge, passing with a stack of dishes from the kitchen to the dining room.

Knot feels safe in the kitchen with the women. Safer still when Lee takes him to his dim bedroom to talk. Seated on the rumpled narrow bed, Lee leans back against one of the stubby dark wood posters and crosses his legs on the bed, feet in new black and white basketball shoes almost touching Knot's right leg where he sits near the bunched pillows at the head of the bed.

From ten to twelve years old, Lee looked, to everybody in charge at his school, like he might be football material, what with those stocky arms and legs and expanding chest; but when he began growing taller, after twelve, it was decided that he would be a natural basketball player. Turned out, at fourteen, that he would be neither and everybody concerned had been wasting their time and Aunt Willie's money besides.

The room is large with a high wood ceiling and plaster walls painted white. The paint has turned the scorched shade of the pulled blinds, the scorched shade of the sycamore trunk before the drum of fire at the corner store. Boxes and stacks of magazines cover the dresser along the wall at the foot of the bed. The closet with no door bulges with shirts, jackets, hanging pants, shoes and more junk in boxes. There is a smell of dirty socks and stale hair oil.

"Bet you don't know who's speaking at church tonight." Lee sits higher, his brown face grows bright.

"Santa Claus, I imagine." Knot leans forward, listening to his heart beating in his throat. What if the bank robber is outside this very minute, having followed him, or in the kitchen with a butcher knife at Marge or Aunt Willie's throats? If he goes out now, Knot will have to try and save them. He spies his reflection, his ball head and pointed face, his skinny body swallowed up by the silver football jacket, in the mirror over the dresser, and the back of Lee's nappy square hair, and decides that really he wouldn't be expected to save anybody, he wouldn't be to blame. If not for the money.

"Don't tell me you still believe in Santa Claus?" Lee swings his feet to the rose wool rug by his bed, sitting up next to Knot. "Well, do you?"

"I guess not." Santa Claus has never been to Marge's house and of course Knot wouldn't believe in him. But it's as good a subject as any till Knot can get off by himself, calm down and hide.

"Swear you won't breathe a word," Lee whispers, "and I

tell you who be coming to Mama's church tonight."

Knot shrugs his shoulders. The dirty sock smell, mixed with the musky smell of Lee's rank bedding, is bothering him, nauseating him. He just wants to be gone. "Why would I care if it ain't Santa Claus?"

"Be like that then. Hick like you pro'bly ain't heard tell of him no how. Pro'bly ain't even heard tell of *The Cause.*" Lee stands, motioning Knot to stand. "Stand up."

Shaky on his feet Knot stands and watches Lee lift the gray-striped ticking covered mattress. He takes out a magazine with a naked woman on front. She is leaning forward with her head wrenched round, smiling at Lee and Knot. They sit on the bed again, side by side, and Lee turns the pages, breathing hard. Knot is breathing hard but not over these sorry wrinkled pictures of naked women who look oiled and used as the paper they are pictured on, which Lee has worn to tissue from folding and unfolding.

"You think that's something, look at this." Lee stretches out his right leg and fishes in his blue jeans pocket and pulls out a coin-like gold foil disk. "Know what this is?"

Knot is left holding the filthy magazine open to a naked reclining woman with her head thrown back on a red lace pillow, hands rammed between her white thighs. "The Cause?"

"You one dumb niggerboy." Lee slides the gold disk back into his pocket and takes the magazine.

Knot still feels light and distracted from his encounter with the bank robber and Lee takes it for lack of interest in the pictures and the gold foil disk. "You ain't queer, are you?" Lee asks.

"I don't know," Knot says, thinking Lee means strange, odd, a misfit maybe. "Might could be," Knot adds.

"Get out of my room then."

He stands, ready to go out and face the bankrobber. When he gets to the door he stops and says to Lee, "You wouldn't happen to leave me your bicycle when you die, would you?"

So far the bank robber hasn't showed up to kill the family. Judy Beth is in the kitchen when he gets back. Peeling boiled eggs at the counter by the dishpan, she asks about school. "How's it going?"

He says fine as far as he knows.

She gives him a wry look. Either her breasts have grown since Thanksgiving or she is wearing one of those push-up bras in the Frederick's of Hollywood ad in Lee's magazine. Maybe rubbing some of that breast cream on every night. Regardless she is prettier in the white blouse Marge bought to give in Knot's name than any of the women minus clothes in the magazine.

Her hair is another mystery. She's always changing clothes—anything new in the house she's got to wear it right away—and every time she changes clothes she changes her hair. Which wouldn't be all that strange if she went from, say, long hair to short hair. You could figure maybe she cut it. But she can go into her bedroom with short loopy curls and come out with silky braids falling from the crown like plaited whips.

Wandering window to window, Knot watches for the bank robber. Getting in the way of the women making dinner. Aunt Willie sends him to talk with the old gray granddaddy before the purring fire in the living room.

The old man is asleep with his head back on the slender headrest of the wheel chair. His mouth is open, exposing his neat red gums. Knot kneels on the couch and peers through the blinds on one of the tall double wavy windows facing the street. The starched crochet of a round white doily on back of the couch bites into his elbows. Still he looks to be sure the bank robber hasn't followed him. Nothing but children playing in yards and on the street. Regardless, he is scared shitless, as Marge would say.

"What you up to, boy?" The old granddaddy's voice is draggy, nasal, rough, but at least he can speak. His eyes are closed though.

At the dinner table, Lee pops half a deviled egg into his mouth, bowed low over his plate. Aunt Willie scolds him, tells him to use his manners like Knot. He sniggers and cuts his eyes at Knot. "*Queer*, man."

The good part comes after dinner, with everybody sitting around the table talking.

Marge pipes up out of a wrought silence, speaking: "I want all of y'all to listen cause I ain't telling this twicet."

They all get quiet, watching her, Knot next to Judy Beth, across from Marge and Aunt Willie, and Lee on the north end of the table next to the feeble granddaddy, whose spoon trembles on its way to his mouth, tongue out like a lizard's to receive the slow-coming mashed potatoes.

"A long time ago I made what I thought was a bad mistake. I got pregnant."

Aunt Willie sucks in, the old granddaddy drops his spoon to his lap. Knot sinks down into his chair.

Marge looks straight at Knot. "Wadn't such a bad mistake, as it turns out. I got Knot."

"I thought...," Judy Beth said.

Marge holds up her right hand to silence her. "I made up a story to keep y'all from thinking I was a hussy, on top of being a sot."

Aunt Willie's eyes tear behind her glasses. She looks down at her lap, shaking her head, and places a hand on top of Marge's on the table.

"Worse thing I do was not own up Knot was mine— ours. He's a fine boy, and if I could be half as good a mama..." She chokes up, hangs her head.

"You are," Aunt Willie whispers. "You are."

"No. No, I'm not." Marge squares her bony shoulders, sitting straight and sober-faced. "I don't even want to start thinking at this late date about all I ain't done—what I done's another matter and not worth bringing up."

Knot feels his face growing warm, blood flowing throughout his body and loosening it. Bank robber retreating to the back of his mind.

Judy Beth stands, leaning over him, hugging him and overturning his glass of tea. All listen to it trickle from the white tablecloth to the dusky rose rug under the table. "And just when I was about to get a crush on you." Judy Beth laughs.

She smells like oranges and rain.

"Okay," Aunt Willie says, reaching across to mop at the tea with her napkin. "Knot is a member of this family and let's treat him like it."

Everybody hugs him, even the old gray granddaddy wheeled over by Judy Beth in his chair.

Lee sticks out his hand to shake. "Ain't no queers in this family, no niggers neither," he whispers, "You okay!"

"Soon as school's out," Aunt Willie says, "we'll be looking for you here on Troupe Street, Knot. You *and* Marge."

Knot's heart aches knowing he probably won't come now. Can't come now, not with the bank robber close by. He comes within a gnat of saying so and telling all about the money. But if he tells they will be terrified that the robber will break down their door and hold them hostage till Knot gives back the money he stole.

No. He has to wait till summer and hope he has grown muscular and brave in six months. Not to plan or expect but maybe sneak into his prayers a plea for divine help which is what it will take to get him out this mess.

According to Aunt Willie her neighbor across the street had stayed up braiding her hair all Christmas Eve night and into Christmas morning. Didn't even stop to put out Santa Claus for her four children. Why? To look her best for the special visiting speaker coming to Aunt Willie's church on Christmas night.

Another woman Aunt Willie knows has a hairstylist coming to her house to comb out her hair before church.

This excited whispering between the two sisters, Christmas evening, keeps Knot tuned in, eavesdropping from the hall while they hurriedly warm up leftovers for a quick supper.

"Honey," Aunt Willie says out loud, "y'all need a TV. Then you'd know what's going on."

"If he's all that big, why is he coming here?"

"To get people to register to vote, for one thing."

"What we wanta vote for? Ain't nobody but a bunch of white's running. Ain't nothing to us."

"Hush yo mouth, girl!" Aunt Willie slaps Marge on the rump. "We don't vote, ain't nothing never gone change."

"Ain't nothing change for me no how."

"Maybe Knot then. Think about our boy."

Our boy. Knot takes a deep breath, feels warm all over. Would Aunt Willie still say that if she knew about the stolen money? If the bank robber kills Knot, will he be insured now and have a proper funeral?

Judy Beth has been standing before the bathroom mirror so long Aunt Willie has to threaten her with a switch. She smells of flowery musk perfume and Aunt Willie makes her take a bath.

Knot, listening to the sisters in the kitchen, can hear Judy Beth crying low and splashing water in the deep claw-foot bathtub down the hall.

Even Lee is primping in his room—off-limits to Knot now, cousin or no cousin, or so he fears. He hasn't tried to go into Lee's room for fear of nothing having changed since Marge's announcement. If Lee should order Knot out now he thinks the good feeling, the glow, might go and never come back. All he has now will be un-had. He will be Knot-no-name again.

The old granddaddy has been fed, given his medicine and put to bed. Aunt Willie and Marge too are saying what a shame it is that he can't go to church and hear and see this speaker he's admired so long (they don't call the speaker by name, just "he" or "him").

Yes, Marge and Knot will be staying the night at Aunt Willie's, going to her church and sleeping over.

Marge and Aunt Willie put supper on the table in the

dining room, literally grabbing a bite, then off to get ready for church. Like two girls giggling in Aunt Willie's bedroom down the hall while Knot is eating leftover roast chicken and feeling left out and confused but happy, in spite of the fact that this very minute the bankrobber could be seeing Knot at the table through the tall facing windows growing black with night. Knot's squiggly reflection in the wavy dark glass is so eerie when he looks up from his plate that he has to wag his head to be sure it is his image and not the bankrobber peeping in, pointing a gun instead of the fork Knot is holding.

Supper tastes nothing like dinner, the warming-up has yielded a tepid, strong taste and smell, especially to the potatoes. The scorch from the warming has saturated through, concentrated; the potatoes are too cakey, the texture of wet cat food following a blowing rain on Aunt Willie's back porch. The green beans taste like the potatoes which tastes like the cornbread and the brownish-yellow squash. It occurs to Knot that in their haste Aunt Willie and Marge have warmed the leftovers, one after the other, in the black iron skillet that is wiped dry, oiled and never washed, then returned to its resting place in the big white oven till next meal.

Judy Beth is over crying and is fussing with her mother about the earrings she is wearing.

"No, high-heels either, young lady. I mean it." Aunt Willie's bare feet pound the floor, from the bathroom, to Judy Beth's room, to Lee's room.

"Sister," yells Marge, "you got any decent nylons I can wear?"

"Honey, ain't no nylons been on this place since I don't know when." She laughs, excited.

Judy Beth pipes up. "I have a pair you can have, Aunt Marge."

She's too young to be wearing nylons, according to Aunt Willie, which Knot predicted and agrees with. Her getting older means she is getting smarter, prettier, too smart and pretty for him. Besides, now she is his cousin and that beats being his girlfriend by a mile.

Judy Beth and Marge start giggling and Aunt Willie says, "Don't put that thang on her head."

"Do," Marge says. "Beats the hell...heck out of this orange wig I been wearing."

They all laugh.

Aunt Willie calls out, "Knot, get in here and get dressed."

Knot sits up straight at the table; he hadn't expected that.

Judy Beth tells Lee he stinks—"Phew! What's that cologne? Mama, make him bathe."

No time.

"It ain't fair," says Judy Beth.

"Never *never* NEVER say that again." Aunt Willie bounds to Lee's door, speaking to Judy Beth. "That's the biggest excuse in the world for not amounting to something."

"Get yo head out a my mirrow," Lee says to Judy Beth. "Think you change all that much from yo mirrow to mine?"

"What time is it?" Marge wants to know. Sounds like she's talking in a closet.

"Knot, get in here and get dressed," Aunt Willie shouts. "Now where is that good-for-nothing promised to stay with Daddy tonight?"

"Knot could stay," Marge says, popping out of the closet.

"No!" Aunt Willie shrieks it. "Knot of all people should be on hand to hear him."

Marge says, "Maybe *he's* the one's been sending the money."

He—capital H—as in God.

෫ • ෨

The great white church on South Troupe is lit by three crystal chandeliers and hundreds of red candles. Outside people are surging toward the door, and inside along both aisles, looking for seats. So much talking it sounds like hands clapping.

Judy Beth squeezes first through the crowd in the open double doors, teetering in navy velvet high heels with a wide headband to match her shoes. Her cooped hair is now shiny and straight, longer on the sides than in back. Then Marge— Marge, strange-looking with loopy stuck curls covering her gold crown. She has on a low-waisted red wool dress, banded at her slim hips, with a pleated skirt to her knees. Aunt Willie is next, plain as ever, but with dabs of pink lipstick on her stung lips. Lee in a navy suit follows Aunt Willie, and then Knot wearing one of Lee's starched and ironed blue oxford shirts and khaki pants.

Inside, all seats are taken, so Knot and his family are forced to sidle along the back wall to their right. There they stand with their backs pressed to the cool white stucco for people pushing past.

A woman ahead on the raised dais of the pulpit is wearing a white robe and singing in a husky but trilling soprano, the choir behind her joining in on the chorus. No piano music, but background string music coming from the boxy black speakers hung high along the upper walls near the vaulted beam ceiling.

Soon the entire congregation is singing—"We shall o-ver co-ome . . ." Over and over, clapping and stomping and moving, trying to find a space not taken in the scroll-back oak pews, along the walls and in the aisles. Little girls in red ruffled dresses, lace socks and black patent shoes are hoisted onto shoulders, lifted up to see.

The clear watery light of the chandeliers overhead dims and dies. The ruby glow of the candles on the sills of the stained glass windows takes its place. The double doors on Knot's left are closed by four men in black tuxedoes. Locks slip into place and the four ushers in black tuxedos stand before the massive oaken doors, at measured intervals, at perfect attention, hands held before them. Still as wax statues, they are almost the same size, handsome, choice men of the church.

At home, at Knot's church, women serve as ushers. He

thinks these men look too serious, too severe. A chill sweeps over him, head to foot.

The woman singing in the pulpit wraps up the hollow, repetitive song with a hum and turns, going to the choir loft behind her, where other men and women form two rows, end to end of the pulpit, end to end at the front of the lofty, spacious church. Waxy smells and perfume hover over the congregation. Men in dark business suits march up and down the aisles looking left and right, speaking into handheld radios emitting whining voices and static. A tall man with a small head and large glasses looks right at Knot but seems not to see him.

Then Knot can no longer see the pulpit for a boy in a little man's suit being lifted up by the man seated in the pew ahead of Knot. Much jostling along the wall, people standing two-deep.

There is a sudden hush, then everybody begins looking straight ahead. All standing, swaying, singing:

We shall o-ver co-ome
We shall o-ver co-ome
We shall o-ver co-ome....

A harmonious lilting song sung over and again, the same lines, the same melody, till at last it rises and swells like the end or beginning of something mighty, some force beyond the known, the recognizable. Love maybe.

Marge, halfway along the wall, between Judy Beth and Aunt Willie, says, "There he is!"

Knot stares down the line on his right and sees her towering hair, like a hardy exotic flower. Her eyes stretched wide as if she's seen Elvis.

"I can't see," says Lee and shoves Knot toward the aisle and the nearest usher guarding the doors. Yes, guarding.

Knot can now see the dais in the pulpit and a tall brown man dressed in black. He is holding up both hands and swaying, singing. Each side of him are four other men, eight all totaled, also swaying and singing with their arms waving in the air. But for some inexplicable reason there is no doubt that the man in the middle, the tallest man, is the focus, the one whose name is at once dangerous and beloved.

The pulpit is so dim and far away that Knot can't make out their faces at first. But three pews ahead, nearest the aisle, sits a man who resembles the preacher from Knot's church. Or the back of his head, his cream-brown thick neck above his white shirt collar, looks like Richard Troutman's.

The man on the platform, the focus, has that same look of celebrity that the preacher had in the newspaper picture, Knot realizes, though Knot has never seen this man in the newspaper before. Or if he has the man didn't matter, because he has no past in Knot's life, in Knot's world, no future to hang a memory on. Till now.

Then the man's face comes clear: serious, pear-shaped with close-clipped receding hair and small tidy ears. But it is his tilted eyes and the gathering of his brow into worry dimples that give him that serene but anguished look, that bespeak of his passion for all sins borne on the cross, his curse of having been lifted above and in charge of ripping away the iron spikes with his bare hands.

Everybody, including Knot's preacher, raises their arms singing till the tall man in the middle at the pulpit lets his arms down, quits singing and the men flanking him step back, hands clasped before them like the four men guarding the double doors.

The other men in black business suits are still walking up and down the aisles, checking side to side, speaking low into their slender black radios.

Everybody quits singing and other than some scattering coughing and a few babies fretting, they are perfectly still, perfectly quiet. Nobody moves.

Knot can now see that the man in the fourth pew up is for sure his preacher.

The tall man front and center, on the dais, raises both arms again, shouting in a distinct and noble voice, "Do you have a dream?"

The congregation rises up collectively, stomping the

floor and squalling, "I have a dream, I have a dream , I have a dream..."

Knot can barely stand he's so caught up and woozy. His ears are storming so that he can hardly hear. Besides, there is so much racket around him from the caught-up crowd. There's a feeling of swelling nigh to bursting through the walls of the locked-down church. The candles in the windows flicker, flicker, reflecting on the richly-tinted stained glass—Mary, Mother of Jesus; Jesus on the Cross; a dove, a lamb—double flickering from the excited breathing and chanting. But one word reaches Knot's ears over the speakers and in the chanting of the crowd: "equality." He must have heard it before but his ears hadn't been hearing ears then. Either that or it had seemed not to pertain: when you're hungry only food matters, when you're cold only heat matters, when you're scared only safety matters. He's never yearned for anything really, except a bicycle and belonging to Aunt Willie and them. He chokes back tears of joy, warmth welling from his body to his face. These men are the father he's never known, not even by name, including Richard Troutman, the preacher, who Knot feels he is seeing for the first time, recalling his having urged the people of his church to get out and vote, to work for "The Cause"— equality.

This is Knot's first time seeing Negro men in important roles, his first time seeing Negro men act like white men. He never knew Negro men *could* act white. He never knew they could look, act and be so important. Up till now Knot has believed that the waterman and the sheriff and Sammy Bruce and the presidents chalked up on the blackboard by his white teacher ruled the world.

Chapter 8

Marge has made it without a drink all through Thanksgiving and Christmas holidays, and Knot thinks if she can make it through New Year, he can consider her cured. But on New Year's Eve, before noon, last day of 1964, she begins wandering the quarters, sudden friends with her enemies, and nipping with them.

Cold and drizzly as it is, everybody is out standing, rotating around the yard fires. Great blazes fueled by club-like pine knots, smoky lighterd stumps and shed oak limbs, even a couple of broken tables and chairs. Whatever is available, whatever will burn.

They've got burning on their minds and the leaning winds of black smoke are proof.

Cee Ray in a navy knit cap rides his blue bicycle end to end of the crescent road. No Vette in front of Knot's shack, no new or old bicycle either. So, no rich auntie in Valdosta.

Knot has other things on his mind.

Such as Marge scooting her white kitchen chair close to Winston Riley's, sipping from his paper-sacked bottle of whiskey and sharing smokes. Others mingling around the fire now built high and thriving on the frozen gray dirt a few yards from Marge and Knot's shack. Pairs of men and women gravitate from the fires to the shacks, shut doors and no children allowed. Only the old ladies parked in chairs before the fireplaces and TV sets. And haven't they seen it all before? Still, they grumble.

Cee Ray's sister, the little crippled girl, slides on her bottom up and down the doorsteps of her shanty, unseen as the grownups walk over and around her. Once she tumbles from top to bottom and one of the old grannies fetches her up by the crisscross straps of her red corduroy overalls. Brushed off, she grins and begins her usual journey up and down the doorsteps on her bottom. Pigtails by the dozens sprout from her small round head.

Blaring music piped from automobiles, laughing and hooting, cars roaring away and later roaring back. Tough-looking boys and men with their legs crossed lean on the cars, drinking, joking, talking about the boastful boxer Cassius Clay beating good ole Sonny Liston. They talk about women—who went with who. They talk about the war in Vietnam, where they never have been but might have to go—Cassius Clay being one of them but none of them, he probably won't have to go. Good-naturedly they exchange swipes. Next minute a fight could break out among them. In spite of the wet cold, they wear their shirts open to reveal the rippled muscles of their chests, sleeves rolled and lots of gold, pants so tight they wrinkle at the thighs.

Close to dusk and even the dogs act drunk, yipping and chasing and dodging the men's iron-toed work boots. The weather is doubly cold but no drizzle now, just mean low clouds threatening sleet.

Must be a hundred people or more. Two huge fires burn, and Marge is now rared back in a kitchen chair before the fire in front of Cee Ray's shanty. She looks blank-eyed and alone and mad even; it's as if her eyes have turned around and are looking inside and don't like what they are seeing.

A fight breaks out before the fire in front of Knot's house. Two men shoving and socking each other and scarffing up the fouled dirt. Everybody gathers round them, egging them on or trying to part them. Knot can't tell which from where he sits at the window inside his neat closed house. Fire singing in the heater, other side of the room.

All day the clouds have kept the quarters world gray and gloomy, despite the frolicking, so that by dusk the fires only seem brighter, the rest of the shanties and dirt and trees the same dull shade of gray, save for a few houses with chains of restless colored Christmas lights flickering in windows. Nothing changes. Everything changes.

The old ladies wander from their porches over to the fight, everybody shouting at once. The old ladies look hurried and cold, bundled up in coats and head rags. Worn faces pinched with fear.

Children play but keep their distance from the adults. Now and then the fires draw them to their heat but these children are wise to the ways of adults at the bottle, wise to the fact that glad voices can turn gruff and people they know can turn into strangers, scare-boogers loosed from nightmares.

Gradually the crowd around the fight drifts away toward the barbecuing pig, under the low-hanging branches of the old oak across the school-ground fence, revealing Marge and another woman left quarreling around the fire in Cee Ray's yard. The other woman looks like Winston Riley's girlfriend. Her silhouette is hip-heavy, bosomy, what the boys call stacked. Marge, skinny legs poking from the dipped tail of her heavy black overcoat, is stalking circles around the girl with her hands on her hips, wagging her head. She stops, leaning into the other woman, still with her hands on her hips, and looks like she is about to spit. But instead she walks away, vanishing into the shadows between the fire in front of Cee Ray's house and the glowing coals of the barbecue and lit cigarettes between lips.

It is pitch black between fires now and Knot watches the crowd gather at the barbecue. He is starving, has eaten only a peanut butter sandwich this morning. He can smell the oaken searing of the pig, the dripped grease frying on the coals. Nothing he would like better than some barbecue, but he's too tired and disgusted to go out.

He starts to get up and turn on the overhead light, left off since he sat down at the table to watch from the window. Truth is, he is terrified of drunks. Terrified of weekends and holidays in the quarters. The Marge at Aunt Willie's at Christmas is somebody else, not this dark sullen woman, alone even in a crowd, who he's been watching all day, worried sick.

Cee Ray is still riding the bike, firelight to firelight, and then shadows, steering with one hand and chomping down on spare ribs with the other. Nothing bothers Cee Ray, but Knot no longer believes that a bike is the cure for loneliness, fear and boredom. To look out the window now, he can almost fool himself into believing that he is back where he was before Christmas, but he's seen a different way. Maybe he was better off before he knew better. Maybe he could join the children playing, eating, laughing, living, had his ears never been opened, had his eyes never seen. What will happen now that Marge has slipped? Is he trapped in this dark madness until he can grow up and leave on his own? Yes, no doubt about it, he will leave when he can, he will be a man like the men he witnessed at Aunt Willie's church. He will be like the preacher, who all day Knot has dreaded driving up and finding Marge and the others in their backslid condition. The shame of it all!

It comes to Knot that as long as he is ashamed he is part of it. He is one of them.

Suddenly the fire in front of Cee Ray's shack burns brighter, higher, braiding tongues of fire splitting, flaring and reaching like fingers of fire around a washpot. He opens the front door and stands, watching, listening to the laughter and loud talking at the barbecue under the oak. But the screaming of the fire before Cee Ray's shack stands out—human pain at its limit.

Then he sees in the midst of the fire something thrashing, then somebody, Cee Ray-size, standing over the fire, reaching into it, stepping back and reaching again and snatching a burning bundle from the fire's talons. Child or dog? Child.

Knot opens the front door and stands, then dodges back into the room, grabbing the quilt from Marge's bed, and heads out again, running and dragging the quilt, then gathering it in his arms to keep from tripping on it as he runs. Ahead, Cee Ray is rolling the little crippled girl in the dirt. Kneeling, frantically beating at her smoking chest, her glowing rags of red overalls.

The girl keeps screaming, flailing her arms, her stub

pigtails flaring like the points of a gold crown. Screams beyond screaming. Slapping at Cee Ray as he slaps back at her.

Knot fans the quilt out and swings it over her, and he and Cee Ray together begin wrapping her up in it, muffling her screaming. In the light of the fire Knot can see Cee Ray's mouth is greasy; his eyes are the eyes of a terrified, tortured animal.

"Go get everybody, go get Marge." Knot yells at him. "Get the sheriff to come quick with his car."

He is gone before Knot can see him go. Knot bundles the little girl in his arms, feeling the heat of her body through the quilt. Smelling the stench of her cooked flesh which he tries to believe is the barbecued hog, but there's a big difference, a sickening difference he can't name. The girl is no longer twisting, no longer trashing, but still and silent, smoldering inside the blanket, he imagines. He keeps walking toward the crowd at the barbecue, moving slow, but seeming to move faster as in one accord the crowd moves toward him bearing the bundled child toward them. They come on, the tortured from hell, stricken mute, nightmare in motion.

One of the old grannies steps from the shadows on Knot's right and takes the child from him, wailing and crooning and walking to be walking as the crowd pulls in close around her.

On the outside now, like during the fight, Knot feels himself sinking into the dark. Alone as he has never been alone, and the heat of fear settling inside with the smell of burned flesh.

CR • SO

The next day, at church, the preacher calls on all gathered to pray for the little crippled girl. Then he has Knot take up a love offering for the family—more money than Knot has ever seen in the collection plate. Marge is at home, sick and low but not even bothering to swear that she will never drink again, like she used to do following a drunk. So, no music at the morning service, no long-legged proud woman at the new piano.

Sometime after midnight the ambulance had come for the child, miraculously alive, they said. The sheriff, having come in his car to transport the burn victim to the hospital, ended up arresting Cee Ray's daddy for jumping on his mama, claiming that she hadn't been watching out for the little girl. Around and around the blame went. The sobbing mother said she had thought that the child's grandmother was watching her.

Marge refused to allow the sheriff to take the girl in his car to save time—"Thank you sir but no, we just wait on the amb'lance this time." *This ain't no nigger stabbing here like I seen you haul in before. This a burnt baby with flesh busting out of her.* Sober and solemn and calling up all her forgotten nursing skills, she had seen to the tiny girl inside her house till the ambulance came—lit-white and chrome, sterile against the crowd's filth, their stench of alcohol and guilt, their blackness and the cold of night. Gently placing strips of clean bed-sheeting sticky with pink burn ointment on the little girl's oozy charred body, arms and withered legs, Marge had to shake off the wailing women around her trying to touch the burned child. As if somehow they could make amends for their neglect and heal her wounds with a touch, like Jesus' laying-on of hands.

According to the young white doctor who came out with the emergency team from Valdosta, they would be flying the little girl by helicopter from Valdosta to Gainesville, Florida, a couple of hours south, and the special children's burn unit there.

After they were gone, Marge had walked off into the dark. Nobody knew where.

At church on New Year morning, it doesn't dawn on Knot or anybody else that he is about to be labeled a hero. Then about midway through the sermon on David and Goliath and how David was small in stature but brave and pure of heart, a man after God's own heart, the preacher singles out Knot to come before the church and stand with him in the pulpit. Knot is the one who rescued the little crippled girl from the fire.

The preacher places his thick right arm around Knot's shoulder and grips his right forearm. No jostling motion, like Knot has known in the past when on rare occasions, maybe after church, say, one of the men hugs him for sweeping leaves off the steep, slippery roof and saving the man himself the trouble and danger. No feely squeezing from the preacher, like the men of the church are wont to do, at which point Knot would generally feint and squirm and act goofy to make light of their commenting on his stick-thin arm—no muscle, no flesh. What ails you, boy?

Still, Knot, facing the congregation with the preacher, is unprepared for what the preacher says next:

"I've come to know this young man well since I came to this church last autumn. I've known him for humble and kind. I've played basketball with him and I've eaten at Sister Marge's table with him at my right hand." Here the preacher smiles at Knot and tightens his grip—still no jostling, no kidding. "I've never had to ask this young man to do anything around the church; he just does it and then goes on his way. I've come to know him in a special private way, this young man, but last night he showed me another side of himself. How brave he is, reaching into that fire and risking his life to save a helpless little girl.

"That said, with his permission, I'd like to publicly rename him." He looks at Knot with those kind hazel eyes. "On this first day of the new year, 1965, I'd like to rename this budding hero a fitting proud name. I'd like to rename him David."

Knot nods and hangs his head, waiting for somebody to laugh. Nobody laughs. The hand gripping his upper arm remains firm.

"Take that in the form of a motion, for the record. Do I hear a second?" the preacher asks, taking his hand from Knot's arm and stepping to one side with both hands raised to glory like the men at Aunt Willie's church.

"I second it," somebody says.

"Amen."

"Motion carried."

Knot should tell them now. But after all this fuss over him being a hero he would be letting the preacher and everybody else down if he tells the truth, though the real truth is, inside he does like being a hero, David. He feels important for the first time: David Crews, hero. Something about the four letters with an "O" on the end makes him think of how noble, short and full of glory the word will look on his tombstone. The shortest words, the quickest-said words, say the most. Of course, a hero will have the insurance and a proper Negro funeral.

Now standing behind Knot, hands on the knobs of his shoulders this time, the preacher prays for Knot and Knot can feel the heat of his prayer through his hands, soaking into him. The preacher asks God to guide this young David and keep him from sin, from falling prey to the pull of immorality around him. He asks God to keep this young David pure of heart and guide him down the narrow path of righteousness. "Spare him, Lord, from lust of the flesh and the charms of what might destroy him." The grip tightens and Knot can feel the trembling of the Holy Spirit passing from the preacher's hands. "Keep him honest, Lord, and free of the taint of money. May he do great things in thy name and make you proud, Lord."

Knot squints his eyes shut. No peeping. He sees the alley where he found the money, and the money in the bag he's been filching from. *Broad path of unrighteousness and unrestrained love of money.* His coveting Cee Ray's bike is laid bare. And to top it off, he has stolen Cee Ray's glory. Any minute now, he expects, the power of the Holy Spirit passing through the preacher's trembling hands will turn into a jolt of lightening and boom of thunder at once, body and soul plunging down into hell for the unforgivable sin of blasphemy. Already he is sweating, stiff as a corpse.

Knot is still standing, being blessed, while everybody sings "Blest be the Tie that Binds." Out of the song rises up a chant—Da-vid, Da-vid, Da-vid. And one by one they file slowly up the aisle, hugging Knot-turned-David, saying his name and hugging him, men shaking his hand. Tears in everybody's eyes.

The one person aside from Aunt Willie and her family, who Knot has wanted to admire him, is the preacher. And he is about to find out that Knot is a fake, a liar, a thief. He should tell them now what a coward he is. And how Cee Ray, his enemy, and not he, is the real hero. But Cee Ray of course isn't there and anyway the mistake is such sweet revenge for the bicycle business and it is Knot, not Cee Ray, who has just placed five one-hundred dollar bills, sneaked from the bowels of the old piano in the fellowship hall, in the love offering, which for all he knows could wind up going toward a Corvette for Cee Ray.

Though Knot knows the bike isn't everything; it's still a sore spot, a long-held yearning that continues to fester, simply by virtue of having been there so long.

The good feeling of being a hero doesn't hold throughout Sunday, and by that afternoon, hearing Marge snore from her cot with her back turned to Knot-now-David, he watches Cee Ray, the real hero, riding the bicycle, both hands in white gauze bandages like mittens.

It is quiet in the quarters now. Nobody is out and about, except the dogs and Cee Ray picking over the bones and meat scraps of the barbecued pig from the night before. Cee Ray's whole family is gone to the hospital to be with his little sister—it's too much to expect that she can live without skin. Her entire body has been burned; she probably won't make it. Cee Ray has been left home with his ailing granny, who broke down and took to her bed after seeing her helpless grandchild burned. Still, Cee Ray rides his bicycle, slow and easy, back and forth, round and around.

Early evening and Knot goes out to the road and stands, waiting for Cee Ray riding up the east straightaway, past the school gym and then the baseball diamond. Overnight the clouds and sleety rain switched to bright and cold, nose-running cold. Looking up at the blue sky, it is hard to believe that last night was so miserable. It's as if a whole year has passed and it is another time, another place. Except that he can smell the bitter burned wood and barbecue, reminder of the chaos and the little girl's parched flesh. He feels sick. He has never before felt so sorry for anybody as he does for Cee Ray, who all day Knot has been watching pick over bones from the barbecue, riding just to be riding, for something to do.

Cee Ray stops when he gets to Knot and sits straddled the bicycle, with his white-bandaged paws on the handlebars.

"How's your grannie?"

"One minute sleeping, next minute crying. Ain't nothing I do make no difference. She bless me out, run me out." Cee Ray wipes his nose on the back of his red jacket sleeve—glazy snot streaks. He smells of stale ingrained smoke.

"How's your sister?" Knot asks.

"No word yet."

The sun is almost down behind the treeline in the west and it's colder, cold like mist seeming to drop.

"Hadn't been for you, she wouldn't have a chance."

"Aw, man," Cee Ray says and looks off. A grin plays across his pretty-boy face. "She still on fire when you thow that quilt over her."

"Still and all," Knot says. "I didn't save her, you did." Knot turns to go.

"Hey," Cee Ray says, "you wanta ride this wheel here?"

"Gotta go to church." Knot keeps walking, hands in his pockets, walking. Hoping his sin of taking credit for being a hero has been forgiven and he won't have to take it before the church. But knows better. Besides he had sworn never to take more money from the sack and he has, albeit for a good cause.

Cee Ray rides up behind him, alongside him. "Cold out here, man. Take my wheel here to church."

"Naw, ain't all that far." Knot doesn't want to go, but has to. Really, he has every reason to stay home, with Marge apt to get up any minute and start back to drinking.

"Man, I hate it bout you not getting that car for Christmas. No wheel neither."

Knot shrugs, walking, sun behind the trees streaking in his eyes. "I bout quit wanting one," he says.

"Grannie say the same God give us the money before done give another seven hunderd for Sister."

"Yeah." Knot walks on toward the paved road leading east to west, where he will turn north over Troublesome Creek to the church.

Cee Ray sprints forward, bike chain rattling, zips up to the red light and turns around. Turning again and pacing alongside Knot, then off again. And again. He is still riding circles around Knot when he turns north at the crossing. Cee Ray zips down the dip at Troubesome Creek and back, feet up on the handlebars. Hands in soiled white gauze like boxing gloves.

The sun is gone and it is colder, freezing, but no wind.

Cee Ray weaves on the highway, up to the front stoop of the church house and back to Knot walking along the road shoulder. Ahead, old ladies in heavy dark coats wander from their houses at the old Samson Camp across the road. White light from the overhead florescent bulbs blaze in every window of the little white cinderblock church.

Knot, now walking across the springy dead grass of the churchyard, thinks Cee Ray has gone home, when suddenly the bicycle streaks past and brakes at the front stoop. A sign from God if he gets off and goes inside with Knot.

He does.

He even sits with Knot on the back row, left side, sniffling, wiping his runny nose on his jacket sleeve, gauze wrapped hands laid palms up on his legs. His dark blue denim jeans look soft with filth, new but never washed. Knot hopes and prays he will get bored and leave before preaching starts. He smells of smoke and hog grease.

Instead Cee Ray sits forward listening while various old ladies stand to testify. Mostly they talk of the little crippled girl's being burned, the sorry pitiful life, their prayers for her, then their testimonies twist round to the old ladies' own plights and virtuousness by implied comparison. The mother, Cee Ray's mother, is condemned for neglect without a single mention of her name but Cee Ray doesn't seem to notice and nobody has noticed him. It's as if he's not sitting there

The church has that hollow feel and empty look of all Sunday nights, even on the New Year holiday. The room hums with the white florescence of the tube lights hanging from the ceiling. The Christmas tree next to the empty piano bench and the window decorations of tinsel look cold and done-with, without the colored lights on. But the church is warm, too warm, for all the jackets and coats and headgear. Only the preacher looks fresh for a fresh service. The preacher and maybe Cee Ray in his downtrodden innocence of church ritual and night-attendance slumps. Everybody else is looking forward to a short sermon, eager to be gone. But hasn't the preacher said, often, that those who attend the night service are the real disciples of Christ?

Knot may as well get it over with. He stands, waiting his turn while the old lady ahead of him testifies about how the devil showed up in her sleep and she began praying and he disappeared.

When she sits, pressing her white handkerchief to her mouth to muffle sobs of joy, the preacher says, "David," nodding at Knot. He is wearing a red tie with a gold cross tie pin and dark tailored suit, his white shirt lending to his shining countenance. His face is all countenance, a beam, without distinguishing features.

Cee Ray is watching Knot. Everybody is watching Knot.

"This is Cee Ray," Knot says, turning, pointing at him seated on Knot's left. "He's the girl's brother what got burned in the fire last night. He's the one pulled her out. Not me."

Cee Ray's greasy lips part as if he is about to speak, but

he is either too shocked or too shy. Or maybe too innocent to catch on to the religious significance of Knot's confession.

The preacher says, "I got it wrong, didn't I, David?" He laughs. "At least, half wrong. Forgive me, Cee Ray. I see those bandaged hands now. Glad to have you at church. We can use some young men in this church. I hope you'll come back with David."

Cee Ray's lips are still parted, but his lids are closing. The white lights overhead make the grease in his square scribly hair gleam like diamonds.

Again the preacher creates a sermon out of Knot's actions—still "David" with the pure heart. The real test of a hero is his willingness to transfer heroic action to somebody else. The real measure of a hero is humility—*I'm only a poor man and little known*. Knot is still a hero. But the preacher draws conclusions about both boys, a credit to their community. He warns against being judgmental—judge not lest ye be judged; the judgment you give is the judgment you will get. He warns of piety. The old ladies who have testified don't get it. They nod and nod—amen.

Knot can only think with much trembling that if he is David, that makes the bank robber Goliath, who he will have to defeat. He'd as soon be Knot.

On the way home, after church, Knot rides the bicycle up to the crossing, circling Cee Ray and pacing alongside. Neither speaks. It is almost dark, only a chill phantom of light, starmist and silhouettes of trees and houses. When Cee Ray's turn comes to ride, he zips away with glowing white hands and doesn't return.

ᘒ • ᘑ

Like magicians, four men create a clean concrete basketball court from dirt. Scraping, blocking, filling and screeding, they construct a twenty-by-twenty level square before the jerry-rigged post and goal.

In no time, the concrete is decorated with human hand and foot prints, dog and cat paws and chicken claws—a strange and wonderful mosaic and everlasting monument and testament to all in the quarters having been there. The little crippled girl's name—Rosie—which nobody seemed to have used before her funeral, is scratched into the concrete.

At her wake, two weeks after New Year's Day, she lay in her white casket Saturday through the following Sunday and her funeral at Knot's church. No insurance, since her mother had let lapse a couple of premiums, and if not for the Love Offering, there would have been no white casket or white limousines, no ushers in tuxes or fancy going-home dress for the child in the casket, who looked like a doll. A made-up melted doll thrown in the fireplace during a fit. An angel now, the girl lay in state at Cee Ray's house while people came and went and told their version of the story of the fire. Their part in it. Though nobody owned up to neglect, nobody owned up to having forgotten her.

Evenings, when the basketball boys are at practice, in the lofty white gym on the east side of the school grounds, the children gang on the concrete and make playhouses, play jackstones, ride bicycles and push toy trucks bought with Knot's money.

Everybody gravitates to the concrete stage, bringing chairs and building fires, to visit and watch whatever happens to be playing at the time.

They watch Knot and the preacher, playing one on one basketball. While across the fence and a distance over, balls bounce and feet slap and screech on the gym floor, boys shouting to one another and the coach blowing his whistle. The neighbors laugh and clap and call out, some rooting for Knot but most rooting for the preacher who has made good on his promise to build the court with their donated nickels and dimes. Of course, none has matched Marge in giving.

Knot had tried to swear off giving away more of the money, in order to prevent Marge's becoming too grounded in acceptance and religion. But the concrete court was an itch that wouldn't quit.

Marge was the only one in the quarters who neither attended the wake nor the funeral of Rosie the Angel. She was the only one who took to heart her share of the blame. She never asked Knot's forgiveness for getting drunk; and still she refused to say never-again. She went to church, played the piano, cooked and cleaned her house and the houses of the white women she worked for. She was staying close, walking the straight and narrow.

In the chill evening dusk, gradually the spectators take up their chairs and wander to their houses. And gradually the preacher and Knot quit their game and idle into passing each other the ball for slow-moving concentrated jump shots.

All sound gathers on the court, the balls at the gym like an echo—*blap blap blap*—of the ball on the concrete court. The preacher's voice tuned low, almost secretive, as he speaks to Knot: like this and this. Like this—a demonstration of techniques, tricks with the ball. And always that shuffling dance ending with a burst in the air and the ball shishing through the net.

He teaches Knot "the prance" off court, and "the prance" on court. He teaches him to shoot soft as if tossing a baby through the net to be caught before it landed on the hard floor. Poised, cool, just keeping beat with the ball, a dance. Smooth on court, cool-catting off court. The basketball dancer in action. Keep it clean, go by the rules of the game and you'll have nothing to keep you awake nights.

He stands behind Knot and places the ball in Knot's right hand, middle finger pointing at the goal. "Squat from the hips and snap your wrist, shoot like lightening striking and lay it through the hoop." He begins whispering. "Let that ball wallow through the net. You're a dancer, you know all the moves. You're not doing battle with the ball. Don't whip-up on that ball."

Marge calls out, "Y'all come on and eat supper, hear?"

෬ • ෨

It is almost spring-like, end of January, when after school Knot walks to the church to retrieve the money to take back home. But not all of it.

Standing on the piano bench of the sunny, silent church fellowship hall, he lifts the lid on top of the tall upright piano and reaches over, inside, and lifts the brown paper sack with both hands. The insides of the piano smell musty and old but the money still smells new. *Huckleberry Finn* is tumbled on its side, yellowed pages spread like a fan.

He takes the book out, then the other three books and places them on the piano bench, then begins slapping stacks of bills onto the bench beside the books. When he gets to the halfway mark of the stacked money in the sack, in his estimation, he stacks the banded bills in his arms and carries them into the main part of the church. He goes to the slick pine podium in the pulpit and dumps the money on top, then begins stripping the paper-sacking wrappings from each thousand-dollar stack of one-hundred dollar bills. Lots and lots of loose bills—the dollar-green color and the number 100 having lost its magic to cast a spell on him—to be stacked again on the shelf below the podium, next to the red-felt bedded collection plate and the little white booklets of visitor's slips that nobody ever fills out. He rips a sheet off and with one of the red nub pencils in a cup, he writes: "For the cause."

Surely God will understand. Surely God will know his heart and know what a good cause it is. He doesn't feel guilty about the money he's given for The Cause, he doesn't feel the need to repent. To him the cause represents Boots and her babies, Marge and hers, women and men whose names and misfortunes he's forgotten they've been unimportant for so long.

On his way home, coming up the dip of Troublesome Creek, he spies Becky Bruce sitting on the courtyard railing, facing the post office across the street.

Wearing white tennis shoes, blue jeans rolled at the ankles and a lighter blue short sleeve shirt, she is blowing plastic bubbles with a blue straw. Hatch marks of rose sun shimmer over the growing bubbles. She pinches off a bubble from the end of the straw and lets it go, up into the deep blue sky; then another which floats straight up to the waving American Flag at the north entrance to the courtyard; another out over highway 94 and the white steeple of the red brick Methodist church east of the post office.

Crickets sing in the curled blond grass each side of the road, and there's a smell of winey sap on the air. Jay birds, duped into mating rehearsals, flit and dive in the red-tinged sweet gums atop the cliff where the creek has washed a weed-choked gorge. Paper trash and bottles, never seen in summer, when the green leaves and vines knit bonnets over them, shine from beds of dead weeds and water grass. But still there is birdsong trilling down from the cliff into the gorge.

Knot turns east at the crossing on the post-office side of 94, feeling the leveling out of gravel to concrete sidewalk. Watching the bubbles rise and fly he clutches the sack of money to his body; it feels suspiciously light, dangerously thin. The wallowed-out brown paper might rupture at any moment and what little dab of money is left might spill on his feet with the telling wrappings ripped from the bills left at the church. The top of the sack no longer rests under his chin, but low on his chest. If he doesn't return it to the bank soon, there will be nothing left to return.

The dull winter-green of the great live oaks along the sidewalk are reflected in the bubbles, bubbles the size of birthday balloons; the oaks and the sun and even Knot with a bubble head are reflected in the balloon now floating before him, bursting in his face. SPAP!

He jumps as if shot. The sugary resinous chemical paint smell of the plastic bubble gook carries on the air.

She stops blowing and lowers the toothpaste size tube of bubble gook and the straw to her lap, chewing gum, feet crossed and swinging. Sad-looking that she has scared Knot, either that or on the verge of asking what's in the sack.

"I'm sorry," she says low, barely audible. As always, when faced with iffy praise or condemnation, she shrugs her shoulders and the right corner of her mouth tugs down in a smirk. Who cares?

A long brown car passes, stops at the crossing and goes on. In front of the Methodist Church, Knot heads across the highway and the back road behind the courthouse to get to the school bus shortcut—the straight gravel road from 129 to the schoolhouse. Several cars belonging to people who work at the courthouse are parked in a line, bumper to bumper, on the grass median, their shadows humped up, huge and comic, in the low cast sun.

Nobody is out and about, so Becky stands and starts winding east along the sidewalk, bubble wand down by her side. At the corner of the white pipe railing of the courtyard, she turns, walking faster till she is only a few yards behind Knot. He can see her shadow on his left, long, lean and gliding on the bumpy gray gravel, a carnival giant among the clown cars. That he cannot hear her walking, her footsteps, makes him want to look behind to see if it is really her in caricature, her shadow.

When he turns east again, up the school bus shortcut, and the facing Fifty-ish frame houses, all the way to the schoolhouse—portwine brick and many-sided with a faded black hip roof—the sun is directly behind him and her shadow is gone and in its place, his own shadow, the carnival giant going before him. Knot in Becky's shadow.

Is she gone now?

If she is still following him, why?

When he can no longer bear the wondering, he looks back and sees her farther behind but still following. Chewing, blowing bubbles. She looks like a sad clown at the tail of a parade.

At the empty school ground, he goes through the free-swinging chain-link gate, smelling lead of school-bus yellow pencils and chalk dust. Smelling the sulphurous water of the fountains along the halls. Water fountains at the courthouse have only recently dropped their COLORED and WHITE signs on the walls above the hanging white porcelain drain bowls; Knot never drinks from either fountain. Even at school where there are no signs designating colored from white, he doesn't drink from the water fountains. To be on the safe side. Does he trust integration not to backfire? No. He's not taking any chances. Just as he's not taking any chances, by sidetracking into the school yard, that Becky Bruce might follow him into the quarters and get them both in trouble. Too, he is testing to see whether she is really following him or only out walking.

Across the concrete brick-pillared breezeway that attaches the new flat-roofed building on his right to the old tall bulky main building of portwine brick on his left, he takes a right at the corner of the new classroom addition and stands close along the new-red brick wall. The connected school buildings of differing shades of brick hook around with a dirt play ground in the middle so that Knot is facing the iron gray whirl-a-way and lumbering swing set and high slide, backed by the lower grades' classrooms in a low neat line and slick concrete sidewalk. Sandwiched in between the odd shades of brick, he leans against the cool wall, his shadow under cover of the straight-edge shadow of the eave drop, waiting for Becky to show.

He has almost given up when he sees the shadow of the giant ghosting forward, flat on the foot-tramped ground at the corner just off the breezeway. A bubble about the size of a basketball floats ahead, up and above the circular whirl-a-way, then lodges in the umbrella oak with a wooden bench around it for the teachers to sit during recess and grade papers while watching their pupils play.

Becky is standing at the corner, not four feet from where Knot is standing. She looks left, then right, eyeballing Knot. Still chewing her gum.

He shifts the sack of money higher in his arms and tightens his grip.

"Why you following me?" he asks low.

She shrugs and blows another bubble. Pinches the bubble off where it is stuck and bobbing at the end of the straw and lets it go. The balloon flies the way of the other, over the whirl-a-way, almost lodges in the oak, but rises higher, revolving in the sky with blue and green map-shaped images like a world globe. The silvery tube in her right hand has a blue label and is almost collapsed. The cap is off and the smell is so strong it stings Knot's eyes and nostrils. Or is it her breath?

"Aren't you scared of getting in trouble?" he says.

She looks around. Sidles up to the wall on his left, tucking her shadow into the eave drop, and leans with him. Knee crooked, one foot up and behind, resting on the brick. "I just wanted to know what's in the sack."

"For me to know and you to find out."

"I'm trying." She doesn't sound like herself; she sounds cocky, smart-assed. Her eyes, mostly pupil, are rolled up to where a band of white shows below the thin blue rims of her irises. "It's money, isn't it?"

He laughs out. "Money! Was, I wouldn't be on foot, I have me a bicycle." The answer comes to him, for one thing, because along the curve of the quarters, across the field of reddening bitter weeds, he can see Cee Ray riding his bicycle. He can hear the grinding of the chain.

Knot really wants somebody else to know about the money. Somebody to share his burden suddenly.

He opens the top of the sack, takes out one book at a time and hands them to her. He tilts the sack then for her to peer inside. She steps closer, sucks in air, gasps, exhales.

The sharp resinous smell of the plastic bubble gook is overpowering—school doesn't even smell like school, but a paint factory or a turpentine distillery.

"You can touch it," he says of the money.

Chewing, she shakes her head no. "Where'd you get it?"

"I found it," he says. "Found it in an alley last summer while I was staying with my aunt in Valdosta. Bank robber dropped it cause the police got after him." He doesn't say po-lice, isn't even tempted. In fact, po-lice, that accent on *po*, sounds unnatural to him now.

"You planning to give the rest away?" she asks.

"You can have some. I don't care. The rest goes back to the bank soon it gets summer." He reaches into the bag and pulls out two bundles—two thousand dollars in neat green hundred-dollar bills!—and tries to hand them to her. The bands are stamped with red circles and writing.

She shakes her head no again and hands back the books. Leans into the building again.

"I wouldn't have any use for it," she says, squeezing some of the bubble material onto the end of her straw and shaping it round with her fingers to block air escape through holes that might form in the thinning walls of the bubble when she blows.

He knows what she means. He stacks the books atop the bills again and folds down the top of the softened paper sack.

She blows the bubble, pinches it off and lets it go the way of the others; no wind but the balloon-like bubbles seem to have developed a certain track between earth and sky on this fair mock-spring day. "You ever chew any of this stuff?" she asks and squirts an inch of the clear bubble gel onto her right pinky and wipes it on her blue tongue. Her bubble straw is blue, her shirt is blue, her eyes are blue and now her tongue.

"Make you drunk as a skunk," he says. "You reckon you oughta do that?"

She is chewing, nodding. It occurs to him that's exactly what she is—drunk.

"Hey! How long you been doing this?"

"A while now," she says. "Better than bubble gum." She pulls a full tube from the hip pocket of her blue jeans.

"I ain't into this, I ain't into this," Knot mumbles. He crosses in front of her, to go to the corner of the building where he can hear Cee Ray riding, out of sight, along the road beyond the gate. Knot doubles back without stopping and almost bumps into Becky following him.

"Go on home," he whispers to her. "Go on."

"Where you taking the money?"

"Go on, I say." He starts walking toward the breezeway.

She ducks back behind the building and he can hear her crying. He has every intention of leaving her there but can't. Besides, Cee Ray's jutted head is in view around the corner of the new-building wing, seen but unseeing.

"Don't cry," Knot whispers, stepping back to the wall where he was standing before.

She is squatting on the dirt with her back to the building, chewing, sobbing, slobbering.

He goes over, squats down beside her and places the money sack on his left, where rain has dripped off the eaves tapping out an elliptical line in the raw dirt and concrete crumbles.

"Hey," he says. "You wanta help me hide this money?"

"I don't care," she whimpers, wiping her eyes on the sleeves of her blue cotton shirt, but not crying now. Her lips are puffy and purplish, her usually pink cheeks are no longer pink. Saliva has dripped down her shirtfront creating a darker blue line.

"I can't get the money to the house just yet. Not with Cee Ray out there riding and Marge apt to happen up any minute. Gotta take it to the woods, I guess. Get it later." What he has in mind is to lure her into the block of woods behind the quarters, then point her west toward her house on the south edge of Statenville. Then light out for home himself.

When they hear Cee Ray swerve round at the end of the road, facing 94, rattling back with a spin of gravel toward the quarters, and they can hear no near roaring of automobiles, no sounds but distant dogs barking and children calling out at play, they slip around the corner of the building, across the shadow-duplicated breezeway. Passing through the gate, they make a beeline for the woods across the road. Knot in the lead and hassling like a dog, he's so scared. Becky behind, chewing a new dab of her dope bubblegum.

Cee Ray is moving on up the road, butt in the air and bare legs in tight dark shorts pumping. Dumb to the whole affair, which no doubt he would find interesting since he's been known to make remarks about Knot's "girlfriend"—the white-headed girl in the green truck. "That man gone have yo hide," he would say. Though Knot had never mentioned the girl, but what was true didn't matter to Cee Ray, who generally was known to draw his own conclusions, to pick up on any clue and use it to tease Knot. Lately, though, since his sister's accident and death, he'd been talking less, thinking more, keeping to himself.

Chapter 9

The sun is almost down, just an orange blaze raying around the stout pines, oaks, bays, hickories and poplars. Hazy streaked light undercut by shadows and thick brush. Nets of woody vines and spiked bare trees and switches for bushes that look dead but will spring into green when the season comes for real, when it proves it will stay. Always though there are the evergreen wax-berry myrtle, fanned palmettos and bristly pine tops, plus plats of short grass where frost never falls, the touching branches of the magnolias with their broad polished leaves and the live oaks with their bushy overhang having sheltered the grass.

Weaving through the woods, Knot follows the sun, headed west where he will point Becky toward home. He can't wait to get rid of her; besides with the sun no longer providing heat, he is shivery cold. Shivery with fear. But Becky is happy and loose again. She holds to the tail of his silver football jacket to keep from stumbling to her knees. Briars snag on her jeans. Her feet are dragging in the crisp leaves growing soggy with dew. No jacket of her own and she must be freezing.

He should offer his. But he's in hopes of getting rid of her soon. He listens for traffic on 129—he has to be getting close. He hears the thundering of a semi on 129 and it slowing at the city limits sign, south side of Becky's house. But he's not close enough yet. Still, no point in taking off his jacket just to put it back on. Besides, her wearing his jacket...well, how will that look if somebody happens up? He wishes she would let go of him. Not walk so close.

Hell, if anybody so much as sees him with this white girl, not to mention sees her hanging on and Knot himself bearing a bag of cash, he'll be hung for more than stealing this money.

They are more than halfway between the quarters and

highway 129 and her house, he figures, when the sun drops out of sight. Roughly estimating by the time and space taken up by frequent tours and detours of these woods—play-hunting, going to the store, hiding out from other children and adults in bad moods—Knot figures it's less than a mile. Not that far from the school house to the Bruce house, but Becky is slowing him down, and out of respect Knot has been weaving to avoid the rougher patches of woods, especially the blackberry thickets and snaky, boggy slews.

He can hear the traffic on 129 getting closer, voices he can't make out. Somebody calling. Now he really will have to leave the money in the woods or answer to Marge, who should be home from work by now.

Becky is stumbling behind, stumping over bushes and stobs, cured fat splinters from a blasted lighterd stump and felled trees. Crisscrosses of barkless trees, they have to walk around. And on the other side, a scarred-over dirt pit in a clearing where Cee Ray and some of the other boys had blasted the stump with dynamite stolen from the Samson Powder Company. That had been last year sometime but the smell of blasting powder is still rich and smoky. The chilled air seems to compress the smell, to deepen it, as well as the sharp smell of pine tar from the streaked pines warmed by the sun shining down on the clearing at midday.

The blast of dynamite had been heard for miles. Timber all around splintered as if lightening had struck. Who was responsible? Not Cee Ray with his head bandaged in a bed-sheet, peepholes for his shifting bloodshot eyes.

Becky, behind Knot, is hiccupping, giggling. Still tugging on his jacket, making a game of it.

Stepping high over humps of bombed gray dirt, Knot shakes her free and heads for a cluster of palmettos on the west edge of the clearing. Becky goes over and stands dazed-looking with her back to a hickory tree, to the right of the palmettos. Slowly she slides to sitting position, head down on her arms and hugging her knees, having suddenly come to her senses and feeling rejected, embarrassed, maybe ashamed. No longer giggling, but crying now, she hiccups and gags.

Knot quells the impulse to go to her and beg her to forgive him for being so mean, for shaking her loose and feeling ashamed, afraid, to be seen with her. But it is almost dark and it is cold and he has to hurry, and he can't let her think the two of them together are okay. He can't say where he knows it from—possibly from Cee Ray—but he knows that Negro boys and men are supposed to be keen on the idea of crossing over; their goal, from the white point of view, is to hook up like animals with a white female.

Yes, he can send her walking from here.

He picks out a deer path winding through the woods to 129, and he can see scattered lights of automobiles and houses, so she should be able to see them too. Sounds of light traffic slowing or speeding up at the city limits sign, south of Statenville—just a short walk.

Quickly he places the sack of money in the midst of the sprawling palmetto fronds, at the throat where green palmetto berries are sprouting. Then he scoops up dead branches and pine straw and begins arranging it on top of the sack to his satisfaction—Becky is no longer crying, only sitting there—that the sack is covered by windblown and drifting dead limbs and straw. Nothing natural looking about it but it will have to do. He has to go. The hickory tree with a knothole below the bole where the bare limbs branch out marks the palmetto cluster where he has placed the money. It is dark enough now, heavy dewy dusk, so that the tree and Becky both seem to fade before his eyes.

Moving closer, he can make out that Becky is doping her tongue, chewing, holding to the tube of bubble gel.

It dawns on Knot that the half-empty tube in her fist is not the one he first saw her with. This is the new tube and she has chewed herself into oblivion.

He tramps over to where she is sitting, snatches the tube from her hand and tosses it out over the woods. She simply sits there, chewing.

"You one crazy white girl," he says.

She starts crying softly with her head on her arms on her knees, as before.

He sits beside her, feels her shaking and places both arms around her shoulders. Her tears wet his jacket sleeve.

"I'm sorry," he says. "It's just I'm in this awful fix. I can't leave you here and every minute you're gone from home, they—your mama and daddy—get closer to finding out where you've been. Where you are."

"I'm cold, I'm scared," she says, truly childlike, her slow coarse voice having gone squeaky, cartoonish.

He nudges her upright and opens his jacket, then pulls her close to his broken beating heart, wrapping the right front of his jacket and his arm around her. Gradually warming, she goes limp, snuffling.

"It's okay," he whispers into her clean hair. "It's okay."

In the dark, they are both dark, the same color, and it doesn't matter. Nothing does. He can't send her home doubting whether she can even walk.

But of course they can't stay.

She stops snuffling. Then next minute she is silent and heavy, in his arms, against his chest. Asleep, out, kaput, Lord Jesus!

He can hear Marge in the quarters to the east calling his name. "Knot? Yoo hoo, Knot!" Over and over.

He has to go.

Her voice is like a magnet drawing him, he's so used to obeying without hesitation.

Is she calling him "David" now? Or is it somebody else calling another David. He cannot recall any other boy in the quarters named David, so he credits her with calling the name. "Da-vid? David!" Barely short of a scold.

If it is Marge, who told her about the name change? It has to have been the preacher. Knot hasn't breathed a word. Her knowing his new name, calling it, shocks him and makes him feel naked and vulnerable, though wanted.

He slides slowly, carefully, away from Becky, feeling

her leaning, but not clutching, her arms limp and falling to her sides. One crumpled beneath her as she settles on her left side and brings the other arm up with her hand forming a fist and pressing beneath her chin. Standing, Knot shucks off his jacket and spreads it open over her bare arms, exposed shoulder and back. A familiar yet alien object. Untouchable but vulnerable as he is. He can hardly make out the features of her face, it is so dark; only her white shoes overlapping as she draws up her knees. How she must sleep in her bed, at home. She looks that comfortable, which is the most frightening thing of all, to Knot. She won't be getting up anytime soon and she will freeze if he doesn't come back. She might die anyway—she might be dying right now.

It is truly dark and the dew is risen, dampening the green bushes that brush his pants legs as he sets out across the woods for home. Terrified, slapping aside branches and untangling vines, running and thinking he should turn back. Look out for Becky. Strangely though, she seems safer where she is, safer where her daddy can't lay hands on her.

The bare bulb in the back window of Marge's shack looks too yellow. He can see Marge moving about near the front, making supper. Smells like fried beef tripe.

He waits for Cee Ray to make the long curve to the schoolhouse on his bicycle, both lit by the flickering light of a yard fire, then dashes from the cover of woods, quick across the dirt yards, Winston Riley's and then his own, an understood line which means nothing really. He eases up the back doorsteps and through the door, feeling warmth and smelling the battered tripe frying. A soothing though sickening smell mixed with the inhaled chemical taste of Becky's bubble gook.

Marge, at the stove, doesn't turn around. "Bout time you get on in here. Where you been?"

When he doesn't answer, she turns, holding out a long three-prong turning fork. She is dressed neat in her usual black skirt and white shirt under a white bib apron.

His hands are behind him, holding to the doorknob; he

can't seem to let go of the doorknob.

"Marge, you gotta come quick. I got a girl out in the woods." He breaks up his sentences to breathe. "Can't do a thing with her."

"What girl...what?"

She stoops to silence the hiss of the blue gas flame under the pan. The circle of fire pops, goes out.

"This girl follow me, all messed up. I try to get her home, she won't go, she sick, she scared." Rushing his words, his sentences begin fusing.

"What ails her?" Marge lays the fork down easy on the center of the stove where a platter of golden fried tripe waits for the last piece sobbing grease in the pan.

"She be chewing some old bubble mess. Act drunk."

"Becky Bruce. Lord in heaven, that chile!" Marge looks wild. Usually it is her prerogative to burst through doors after dark with Knot overcome by shock.

She throws up both hands, then begins stripping off her white bib apron, snatching it over her head and spiking her orange hair. Grabbing her thin green cotton jacket off the hook by the front door, she wheels and her feet beat and shuffle on the floor in a terrible desperate rhythm as she crosses the room, trailing Knot out the back door.

Arms crossed and teeth clenched, tilting forward, she takes short, quick steps behind Knot, as if she might overtake and trample him or is maybe hanging back in dread of what she will find when she finds it.

No flashlight and they can barely see in the woods. Starlight overhead seems to grow brighter, shingled silvery light composed of mist, now that they are out of the lighted house and their eyes are adjusting to the dark.

Behind him, Knot can hear Marge crashing through the heavy brush, breath coming quick like her footsteps. Not a word, but he can feel her sorting thoughts, can feel her fear. Knot has to backtrack several times through the woods before he finds his way to the site of the pit created by the dynamite blast. Walking fast now over the humps of dirt and crisscrossed trees, he can see his silver jacket on the ground and then Becky's white shoes. Closer, he can see that she has turned on her other side, facing away, and the jacket has slid from her back. The smell of vomited chemical is so strong it takes his breath. She looks smaller, shrunken, dead.

"Get up, sugar," Marge says low, still hugging her own body, and kneels beside Becky. Then sterner, louder, "Get up, I say."

Becky sits slowly, rubbing her eyes, then scrambles up, rocking on her knees. She looks at Marge, then leans all her weight into her, leaning so heavy that Marge tilts back.

"Get her on the other side," Marge says to Knot. "Let's walk her to the house."

"Her house?"

"Our house."

"Ain't no way, ain't no way."

"You got a better idee?"

"No ma'am."

Marge places the back of her hand on Becky's forehead. "Lil ole thing's cold as ice."

One on each side, they walk her through the woods, hearing dogs barking in the quarters and seeing the spotty lights of yard fires and harsh electric bulbs. Twice they have to stop and hold Becky forward to vomit and each time she commences to cry, but quits after they get her walking again.

They are halfway across Winston Riley's back yard, fully lit by a bare bulb above his back door, heading for their own, and the chute of light from the back door Marge had left open in her haste, when Cee Ray on the bicycle whips between the walls of the two houses and stops before them. "Man, you in *some kind* of trouble now," he says to Knot. "Bossman gone take a stick to you."

"Git on out from here," Marge says. "Now!" She stamps her foot.

&#x21B   ❧ • ❧

Knot is eating—supposed to be eating—not ten feet away from Marge's bed where Becky is lying, moaning and crying. The smell of vomit is so strong and sour mixed with the stringy batter-fried beef tripe that he'll never eat it again.

Marge is mumbling, bathing the girl's sallow face and arms, and scared as Marge must be, Knot thinks she still makes a fine nurse. It's a side of her he hasn't seen that often before and it negates the image of her drunk and dependent on him.

Pushing back his chair, he gets up from the table and goes to the front door, opens it and the cold air strikes him like a club. Marge has stacked firewood to the left of the front door. He loads his arms and goes back inside, closing the door with his foot.

"I gotta go home," Becky says. "He's gonna kill me."

"Ain't no such thing. I ain't gone let him."

"He will." Becky bawls. Her face looks a little bit pinker but her lips are still puffy and purplish. "When he finds out about the bubble stuff, he will."

Knot opens the front door of the heater. Firelight flares on his face, as he shoves one piece of firewood and then another into chinks burned down between the already burning wood.

"Don't overload it, son," says Marge absently without looking, shushing Becky. "All we need's a good housefire tonight."

Knot sits at the table again, watching, sipping his milk. It smells sour too.

Marge talks loud to be heard over Becky's bawling. "I ain't planning on telling yo daddy. We just say you sick. Say I find you at the school, puking, on my way home from work."

Becky sniffles, biting the back of her hand. Wiping her eyes. Her white hair fanned on Marge's pillow looks impossible, forbidden.

"I ain't gone tell this time," Marge adds. "But next time I hear tell of you doing such…next time I ain't holding *nothing* back. Understand?"

"My stomach hurts, my head hurts."

"You lucky you hurting atall." Marge wipes her face again with the wet rag, rubbing. "Bring me a glass of cold tea, Knot. Let's get some down her."

Knot goes to the old white icebox, opens the door and the stale cold air is released on the hot sour room. The tea is as cloudy as milk. Strong boiled black tea, the way Marge likes it.

He pours a glass and takes it to Marge, now seated next to the girl on the edge of the bed. Her head is propped up on the pillow now.

"You scared, Marge?" he asks.

"I be born scared, baby," she says.

He can see it in her reddened eyewhites.

"Now you sit up a little, missy," she says to Becky.

The girl lifts her head from the doubled pillow. "The light...the light hurts my eyes. I smell paint."

Marge places the lip of the tea glass to Becky's lips. "Ain't paint you smelling, it's that old bubble mess fuming up in yo nose." She looks up at Knot. "How much you say she chew, Knot?"

"A bunch of it went up in bubbles, I know that. Bout half a tube I can swear to. What we gonna do with her, Marge?"

"Take her home, that what."

The girl's eyes fly wide. Her cheeky face screws up. "I can't go home now. What time is it?"

"Going on nine or so," Knot says, though not looking at the wind-up clock on the icebox whose ticking he only now recognizes as the source of the racket marking off precious minutes.

"I can't go home now, I can't go back."

"You have to. Your mama's likely looking all over the place, worried slap to death." Marge's gold hair is standing out like fringe on a straw hat.

"You don't understand," Becky says. "It's not just me in danger. If she tries to take up for me..."

Marge looks long-faced at Knot, interpreting. "Her

mama, she talking bout."

Outside, either a truck or car is motoring up the road. No muffler and the sound cuts through the walls. They all listen, wait. Then, "Ain't no other way," Marge says. Her white blouse is clotted with vomit, specks of red and a filmy jelly-like mucous. "You too young to leave home yet, and the law'd likely slap you in a foster home."

Becky turns her head away. "I know it. I can do it. Do you have any aspirin?"

"Ole aspirn's bad on yo stomach, apt to make you thow up again. Get me a rag of ice, Knot. Some soda crackers too. Gotta get something she can hold on her stomach."

When the girl stands, some thirty minutes later, with the knotted white rag of ice pressed to her forehead, she falls back to the bed. She is now wearing Marge's jacket over her filthy blue shirt and it coops down below her buttocks and hips.

"Get her other arm, Knot," Marge orders.

He does it and together they bring her to her feet and walk her toward the front door.

Knot is terrified that Becky might tell about the money and her drunk; otherwise, he wouldn't have to worry. "Marge, I don't know," he says, hobbling along with Becky slumped between them. "He's liable to kill both of us."

"What *us*? " She shoots him a look over Becky's white head. "You ain't stepping foot in that car, hear me? Colored boy and a white girl, huh uh!"

At first Knot is relieved—he will do his homework while they are gone. While he heats water for a bath to cleanse the vomit stink from his body.

But out in the cold dark with only the faint sulfurous overhead light on inside the car, he knows he will go with Marge. No help really against a man like Bruce, but he will be there. Lil ole knot that he is, he will be there.

After they place Becky stretched out and crying in the back seat, Knot gets in on the passenger side, hugging himself, while Marge goes around to the driver's side. He is shaking and it's not that cold in the now-darkened car. He's not as alone with Becky as he was in the woods, but alone. Ticking quiet, ticking cold. He can see a half-million stars through the windshield, the other half million behind him, then no stars as Marge opens the door on the driver's side and the roof light flushes over him. He can smell Becky's vomit mingling with the wooly car seats.

"Out!" Marge says with her hands on her hips and feet planted. "Git out fore I drag you out, you hear?"

"No ma'am," he says and feels tougher. Like Becky, he can take it. Though he figures for a fact that her daddy probably won't kill her but will kill him sure.

Becky is bawling again, gagging again.

"Knot," Marge says low, so low he can barely hear her over the girl's bawling. "Knot, you just a boy...you don't know." She has forgotten all about the name David now—providing that was her calling him earlier.

"I know a bunch of stuff you don't think I know. You don't know me good as you think you do either." He can see the stars again through the windshield and he can see Marge's trim shadow-gutted face and the girl has either fallen asleep or passed out dead. The silence is a terrible relief.

Marge slides her hands on the steering wheel. "I reckon don't neither one of us know the real each other. No more'n we know that gal back there." Marge starts the car. Sounds like a mechanic tuning the engine under the hood.

She backs the car, eyes in the rearview mirror. "I love you for this, Knot...David. But I wouldn't have you hurt for the world." Her hands are shaking so, she has trouble shifting gears.

He wonders if she's craving a drink. Really he might chew some of that bubble stuff himself if he had some.

The headlights, cross-eyed and set low, are now shining on the point across from the school gate where he and Becky had entered the woods that evening. He will take that route when he goes back to get the money tomorrow. If there is a tomorrow. If it doesn't rain. Lord, don't let it rain. Dry money's hard enough to handle in a paper sack. Is this the time to tell Marge about the money? Can he trust her now not to drink it up? Can he trust her not to tell anybody, not to turn him over to law—for his own good, as she is in the habit of saying?

Something about her turning suddenly tender toward him, her calling him David finally, tells him that he can tell her. But it comes to him that telling her, he will cause her to become the guilty one, the thief by adult association with a child, since she is his mother and responsible for his actions. He's heard that somewhere. Or was it that she is held accountable for his sins until he reaches the age of accountability? He is David now, practically grown and accountable since he's seen the light at Aunt Willie's church. He has seen up close Negro men with a purpose, real men, and has no excuse, can never hide behind a claim of ignorance or can't-help-it because he's had no man to keep him straight and set an example. Still, he might need to linger a while longer in his present boy-state: hide under Marge's dress tail, playing up his knotty size. Because for a truth he is a coward when it comes to facing up to Sammy Bruce, not to mention the bank robber.

When they reach the blinking red light at the crossing, turning south, they can see porch lights on all along the highway from the short string of facing houses phasing out just past the Bruce house and the city limits sign. And closer, they can make out the sheriff's dark blue car with a gold star on the sides parked out front of the Bruce house on the right. People wandering through yards with flashlights. Even the pecan orchard is crisscrossed with light beams like shooting stars.

"Uh oh," Marge says and glances back to check on the girl.

Knot looks too. "She's asleep," he says. Lights from the tall poles between the courtyard and the Baptist Church stripe Becky's head and body, change her white hair, her jeans and Marge's green jacket, into gradating shades of lavender and puce. She is curled on her left side, hands folded beneath her face, dead-white instead of pink.

"I'm gone go on by the house." Marge is leaning forward like a criminal about to break through a traffic barrier, peering over the steering wheel through the windshield at the hives of searching men and women and even a few children crossing the highway to and from adjacent yards. Lots of shouting, loud even through the closed car windows. Minutes later, they pass from light into darkness. Heading toward the Florida line and a few scattered lights from farms set back off the highway.

Fog drifts toward them, it seems, spun white clouds and wispy tags, on again, off again. No other traffic on 129 as they motor south with the object of the hunt in the rear seat. It seems to Knot that everybody is out searching and that is why nobody is out driving, why Marge meets nobody or has to pass. She drives slow, stiff at the steering wheel and clenching it with both hands. Usually she drives with one hand on the bottom section, underhanded, with her elbow resting on her thigh.

Knot keeps his eyes on the windshield or stares out the window at the traveling darker tree shapes moving against the dark. He thinks it's entirely possible that somebody searching for the girl will happen up on the sack of money, probably dew-drenched and spilling from the damp dissolving sack. And maybe it's just as well. So far, all the money has brought Knot himself is grief and a few rides on Cee Ray's bicycle. Well, some of it had bought Christmas for needy children. And he has paid Aunt Willie back her stolen money. He hopes. Then there's the little crippled girl's funeral and so far Boots hasn't come back. As for The Cause, the money he left at the church after school, for all Knot knows, Cee Ray or somebody like him, could go in and take it and who would ever know?

He sits higher in the car seat, watching the two-path ramp where Marge is turning in, backing out on the highway.

Heading back toward the lights of the houses plentiful as the stars. The blinking red light of the crossing farther away, fascinating in its ability to charm and distract, when it has been there all along. Knot has always seen it but feels he is seeing it for the first time.

"Now what?" he says.

"Now we stop," she says, sucking in air. "We stop when we get there."

"Maybe we ought to take her to the preacher."

Marge glares at him, her face dull copper as an old penny in the orange glow of the dash light.

"Yeah," says Knot. "We take her there and dump her, the preacher's got trouble."

"Way I hear it, Preacher's got trouble enough coming up when *they* all get here, messing and gomming in our business, showing out at his church."

"They?" Knot knows. "The men from Aunt Willie's church? What's that matter?"

"KKK, that what? Preacher have a cross burn in his front yard; he be run out of this place on a rail for acting up. Wait and see, ain't nobody round here gone show up at the church *but* the Klan. White men want our vote, they pay us in cash or shine, and don't look at me like that—you getting old enough to spot the truth when you see it."

"You mean, us...we...oughta just forget about The Cause?"

Soft fog spirits over the car, enveloping it in white. Then gone.

"*The Cause?*"

"You know, what those men was going on about at Aunt Willie's church."

"You got big ears, boy." She laughs, staring ahead at the lights growing bigger, brighter, but it sounds like a croak coming from low in her throat. "Equal rights—what they call it—won't be coming no time soon." She pauses. A frown screws her features into a tight copper mask. Then speaking low, "Maybe in yo lifetime, maybe. I hope so.

"Now hush! We got a cause up there. *Now.*" She lifts one long finger, tipped out on the end, from the steering wheel, pointing ahead. "Ain't have nothing to do with no thinking. I got enough just *doing*. Try eating *thinking*, try warming yo behind by *thinking*. 'Thinking' what it is and that NACP—whatyoumacallit—be welcome to it. My job be to do for me and mine. I do that, I'm doing good."

The lights ahead are now glaring on the windshield— that close.

"We stop—all they is to it." She seems to be speaking to herself, trying to convince herself.

He thinks he can hear her heart but it is only the hammering under the car hood. "Then what?"

"Then I get out and help the girl out. Not you. You gone lay low and wait. A prayer ain't gone hurt. Just don't show yo ugly mug." She laughs weakly, pats his left knee. "Now, wake Becky up."

He is glad to change the subject, though he'd like to point out to Marge that what she's just said about doing for "me and mine," doing what she can, the best way she can, is what The Cause is all about, in his opinion. It adds up, accumulates, until eventually the whole black race has earned their equality. Same goes for individual whites, Becky included. As for voting he's not sure, but he would imagine it's the same way—his vote, if he could vote, added to Marge's vote and the preacher's vote and Winston Riley's vote, and Cee Ray's vote... And education: What if Cee Ray got educated, grew up and got a job; what if Knot himself went to college? Becky could find her own place someday, her own peace. He wouldn't know how to say all this to Marge anyway, but it's there, stated or unstated, thinking quickened from nothingness, the black void of not-thinking, and waiting to form into words and action.

He kneels in the seat and leans over the back. "Becky, wake up," he says. His voice goes liquid. "Wake up," he says again, but she doesn't move. "She's sleeping like the dead," he says to Marge.

"Shake her," Marge says.

He starts to, then draws back his right hand as if nearing the head of a snake.

"Go on." Marge elbows him. "We about there."

He places his hand on Becky's arm—it feels so strange, touching her—and shakes it.

"My head!" She unfolds like a paper doll and props on one elbow. "Where are we?" Eyes still closed.

"At your house."

She sits straight up, looking left, right and ahead. Her breath smells like vomited pine tar. She starts to cry, low mewling that deepens into sobs.

Knot smoothes her poofed hair. "Don't cry. Don't be scared."

"Sit down, Knot," says Marge, slowing, braking. "Sit down and stay down."

He does what she says. Staring ahead at the lights. At Sammy Bruce standing at the rear of the sheriff's car, on the road shoulder, in front of his house. The car is parked between the two large live oaks that start a chain of similar oaks along the left side of the highway all the way up to where 129 divides and joins 94 behind the brief string of stores and the crossing with the blinking red light. The long-waisted, tall sheriff in his blue uniform, leaning against the bumper of his car, usually terrifies Knot, but Bruce with his pulpwooder shoulders is scarier. His hips are cocked and his thumbs are hooked in the belt loops each side of his waist. With each word spoken his head juts and lifts like a barking dog's.

The Bruce's small white-painted porch looks starker white with the ceiling light on, reverberated light, a bounce of white that sheds onto the yard and the short concrete walk and people grouped and talking, others gathered round the sheriff and Sammy Bruce.

Nobody is wandering with flashlights now that Knot can see. It's as if they have found the missing girl which is of course not the case, so the next most logical assumption is that they have turned up a witness who has told them the girl's whereabouts, or where she was last seen. Cee Ray?

Marge turns left at the glaring black and white city limits sign and eases up between a red car and a pickup parked just off the ditch, south of the Bruce house, facing the pecan orchard. On the flat of the outer yard, running to ditch, which Knot has raked when he was happy and innocent.

Like a flash, Marge is out—the overhead light trips on and off. Then she opens the back door and starts mumbling raspy but soothing words to Becky, still crying.

Knot, scooched low, can see Marge's head in the side mirror as she passes behind the red car on his right but he cannot see Becky's. When they are gone, he listens for an explosion of voices and doesn't have to wait long.

Mrs. Bruce begins sobbing openly—he can pick out her voice—but it's happy sobbing, muffled by hugging. She's just glad Becky is okay. Bruce booms questions. Where the hell you been? What the hell happened to you?

Marge is talking, mumbling—found her sick on the school playground heading home from work. Did she say that, or does Knot only imagine she said that?

Knot is facing the star-glazed pecan orchard, commotion of talking and shouting in a circle at his back, next to the highway.

He thinks about a mama quail he walked up on once with his B.B. gun. She had looked winged, crippled. He could have shot her a dozen times and took her home for Marge to fry. But he only followed her off into a patch of pine saplings till he lost sight of her. On the way back to the woods road, he found her scattered speckled chicks, scraps of flesh, bone and feathers, cheeping and wandering. Everywhere he stepped, there was a chick.

Bruce is over-talking Marge, so she talks louder. Either bluffing or losing it.

Suddenly: Everybody is shouting at once. Mrs. Bruce says, "Don't bother her!" Marge shouts, "Be shamed of yo'self! Lil ole chile and her sick." Nothing from Becky not even her sobbing which is stuck in Knot's head and maybe that's what sets him off. Maybe her "taking it" is what causes him to snatch open the car door and sail out, slamming it hard enough to break the glass, hard enough that he can hear shouts toning down to murmurs and see every head turning his way as he steps from the shadows into the relative light, floating, it seems, about a foot above the crisp frost-killed grass. His fingernails dig into the palms of his hand.

Marge says, "No," as if he has already gone too far to be rescued.

And he has.

"Leave her alone, you old bully," Knot shouts.

Everybody is staring at him. Becky and her mother with an arm about Becky's waist step back to the huge oak trunk and Knot takes their place before Bruce, staring up into the face of the huge white man he has just called an old bully.

All talking at once, the crowd parts and the scary sheriff in uniform steps between Knot and Bruce. Maybe blocking the blow about to be delivered which Knot has already braced himself for. He does for a fact float, absence of earth under his feet, as Marge steps behind him and hangs both arms around his waist and presses him to her bony body, carrying him from the light to the shadows.

Chapter 10

The next morning it is raining, a slow cold rain in which to drift into deep sweet sleep. Till Knot remembers. First, his craziness, coming up against Bruce and then that it is a school day, and then that the money…the money is still out in the woods, getting soaked.

Marge has gone to work and there is a slow fire in the heater, ticking down with the ticking of the clock and the rain on the tin roof. Meaning Marge has decided not to wake him to go to school. Either he doesn't have to go today, or can never go back again.

What will happen?

He gets up and pulls on his puke-sour brown jeans and goes to the dim corner behind the wood heater, to the right of the front door. The panes of the window next to the heater are so polished they gleam, save for the single pane on the upper right corner with its brown cardboard mend like an eye patch. Outside is drear, solid gray, and the rain is ongoing, steady and lacking neither breaks nor wind-driven bursts of rain.

In the corner is a large stuffed green plastic garbage bag full of other bags, mostly paper. He dumps them, then kicks them into a pile to prevent them creeping too close to the heater. Behind the heater is where the heat feels fiercest, smells hottest. Marge being Marge and neat now, of course Knot can't leave the bags where they are. He scoops them up and stuffs them into one of the paper sacks, sets them in the corner. Then he rolls the plastic garbage bag and places it inside his T-shirt. His belly looks like Bruce's. He takes the jacket handed down by his cousin Lee, slips it on and goes out. Closing the door easy and checking all around. Smoke feathers up from the leaning and crumbling chimneys of the other shanties. Knocking about inside, TV voices and real, but nobody is out.

The sky is the color of the smoke and the rain has set in, falling in clear thin ribbons. Cold, and he dreads going out in it. Dreads the soggy pale mud and sandy-bottomed puddles, remarkably clear and clean and dimpling with rain.

He is amazed at how near the cluster of palmettos hiding the money is to the quarters. Yesterday, it seemed that he and Becky had walked miles through the briars and brambles he is now walking through. Or maybe he is so scared that the money won't be there that he is walking faster. Of course, poor sick Becky had slowed him down. Strangely he doesn't feel scared, only relieved that the money is still where he left it. Sodden, but there.

He kneels at the base of the palmettos and begins reaching into the soggy sack and transferring the bundles of bills to the green plastic bag, shielding it with his body partially blocking the eastward-slanting rain. He had started out counting the bundles, but has lost count before he gets done, spellbound by images of Becky, maybe beaten to death by now.

But he reasons that with all those witnesses around, Bruce probably didn't bother her. What will happen to her as a result, who can say?

All around the palmetto cluster are the bands ripped from the money stacks he left at the church. They look like corn shucks, or fall leaves even. That is, until you see the red stamps on the bands and the hair-raising $1000 markings. That is, unless like Knot you have been seeing the markings for so long that they are no more than figures in a written math problem, hypothetical, White: *If Mr. Sims has $1,000 and he puts it in the bank on savings, at 3.1% interest, how much will he have earned within five years?*

After he has gathered all the bands and put them in the plastic bag with the money, he twists the top and starts out of the woods. It seems heavier than when he carried it from the church yesterday. Heavier and in need of lightning. Begging to be given away. Heavy as his head but growing lighter with the knowledge of who next to send the money to, and why hasn't he thought of it before.

At the shack, he goes inside, sets the bag down on the floor next to his cot. He sits and opens it and picks out two bundles. Strangely crisp and dry. He places them on the cot and fastens the top of the bag again and shoves it under his cot, not to be moved again till he can return it to the bank. "So help me God," he says.

Judy Beth had drawn Marge's name for Christmas and probably with Aunt Willie's money, paid back by Knot, she had bought Marge a new pair of flat white shoes for summer church wear.

Knot goes to the hanging clothes next to the bathroom door and pulls the glossy black shoebox from beneath the drapes of Marge's skirts, opens it and takes the shoes out. They look like boats. White tissue paper is stuffed in the toes and in each there is a pale flat narrow wood paddle wedged between the paper in the toes and back to hold the shape. The shoes smell new and white. The soles are spotless and they seem more for looking at than for wearing. He cannot picture Marge in them.

Wet in his soured jeans he sets off walking toward the school carrying the shoebox with two thousand dollars in it. He has wrapped it tight in paper sack and taped it and addressed it to Doris Bruce, ready for mailing with borrowed change for postage, including the quarter Marge gave him— more than the two of them combined is worth, Bruce had said.

At the schoolhouse, the little kids are lined up along the sidewalk of the lower-grade wing, all set to go to the lunchroom, holding out their hands to dare the cold rain, meaning it is around eleven o'clock. Sour smells of milk and yeasty bread carry on the raw air. Puffed vapors from Knot's mouth gauge and reveal his panic, like smoke flares sent up to tip off the law and Sammy Bruce to his whereabouts. Like midget prisoners out for break, the children are smoking too. Their shivering and stamping and hugging themselves remind him of how cold it is, how cold he is, how warm it was yesterday and how different he was then.

He is almost to the post office—bright red wet bricks but gloomy in the rain—before he thinks about the fact that he'll have to have the package weighed and stamped by the postmistress. He stops. A pulpwood truck roars past, spinning rain on the asphalt and gravel. Knot doesn't even look at the driver but figures what are the chances, how unlikely and unfair at this point, that it is Bruce? That the truck doesn't try to run him down is proof it isn't Bruce. But just in case, Knot edges closer to the courtyard railing.

No, he cannot use the post office. Everybody in town will know by now about him bowing up to Bruce and maybe even be pairing him with Becky. Likely somebody had seen her tailing him to the schoolyard yesterday.

He steps over the white dripping railing and into the courtyard. Then heads for the walkway behind the courtroom, through the breezeway and between the sheriff's office and the jail. Listening to the rain on the oaks and his sneakers squeaking on the wet concrete and then an unseen jailbird calling out to him.

"Come here, boy. Come talk to me."

It seems entirely possible that this man could be him in a little while. But he doesn't look back, walks faster out into the rain and across the school bus shortcut, to the back of the garage: junk cars, oily mud and hammering inside. A grease gun hisses and a man in a yellow helmet and goggles is bent over a greasy iron trailer frame, welding. Fierce arcs of light the color of lightening.

At the aqua concrete- block cafe, facing 129, Knot takes the dirt road past a vacant lot on his right and the white Baptist Church on his left, past a big rundown unpainted house on the end. He has to climb a rusty wire fence to get to the woods between the quarters and the Bruce's house.

He has to be crazy; he has to be out of his mind. He goes on, glad for the cover of wet trees and brush and even the briars snagging his pants legs. But freezing now. He can't stop shaking. He can hear the dogs in the quarters barking.

He can hear traffic slowing at the south city limits sign and the Bruce house. So he heads west, traffic sounds growing louder, clearer. A door slams. He can smell smoke from chimneys and cooking—smells like ham-hock vegetable soup. He is starving which makes him colder. His brown jeans have almost ceased to smell like puke.

He can tell by the break in roof peaks of the houses, woodside of 129, that he is nearing the lane leading to the place where he will leave the box of cash. Tall gum trees, bare of leaves, mark the spot and he is still under cover of woods when he comes in view of the small white frame house across the highway. He listens for traffic, north or south bound, through the ticking of the rain on trees, nothing, and Bruce's green pickup is not parked on the left side of the house where Marge had parked last night. The two houses on each corner of the lane at the highway have smoke rising from the chimneys. People at home but he will have to take his chances. Don't run, walk. A Negro boy running will draw the law. His jaw aches as he walks with the box under his arm, drenched and freezing, terrified.

Negro men and boys have been shot for doing less.

Don't stop walking.

Don't stop till you reach the porch and place the package on the floor, sliding it toward the closed front door so that Mrs. Bruce or Becky will have to trip over it, going out, before Mr. Bruce can get hold of it.

Then he is actually doing it, placing the box on the wet gray porch floor and shoving it toward the door, almost without stopping, heading back up the lane—don't run! Backlog of sounds—Becky talking to her mother. Had he only imagined that? No. Of course, Becky hadn't gone to school either.

When he gets back to the gum trees at the end of the lane, a north breeze breaks loose great droplets of rain. He turns to wait for a few minutes, as long as he dares, to maybe see Becky or her mother step out on the porch and retrieve the box. But he can't see the package. It is gone or either the brown paper has blended in with the gray floor. He prefers that the package be gone and turns toward the woods with that picture in his head. He has done all he can do. The rest is up to Doris Bruce.

That evening, Marge brings word from Miss Iris, the widow-woman she has worked for that day, that after Knot and Marge left the Bruce house, the night before, the sheriff had ordered everybody else to go home.

What happened next is anybody's guess.

ભ • ૪૭

Knot goes back to school the next morning with a warning from Marge not to talk—the less said the better. He hadn't expected Becky to be there and she isn't. Her empty desk says it all.

The night before Knot had dreamed that she and her mother were getting on the Trailway bus that stops once a week at the store across from the southwest corner of the courtyard and the school bus shortcut. He was inside the bus, sitting about midway the rows of seats and Doris Bruce had stopped and patted him on the head. Becky, behind her, stopped and smiled. When she stepped forward toward the back of the bus a huge bubble appeared, trailing Becky. Sammy Bruce's warped face in the iridescent gleam. The bubble popped and Knot woke up.

At recess, in the cold clear sun of the playground, near the same spot behind the new building where Knot and Becky had stood only two days before, a group of girls have clustered to talk. When he passes, hands in his pockets, they shush each other and stare after him.

The teacher with the moon-glazed hair and papers on her lap is sitting on the bench built around the brittle old oak trunk. She is wearing a maroon wool coat buttoned up and a paisley scarf around her neck, ends tucked into the top where the wide lapels come together. She motions Knot over, then slips to one side for him to sit.

"Knot, you haven't turned in your math homework for the past week. You want to tell me why?" She is grading papers, doesn't look up.

"I didn't do it, ma'am."

She looks up. "This have anything to do with that business about Becky Bruce?"

"No ma'am."

She looks down, checking math problems with a pen that writes red. Her chin folds. "I'm here if you want to talk."

"I don't." He hopes he doesn't sound smarty. "I mean I wouldn't know what to say."

"Did you know she's leaving school?"

"No ma'am." He holds his breath.

"Her daddy says he doesn't want her around you."

"Where'll she go to school, you reckon?"

"There's talk she might have to move to her aunt's in Valdosta."

Knot exhales.

"Her mother disagrees though."

Knot sucks in again. "He always gets what he wants. It'll go his way."

"Maybe not. Her mother says if Becky goes, she goes."

"To the aunt's house?"

"No, that's his sister, not hers. Get that homework caught up, hear?"

"Yes ma'am." He starts to walk away.

"Oh, and one more thing."

Uh oh, she's onto him having a hundred-dollar bill in his fist and not a dollar the day he tried to slip it into Becky's book satchel.

Her sharp green eyes are on him when he turns but she is smiling. "I really like that you are signing your name David now. Suits you better than Knot. But you're going to have to clean it off your desk before school lets out for the summer. Okay?"

CR • &O

David has been at Aunt Willie's two whole days before he gets the time or courage to take the money back to the bank.

Yesterday morning, he had gone with Aunt Willie to take the old granddaddy to the doctor, whose office is downtown, southeast of the First National Bank on the diagonal interrupted by a traffic light. While Aunt Willie sat fanning the granddaddy, waiting for the doctor, David looked out the upstairs window, figuring how to return the money without getting caught. The old man was sweating, in great pain and needing his shot, but still his long thin legs in creased gray twill remained still, feet flat on the floor, while two small children belonging to an idle fat lady romped around him on the couch. His hollow nickel-colored eyes hardly blinked. The children were after destroying the magazines stacked on a corner table to the left of the brown vinyl couch end where the granddaddy sat.

All aquiver and up tight from battling her daddy's pain, Aunt Willie said, "Y'all go on now, go set down like good chirren," motioning with her hand fan toward the other side of the room, another couch and their mother bogged serenely in the deep cushions.

A housefly lit on the granddaddy's nose and he lifted his right hand, slow as if not to further rile his pain.

Pigeons fluttered to and from the thick wood windowsills and car horns honked below. The door-size solid-glass window was raised where David was standing, leaning out above a white-painted iron radiator, same smells of fountain cola outside as in, which David would never understand. He could hear the doctor laughing in his office beyond the next wall. Laughing louder than Sammy Bruce talked.

The doctor was large and pale and had soft hands that smelled of alcohol and looked gentle but were rough. David had seen him that one time for what the doctor called "coronals" up and down his neck, but Marge had called "knots." A shot in each coronal, and the name Knot, and Marge calling the coronals *knots*, tickled the doctor so that his great belly began to rise like dough. Then he let David fish a Dixie cup of peppermint in cellophane twists from the bottom drawer of his white refrigerator, otherwise neatly stocked with rubber-stoppered vials of liquid for other shots. The sight of which turned the sugar taste to quinine in David's mouth.

The paddle fan overhead whirled slow. Still, the oatmeal stucco room was too hot, but David in the window felt cool. If he turned though he would grow hot with transferred pain—he loved his granddaddy for his dignity, strength, and kindness and just because he was his granddaddy.

"Ferman Crews," the nurse called, standing in the doorway of the office.

Ferman Crews. David Crews.

David forced himself to watch the old man slip toward the edge of the couch, try to stand and fall back. The nurse in her white silky uniform and soft white shoes, stepped out and around to the other side of the old man to help Aunt Willie pull him from the couch. He waved them away, and slowly began to inch forward again and rise with his knees trembling. David knew never to try and help him, he understood. Yesterday Granddaddy had given up his wheelchair, saying he would stand like a man till he lay down to die. It wouldn't be long.

"Lady," he said to the woman on the couch reading a *Readers' Digest* with the children crawling over her hairy crossed legs, "I was you I'd take a holt while they's still time."

After he had vanished behind the white door with Aunt Willie and the nurse, the little girl asked her mother, "What did he mean by that?"

"Busybody! Just a old man don't know his head from a hole in the ground." The woman went back to reading.

David smiled, again canvassing the streets below and casing the bank front as if for a heist. Maybe he should return the money to the alley, east across the street from the bank, but he feared it might fall into some other boy's hands and he'd be cursed forever like Knot with having to see all the things he had the money to buy but couldn't buy for fear of getting caught.

So far, David has seen no sign of the bank robber, who he had last seen at the corner grocery up the street from Aunt Willie's on Christmas day. He has ridden Lee's bicycle up and down the street, looking, and returning the long way, one block over, riding out a square, in case the bank robber should spy him and follow him back to Aunt Willie's house.

The afternoon he sets out finally to return the money to the bank, he has to pass right by Aunt Willie standing at the counter under the kitchen window.

"Where you off to, David?" she says.

"To the library." He can hear in her voice that she's been crying. He hugs the sack tighter. On top of the money stacks are four paperback books and the money has been transferred to a paper sack again.

"Well, don't be gone long if you want to go with us to the funeral home. Your mama'll be here any minute now."

She calls him David as naturally as she ever called him Knot—Marge's doings. Whatever, as long as she doesn't start drinking again, though he figures she has no intention of moving back to Valdosta; and for a fact, the name David does sound more ambitious and kinder than Knot.

Will David stay? Maybe, maybe not. He can if he wants to but he may not want to now. Marge is still his and he is hers. They're a family. And really he's beginning to like her, to look to her for his needs. Spending time with her because he wants to, not because he has to. Besides, if he keeps improving in basketball under the coaching of Richard Troutman he will make it on the first-string basketball team in a couple of years. His chances for playing are better at his own small school; in Valdosta his competition will be greater. And too without his own personal coach, protector and friend he would be lost.

After hearing that Doris and Becky Bruce would be leaving Statenville, for sure, David had been terrified that Sammy Bruce would be out to get him, to make him pay for daring to come up against him, and especially for defending his white daughter, regardless whether they were slipping around together behind his back or not.

Marge, toting her shotgun, stayed awake nights to guard David. She even threatened to send him to Aunt Willie's in Valdosta—dream come true for David, but so had his nightmares come true concerning some boogerman after him. Finally the preacher had stepped in and gone to Sammy Bruce—living alone since his wife and daughter had gone. Troutman warned Bruce that if he ever laid a hand on David—"Yes, David!"—he, the preacher, would see to it that he, Sammy Bruce, would live out the rest of his days in prison; the NAACP would back him up—"Yes, the NAACP!"

What was rich, what was ironic, was Sammy Bruce looking like a balloon with the air let out without his wife and daughter to tremble every time he stomped his foot. Probably his humbling had little to do with the preacher's threat—law was white and overpowering, especially in the rural south, the preacher had explained to Marge and David. The big blustering man who had paid them a quarter between them was simply shocked and lonesome, so caught up in his shock and lonesomeness he didn't have room to spare for other emotions. Certainly no room for emotions concerning a nothing boy known by the name of Knot.

Cats laze in a stupor along the edge of Aunt Willie's back porch, rich cream and sleek as mink. But not for long.

Going out the back door, David hears thunder way off in the west. He kicks the stand up on Lee's bike, places the sack in the basket, and when he gets to the start of the drive at the street, he can see over the roof peaks of the tall houses across the way gray scalloped clouds.

If it rains on the money sack, he is doomed.

Hurrying now, heart thumping in his chest, he pedals up the street, eyes on the corner grocery on his right, turn on his left. Happy, happy, happy that the bank robber hasn't shown, so relieved he forgets about the weather for a few minutes. Though for a fact he does dread letting the money go; he's given so much of it away that he's long quit counting for fear taking it back is practically pointless. But he can't stop thinking what is one more bundle subtracted? Who will know? What if he should hold some back to pay for a big fine funeral for his granddaddy? Who would blame him?

Maybe Marge, Aunt Willie, the preacher, the world would.

Don't cheat, play by the rules and you'll have nothing to regret.

It is enough to have been granted a real name; it is enough to have been granted a real family.

From the doctor's office, his granddaddy had been sent straight over to the hospital on the north side of town.

Last night David had gone with Aunt Willie to sit up with him. Tubes trailing from his shrunken body and both arms straight down by his sides and taped flat to wooden paddles to keep him from yanking on the IV lines feeding him dope, he looked peaceful as if finally the pain had been reckoned with and he was the victor. But not so the cancer.

While Aunt Willie was out of the room, David had crept to the bed. Just standing there, not speaking, he had watched the old man. His eyeballs were darting beneath his thin wrinkled lids, lips parted as if to speak. All evening he'd been mumbling, since they'd started the morphine drip, maybe dreaming.

"I say she better take aholt while she can," he all but hissed.

"Yessir," Knot answered, "I'll tell her again for you." Then he touched his granddaddy's cool, dry withered cheek.

His eyes parted like his lips, rims of old nickels. "You done all you can do, now don't do no more with it. Take it back."

David stepped away a couple of feet from the bed, watching, waiting for what would come next. He started not to speak but had to know. Had to. "Take what back?"

His granddaddy's voice had gone to dust. "That money." He knew!

How?

Had he seen, had he figured it out? Had the bank robber told one of the old men at the corner store or been asking questions about David, who he was, where he lived, and the man had told David's granddaddy? Not *who*—the man who told probably wouldn't have known David's name, who he was, who he belonged to. Or maybe he had. Or maybe the man who maybe told his granddaddy had repeated what he'd heard about the money, the story of the money, and David's granddaddy, who certainly *did* know his head from a hole in the ground, had pieced it all together as he sat quietly, profoundly, waiting to die.

David has to force himself to pedal cool and easy, though huge raindrops are plopping and dotting the paper sack. He is on Patterson now, heading along the sidewalk toward the bank. Clouds directly overhead and people dashing to their cars and inside shops.

Crossing the street, brown sandals slapping at her heels, a young blond woman with fat hair, wearing a short wild-print tent dress, has to gather the tail of her skirt to keep it from blowing over her head.

He tries to affect the look of just one more sorry black boy, too dumb to get in out of the rain. Just as he is about to swerve up to the gray stone wall and make his deposit, a clean-cut white man, the opposite of the bank robber, the kind of man who *belongs*, the Mr. Sims in the math problem with $1000 on savings—saunters out of the bank with a black umbrella and gazes right at Knot-turned-David.

He pedals on, weaving between two women with white shopping bags over their up-blown hair. And on around the corner and up West Hill, traffic banking on the street, waiting for a green light.

He hears the rain coming harder and sees it like a white fog sweeping down the street. And sudden as the money, he is drenched, the bag is drenched. Dark-wet and sodden. Dampened dust and that fountain cola smell that he can never understand. A newspaper scuttling ahead of the rain is stamped flat onto the sidewalk by the heavy drops.

If a man is called to be a street sweeper, he should sweep streets even as Michelangelo painted, or Beethoven composed music or Shakespeare wrote poetry. He should sweep streets so well that all the hosts of heaven and earth will pause to say, here lived a great street sweeper who did his job well.

Water sluices from shop gutters and streams between the gullies off the sidewalk curb. David isn't sure but he thinks he spies a cash-green corner peeking through the sack in his bike basket. One thing he has going for him though is nobody is out on the sidewalk. The traffic on the street has thinned out to nothing and the crystal lights inside the shops seem to draw attention from the dark rain and dark boy on the bicycle.

This is it. David can't keep riding around with the stolen money in a dissolving paper sack. He gets off the bicycle, walking it alongside. A jaunty loping walk that even he himself half-believes.

At the night depository, he leans the bike against the wall and steps up to the basket with his back to the street and lifts the wet bundle and hugs it close to his throbbing heart. With one hand he pulls open the shiny wet metal night depository drawer and with the other begins reaching inside the dissolving sack and pulling out and shoving, hand over fist, the bundles of money into the slot. He has only to let the drawer close twice—that's how fast he is. *Or* that's how little money is left.

He is on the bike and off down the sidewalk, swollen wet wadded sack and paperback novels alone in the basket, almost before the night depository drawer withdraws, forming a solid wall again. Cool and easy, just one more sorry black boy, too dumb to get in out of the rain.

The End

Janice Daugharty

CR • SO

Discussion Questions For Readers

1. If your name was Knot and it got formally changed to a noble name like David, how would that affect you?

2. Look for facts, or reasons, within the text that validate the title.

3. The "old gray granddaddy" is a key player in Knot's emotional and social development from boy to man, as is "the preacher."
What are some of their qualities, their actions, that inspire and influence and bring out some of the same qualites in him?

4. Life lessons learned by Knot come from the unfair as well as the fair people in his world. List some and explain how and why.
Do you think that young people today are frequently denied such lessons because of sheltering adults who don't want to see them hurt? (two questions, maybe)

5. List some dominant details from which the plot pivots.

6. Character and plot work together to create the story. How might "The Little Known" have been a different story if, for instance, Knot had walked out of the alley and handed the bank-robbed money over to the police?

Work from here on different scenarios to create different stories (might use for paper assignment).

Another example: What if Marge had stopped drinking sooner and moved back in with Aunt Willie, putting Knot and his money in close and dangerous proximity to the bank robber?

LaVergne, TN USA
20 August 2010
194086LV00003B/37/P